WITHDRAWN

Glitterbug

Also by Tony Kenrick

Neon Tough
China White
Faraday's Flowers
Blast
The 81st Site
The Nighttime Guy
Two Lucky People
The Chicago Girl
The Seven Day Soldiers
Stealing Lillian
Two for the Price of One
A Tough One to Lose
The Only Good Body's a Dead One

Glitterbug

Tony Kenrick

Carroll & Graf Publishers, Inc.
New York

First Carroll & Graf edition 1991

Carroll & Graf Publishers, Inc.
260 Fifth Avenue
New York, NY 10001

Library of Congress Cataloging-in-Publication Data

Kenrick, Tony, 1935–
    Glitterbug / by Tony Kenrick. — 1st Carroll & Graf ed.
    p.   cm.
    ISBN 0-88184-748-8 : $18.95
    PR9619.3.K49G57   1991
    823—dc20   91-27598

Manufactured in the United States of America

A nice story came in the other day from an old pal, Charlie Griffiths, who runs Herefords on thirty-five acres just south of Vershire, Vermont. Charlie tells us of a smart neighbor of his who was changing the cotter pins in his milking machine. He got the left-side pin in okay, but flubbed the other one. The pin rebounded off the depressed spring, shot into the air, and vanished. The farmer looked everywhere for it, and he keeps a clean barn, according to Charlie, but it seemed to have gone for good. Charlie's neighbor was in a mild panic; it was going to be tough to find a replacement part in town, it being a Sunday, and he had a herd of animals coming in heavy. But he got an idea. He removed the left-side pin, pressed it down onto the spring, as he had the right-side one, and released it. But this time he kept his eye on it, and watched where it landed. Sure enough, when he went over to retrieve it, there was the missing cotter pin lying within an inch of it. Now that's Yankee ingenuity!

From *Down East* magazine, June 1988

PROLOGUE

About fifty years after the death of John Milton, the great English poet, one of his many imitators wrote the following: "Above all gifts give me the ability to relive my life so that I might expunge the errors and calamities that afflicted it." The author's name appears to have been lost so I can't tell you who wrote that. But I can tell you that he or she was probably right. The chance to relive your life is a precious gift, and the reason I know this is because I was able to do it, in a manner of speaking. Getting the chance didn't come free, and it certainly wasn't easy. I came very close to having my eyes shot out, not to mention being blown into little pieces. Plus I was left looking like something you'd find in the back of a junked refrigerator—on not one but two occasions. And, in addition, I was dragged through an emotional gutter.

Physical torture, mental torture. I'm not sure which is worse. I've put the story down here more or less the way it happened; more, probably, than less. I've embroidered a bit and taken in a seam here and there to make the story move faster than it actually did because, in spite of what you might hear to the contrary, the majority of investigative work is a dull, slogging grind. The attentive reader will note that it would have been hard for me to have made some of the observations I profess to making due to a particularly severe problem I was suffering from. However, the forgiving reader will accept this as one of the many exigencies of storytelling.

CHAPTER ONE

Coming out of it.

Light popping as if a kid were playing with louvered blinds. Focus brought me white sheets, white walls, the white rod of a bed rail, a seated figure in a crisp white uniform: a nurse. She was examining a fingernail, a stern-faced, middle-aged woman who looked up when I blinked as if my heavy eyelids had squeaked with fatigue. She rose and moved out of my vision, walked out of the plain white room I was in, apparently unconcerned with my immediate health which, as feeling and semi-awareness swam slowly back, didn't appear to be all that terrific. I took drowsy inventory: my ribs ached, and were strapped beneath my open pajama top. One arm had a plastic tube attached to it leading down from a bottle of clear liquid. My other arm was bandaged all the way to my wrist, the elbow throbbing. Below the waist the news wasn't too good, either: both knees were bandaged, and my balls ached and were painfully tender.

I thought that was about it until I became aware of a constriction on my head and under my chin. I raised my free arm and felt around. I was wearing a large gauze hat that came down over my ears. That was bad news, but there was worse to come: I hadn't the slightest idea of where I was or what had happened to me.

And even more disturbing, I didn't know who the "I" or the "me" was.

I didn't know my name.

If this was a dream I didn't like it. I tried to wake, but I felt enormously tired, and my eyes didn't want to pay attention.

The dream dragged on, an aural dimension entering into it.

I heard footsteps, then a quiet, modulated voice.

"Good morning. How are you feeling?"

I eased my wrapped head toward a white jacket worn by a smiling man with silver hair, a silver mustache, and fine golden eyebrows; a face made up from precious metals.

"Not so hot."

"I'm Doctor Wein."

"Can I have a drink?"

He handed me a mug from a side table. The liquid was cool and marvelous on my parched throat, and I had no trouble identifying the taste: orange juice. So I still remembered basic things.

"Your name is Wein, right?"

"Correct."

"Then it's just my old memory that's gone."

"Ah." Wein's metallic eyebrows inched inward; he didn't look as if he'd been prepared for the news. "What don't you remember?"

"Anything. Everything."

"You don't know your name?"

"No."

"Do you remember what happened to you?"

"No."

"Well, then." Wein pressed perfectly white teeth against his lower lip, then moved his head in a negative shake. "That's really too bad. There was no way of knowing your true condition until you regained consciousness. And, of course, amnesia's always in the cards in cases like yours."

"What is my case? What happened to me?" As well as

renewed fatigue, a slow shock was creeping up on me. This was for real! I really was a wreck in a hospital bed. While my sluggish mind wrestled with that charming little truth I watched Wein run a few simple tests: moving his fingers in front of my eyes, holding a wristwatch close to my bandaged ears, pressing the cut edge of a key against the soles of my feet.

"You were conscious a little while ago. You don't remember that?"

I did have a hazy recollection of waking up before and talking to somebody, perhaps the hard-faced nurse, but I couldn't pinpoint it.

"I'm not sure. Please. Tell me what happened to me."

"You were thrown from a car. You belly-flopped on the road. Two fractured ribs, multiple contusions, and a severe head wound when you bounced up against the median guard. The highway separator," Wein added, assuming, correctly, that I wouldn't know what he meant by a median guard. I got a quick mental picture of me crashing headfirst into a hard-edged metal stump and closed my eyes on the image.

"You received emergency treatment at Jamaica Hospital, then were brought here to Lenox Hill where my colleague, Doctor Blanton, performed surgery."

"Surgery? You mean he sewed me up?"

Wein's face was starched by a kind of bland seriousness when he broke the news.

"You've had brain surgery."

That stopped my questions. Brain surgery? Christ!

"You were comatose when you were brought in. A CAT scan revealed intracranial trauma. We operated immediately and removed a subdural clot from the left-side frontal lobe. Surprisingly there was no skull fracture. However, as we've

11

just now discovered, your injury has resulted in retrograde and posttraumatic amnesia. Just how deep and long-lasting this is we'll determine when you've healed a little more."

I heard Wein perfectly, heard what he said and understood half of it, but that fifty percent was a killer. I wasn't just temporarily bemused, my memory had been smashed out of my skull.

"It's permanent then, is that what you're really saying? My whole past is gone?"

"I wouldn't be that gloomy. The memory function is still a bit of a mystery to us. We think it's electrical movement between synapses, sparks flying between two contact points, if you like. Damage one of the contacts and the spark won't bridge. However, if a contact is merely dislodged, bumped out of alignment, so to speak, it can right itself any time, and memory is restored."

That sounded a little better, but it was still calamitous news.

"If I were you, Mr. Parrish, I'd look on the bright side."

"That's my name, Parrish?"

The nurse with the severe expression returned. Wein murmured something to her, and she produced a key and unlocked a drawer, extracted a wallet, and passed it to the man in the white coat. Wein handed it to me. With the movements of a sleepwalker I dipped into it with my one free hand. The first thing I found was all I needed: a photographic ID issued to Jeremy R. Parrish. It showed a guy in perhaps his mid-thirties with a strong-boned face, dark eyes confident to the point of challenging, a truculent tilt to the head. There was no way I was going to believe this guy was me; he looked like he was ready to start an argument. I asked for a mirror. The nurse found one on a side table, and held it up to me.

What a sight! Both my eyes were black and swollen, a heavy strip of plaster layered my nose, and with that crown of white gauze enlarging my head, it was hard to tell what or who I looked like.

"My God, I look half dead."

Wein's mustache stiffened slightly, no doubt because he thought I was being a crybaby. His expression said that he saw people every day without limbs, without organs, and here was I merely without a memory.

"You're getting off lightly, Mr. Parrish. An injury such as yours could have resulted in extensive brain damage. It could have left you blind, or dumb, or paralyzed—or all three." He gave that little lesson some time to sink in then said, in a more sympathetic tone, "We'll run some tests in a few days and check the parameters of the memory loss. Do you remember Sharon?"

"No."

"Tom?"

"No. Who are they?"

"Sharon's your girl. Tom's your brother. They've both been here on and off ever since you were brought in. I'll call them and tell them the good news."

Good news? He was speaking comparatively, as he'd explained, and of course it could have been worse; but to me the blankness in my mind was fearfully scary, I didn't *know* anything, had neither family nor friend as far as I knew, no matter what Wein said. In short, I was lost in the world because everybody in it would be a stranger.

"I'm sure one of them will come and see you this evening," Wein concluded.

"Could they come now? Ask them to come now."

That brought a tiny golden smile.

"I'm afraid not. You'll be asleep for the rest of the day."

"Asleep? I don't want to sleep. I'll sleep when I can remember a few things." I tried to push myself up on one elbow, but just that tiny piece of exertion and my body was pulsing as if I'd been whacked all over with heavy sticks. I fell back, fatigue like a swamp sucking me down. Wein's voice shrank in volume, then enlarged, gonging in my woozy head.

"You've got a lot of healing to do, Mr. Parrish. You'll feel extremely tired for at least a week. It takes the brain a little while to recover from being disturbed. You'll have trouble concentrating, and there'll be some confusion now and then. But after that you should see a marked improvement. Things will get closer to normal. So try not to get depressed. You'll get better, but it will be a gradual thing."

"How long? How long before I'm on my feet?"

"I'd say the prognosis is good. You're thirty-five with no excess body weight. You have an athletic build. As a general rule, the healthier you are going into surgery, the faster you recover."

Wein spoke to me a little longer about my condition, being cautiously cheery, told me he'd be back later, and left the nurse to administer some medication. Her humorless face was the last thing I saw before I drifted off. It wasn't conducive to sweet dreams, and I certainly didn't have any.

I was in a foreign country, in a store, trying to buy something, and they couldn't understand me. More to the point I couldn't understand myself as I was speaking a language I couldn't identify. I knew this was a dream for sure, although I would gladly have gone on living in it rather than face the reality that waking up brought. I'd half convinced myself that there was nothing at all wrong with me until my bodily hurts took over, and I heard the distant sound of a woman's

14

amplified voice paging a doctor. However, when I opened my eyes things had improved. The grim-faced nurse had been replaced by a far more attractive sight: a pretty woman in her late twenties.

"Hi," she said. There was warmth in that single word, and a look of love in her gray-green eyes. She had a full underlip and a fine, strong nose that escaped sharpness on account of the dimpled fullness of her chin. She leaned down to me, pressed those ripe lips softly against my cheek. The smell of her skin twigged something in my dead memory: a summer field? Summer flowers?

"You're Sharon?"

Disappointment lanced into her eyes; maybe a little hurt, too. It was clear that she'd been banking on me recognizing her. She nodded and tried to smile brightly, but it didn't work.

"Did Wein tell you about me?" I asked.

"He said your memory could come back any time."

"Or never."

"He told me that, too. But the important thing is, you're out of danger. And you don't have any—" Tears started in her eyes. She tried to hug me which was a bit of a chore being as wrapped up and immobile as I was. "Nobody could even guarantee you'd even wake up."

"I feel as though I haven't," I said into the sweet scent of her hair. "I have so many questions . . ."

She moved back, speared a finger at a cheekbone, and made a better job of a smile. "Doctor Wein said that the smallest thing could jog your memory back into place. A smell, a taste, the sight of something, the sound of something. A big or small event in your life."

"Let's start with a big event. What exactly happened to me? Where was I going?"

"We're not sure. You didn't discuss your work with me much. But you had a packed suitcase with you, so you could have been going to the airport."

"What is my work?"

"You're a skip tracer."

"What's that?"

"You find people who've walked away from their responsibilities."

"Who do I work for?"

"The Acis Corporation. Your boss is a man named Al Charmain."

None of this rang any bells, not the slightest tinkle.

"How long have we known each other?"

"Seven months. We've been living together for the last five."

"Whereabouts?"

"East Twenty-ninth."

"And my family?"

"There's just your brother, Tom. He'll be here tomorrow." Sharon took my half-bandaged hand gently in hers. "Everything will come back, darling. It just may take a little time."

Well, nothing came back in the next twenty minutes, during which, between small, ten-second mental lapses, I continued with my questions. Not a single answer sparked any response; it was like discussing the unmet patient in the next room.

It must have been depressing for Sharon, too, although she was extremely supportive and cheerful. I wasn't sorry when a nurse—one I hadn't seen before—arrived to shoo Sharon away and give me some medication. Sharon kissed me, told me she'd return the next evening, and left me drowsily beginning to feel the effect of the pills I'd just taken. I had a crystal-clear lucid period before I dropped off, and was able to see the true absurdity of my situation: this lovely woman whom I'd been living with for five months, and who clearly loved me, evoked nothing even close to the same response in me. And yet I must have loved her in return, or I assumed I had, but the memory loss had wiped out emotional recall as well. As for all the information she'd given me, I wasn't thrilled with it; especially my job. It would have been easier on my state of mind had I woken up to find myself a man of importance, of some lasting value, but a skip tracer? It sounded a little demeaning going after people who couldn't pay their bills. The job seemed harsh and tough, and again I had to wonder about what I was really like, because that kind of job suited the face of the guy on my ID, but it certainly didn't fit the way I felt about the world.

Around about then I realized my lucid period was all over. Hell, what did I know about the world? So far it consisted of a hospital room, a doctor, two nurses, and a girlfriend. So who was I to say how I felt?

Who was I anyway?

Jerry Parrish, tracer of missing persons.

Big deal.

CHAPTER TWO

I woke up next morning feeling a lot better mentally; the fuzzy periods were much further apart, and I found I could focus my thoughts on something and not lose sight of it.

The improvement put me in a better frame of mind to receive a new visitor: Tom, my brother.

He was a big guy like me, and I thought I could see some resemblance in his face to the one on my ID, a face I was still reluctant to lay claim to. Tom must have come from the sunny side of the family because he hardly stopped smiling.

"So," he said, dwarfing a small chair, "the sleeping beauty awakes."

"You're Tom, huh?"

"That's me."

"Did you talk to Doc Wein?"

"Sure. Talked to Sharon, too. They tell me you have a bit of a memory problem."

"You might say."

He spread his large hands. The grin on his face said that he thought this might be some kind of huge joke. "You sure you don't remember me?"

"I'm sorry."

"*You're* sorry. You owe me a hundred bucks. *I'm* sorry." He had a big, booming laugh; he seemed like a nice guy. "Boy," he said, showing his large teeth, "I'm one guy I thought you'd never forget. I was the big brother who was always tough on the kid. I must've given you a thousand Chinese burns. Tied you to a post in a rainstorm once. You don't remember that? I lured you out into the backyard for a

19

game of Indians, tied you up and ran inside and watched you getting soaked."

I had to smile at the guy, and the anecdote. "I don't remember."

"Billy Hepplewhite? How about that name? You and me and Billy used to raid old man Atwell's apricots, and one night he fired a load of saltpeter at us. You're not gonna tell me you've forgotten an assful of saltpeter, are you?"

I just looked at Tom, but he rattled on, trying for something that would hit the mark.

"Okay, how about the '73 Chevy we went halvies in? We'd double date, go to the Highland Drive-In, me and Evlyn Spink, and you and Janeen Frawley. She of the beautiful boobs? Jesus, if you can't remember a pair like that, there really is something wrong with you."

He laughed again, a little too tightly this time, as if he were covering for that last phrase.

"Where was our home?"

"Upstate. Jamestown. Hot summers and snowy winters. Our folks had a small farm and a big house heated by a Stanley stove. You and me cut about ten years' worth of wood for that thing. You must still have the blisters; I know I have."

"Tell me about our parents."

He pulled something from his jacket pocket: a small photograph in a cardboard holder. It showed a man in a plaid shirt and a straw hat peering uncertainly at the camera. Next to him stood a woman in a faded flower-print dress. They were both in their sixties maybe, both carrying things. In the background was a wood-and-wrought-iron veranda belonging to a rambling clapboard house that needed painting. I stared at the print, my spirits sinking. If I wasn't going

to remember my folks, I wasn't going to remember anybody.

"Papa died in '78," Tom volunteered. "Ma, three years
later."

My lack of recognition saddened my brother, and the
smile went out of his eyes. This was clearly supposed to be
his ace in the hole. He'd more than likely been expecting
my face to light up in sudden recall and for everything to
come flooding back.

I handed him the print.

"What do you do, Tom?"

"I manage the A & P in Bronxville."

"The A & P?"

"It's a supermarket." He tried another tack: recent memories.

"I got a store discount off a turkey last Christmas. You
and Sharon came up for dinner. Karen cooked it. Karen, my
wife. Your sister-in-law." He stopped talking, and some silence built up between us. He got to his feet and gently
punched his fist toward my shoulder. "Hang in there, kid.
It's just the shock of the surgery."

"Sure," I said.

Tom came to visit twice a week, bringing his wife on a
couple of occasions, a big-boned pleasant woman who fluttered maternally around me, constantly asking me was there
anything I wanted. You bet there was, but it was still refusing to put in an appearance. Sharon came every evening,
and between my two main visitors I discovered just about
everything there was to know about Jerry Parrish. I also had
some Get Better phone calls from my boss, and some visits
from friends whom, of course, I didn't know. But I found I
could fake it if I just stuck to generalities—hospital life, the

accident, my exterior injuries, etc.—and if anybody recognized my major problem they didn't let on.

I spent six weeks mending in that hospital room, and during that time Sharon arranged for a tutor to come for a few hours daily. It was Wein who suggested it. His position was that while I should remain confident of recovering my memory, there was no telling when that might happen and, in the meantime, I was functionally dumb. So I went to school again. I studied four basic subjects: American and World History and American and World Geography. As Wein explained I hadn't forgotten the natural, instinctive things: breathing, eating, speaking. Everything my body had learned to do would still be with me, but just about all of my acquired knowledge was on hold.

I found out that a person doesn't have to be a mental whiz to have stored a lot of facts over a thirty-five-year time span. I had to relearn everything and everybody: Washington, Lincoln, Alexander the Great, Julius Caesar, Louis XVI. We did a little literature, too. I met Huckleberry Finn, Sherlock Holmes, Captain Ahab, Robin Hood. When I started I didn't know whether Los Angeles was east or west of the Mississippi, or what the Mississippi was, or how to spell it. I didn't even know whether I lived east or west of Fifth Avenue.

I read lots of magazines and newspapers, too; found out what was happening, and who was making it happen. Plus, I had access to TV videos on the natural sciences. Most of the programs were designed for sixth-graders, but they were perfect for somebody like me who couldn't tell an elephant from a giraffe. About three days before I was due to be released, Wein and his team ran some final tests on me for which they had to knock me out. I don't think the tests told them anything they didn't already know, but I had to assume they were worth trying.

I spent the last couple of days getting my land legs back, walking the corridors, chatting to people, moving slowly around the wards. I was feeling fine physically: my ribs and my abrasions had mended, and all my bandages, except for the one on my head, had been removed. This bandage was a lot smaller than it had been. It was only there to protect the ridge that had been raised on my scalp by the surgery. It ran across the top of my head from one ear to the other, and I was ordered to keep a dressing on it for some time yet.

My black and swollen eyes had long lost their bruising, and the break in my nose had been expertly repaired so I was back to looking something like my old self. Although when I say that it's not strictly true. While the face in my mirror was now revealed to be the same as the one on my ID, there was still a difference in . . . what shall I call it? Attitude? The spark, the force, the truculence, if you like, was gone from my eyes, gone from the set of my jaw. I was happy to see the change; head bandage and all, I liked my new look better.

Doc Wein popped in once after the final tests, wished me luck, told me not to try out for the Yankees straight away, shook my hand, and left. I never did get to meet the surgeon who'd performed the operation, nor did I get sight of his no doubt enormous bill, or any of the hospital costs. Everything was taken care of by the Acis Corporation's insurance plan—a good thing because, otherwise, the shock of six weeks' hospital expenses would have put me right back into bed again.

On the great day of my discharge Sharon arrived with some of my clothes, the ones I'd been brought in wearing having been ripped to shreds and covered in blood.

Sharon looked terrific. She had a full figure, and the clingy dress she wore showed it off in a politely sexy way. So with this good-looking woman on my arm, and wearing jeans and slip-ons, and a cotton jacket, plus a head bandage like a pirate's bandana, we went out into a spring Sunday afternoon in New York City. It was a fine day with high blue skies, and it seemed like a great start for my new life.

But the great start didn't last very long.

Less than twelve hours later the first long, dark shafts of doubt began to creep toward me, and my brave new world took on a serious wobble.

CHAPTER THREE

Home turned out to be a huge loftlike apartment above a street-level stationery store that Sharon said had once been a Greek restaurant.

We rented the apartment from a painter who was on a more or less permanent working vacation on the Cape. The place wasn't zoned for residential living so it was a touch illegal, but, according to Sharon, the rent we paid, versus the amount of living space we had, made it a real bargain in spite of its limited amenities. These turned out to be a tiny open kitchen, and a bathroom that was little more than a sectioned-off area containing a john, a handbasin, and a metal shower stall. But the living room was big enough for a running track, and the dining room/bedroom not much smaller.

One closet held my clothes, and a shelf made of house bricks and sawn boards supported my stereo and tape collection and about twenty books. The books were mainly paperbacks—thrillers mostly—plus some large-format hardcovers. The music, when I played a tape, was nothing out of the ordinary as far as I could tell. I poked around among my things, finding very little of interest and nothing of any possible sentimental value. When I mentioned this to Sharon she told me that I'd never expressed any interest in owning things, preferring to travel light. There certainly wasn't much to show for thirty-five years of living.

"What were my hobbies? Didn't anything fascinate me?"

Sharon was rattling things in the kitchen. She came out

carrying two coffee mugs, a frown seaming her high fore-head.

"You mustn't talk about yourself in the past tense, Jerry. You keep doing it."

"Yeah, you're right. It's just that I'm having a little trouble getting to know myself." I picked up one of the larger books, a gun catalogue. "Do I like guns?"

"Yes, you do."

"Do I own one?"

"I don't think so. I certainly hope not. I hate the things."

"What else do I like?"

"Sports."

"Which ones?"

"Football. Boxing. You watch them on TV."

"A real intellectual, huh?"

She handed me a smile with the mug of coffee. "Mascu-line pursuits, that's all. You have a fine curiosity about a lot of things, but you're just not a collector. Your interests aren't reflected in your belongings."

We killed the remainder of the afternoon just lazing around the apartment, Sharon listening to music while she worked on a painting—it was just a hobby but to my un-trained eye she was damn good—while I rested and leafed through my gun books. They were full of photographs of deadly-looking revolvers and automatics, lethal shotguns, and fat-barreled rifles. If I'd been attracted to these things before, I certainly wasn't now. And that was interesting in a disturbing kind of way: I was beginning to wonder if my head injury had changed more than just my recall ability.

We went out for dinner; to a little Lebanese place down the block. It was on Lexington near Twenty-seventh; I'd decided to read the street signs wherever I went so as to get to know the city again. A short, dark-skinned man with rheumy eyes and a heavy body greeted me in what I assumed was a Middle Eastern accent.

"Mr. Parrish. Too long. Where you keep yourself?"

"I've been away on business."

"Bizniz. Always bizniz," he said, his morose eyes flicking to my head bandage. He signaled an elderly waiter. 'Our bes' table for these good peoples."

The waiter fussed over us as if we'd been there many times, which Sharon said we had.

"We practically own stock in the place," she told me after she'd ordered our usual drinks. Mine turned out to be a gin and tonic, although I had to ask Sharon what it was. It was my first taste of booze in my new life, and I found it bitter and sweet-scented at the same time.

"I think I probably missed this."

Sharon laughed.

I scanned the menu. "What do we usually choose?"

"The chicken for me, the beef for you."

We got the food organized, then sat sipping our drinks. The place was candlelit and pretty, the customers looked much like us: couples, local people who'd hopped around the corner instead of cooking in. Sharon was cheery and smiling throughout dinner, but I could tell she was putting on a brave face. I think she'd been hoping that the return to the apartment, the sight of my own things, the neighborhood, this little restaurant, would punch a hole in the blank wall inside my head; especially the restaurant which she said we always came to for little celebrations. But none of it meant anything; I was still as memory dead as ever. Worse, in fact, because the things I was supposed to like or be interested in just didn't attract me. Like my beef dish, for example. I didn't like it at all. I'd had beef in the hospital— and, granted, hospital cooking had to be pretty ordinary—

but if this had been my favorite dish it certainly wasn't any longer. On the other hand, I'd tried the chicken Sharon had ordered, and loved it. So it appeared that my injury had altered the signals my taste buds sent to my patched-up brain. Another piece of evidence of the difference between the old and the new me.

We left the restaurant around nine, bowed out the door by the sad-faced owner, and strolled south in the pleasant temperature. Sharon wanted to take a look in a store that specialized in Haitian masks, something which she said she liked. I knew from my book learning that Haiti was in the Caribbean somewhere, although I couldn't have drawn an accurate map.

The first of the incidents that later nagged at me happened just after we'd window-shopped the Haitian store. We'd taken a circuitous route back to the apartment, and it was around Twenty-fifth, I think, that I heard a voice call out, "Hey, Jack!"

I looked around. On the opposite sidewalk, outside a bar, a guy was smiling at me. He was my age, wearing jeans and a striped sweater and carrying a full grocery sack. He seemed to be waiting for me to greet him in return, and when I didn't, he opened his mouth to say something else but didn't get the chance: a big guy in a leather jacket, striding down the sidewalk, bumped into him and angrily told him to for crissakes look where he was going. The man in the striped sweater claimed he'd just been standing there and hadn't been going anywhere. The other guy didn't want to let it go at that, and started to argue belligerently.

"Come on," Sharon said, taking my arm. "That bar gets some real lowlifes. Drags down the whole neighborhood."

We walked on. I glanced back at the altercation as we made the corner. The guy in the sweater had taken a sauce

28

bottle out of his grocery sack and was telling the leather jacket to back off. The incident stayed with me for a while although Sharon seemed to shrug it off as just one of the negatives of living in the city: the quick and sudden violence that could pop out of nowhere. I'd forgotten about it by the time we reached the apartment because I had something else on my mind, something that I'd been thinking and wondering about for quite a while now. And it was simply this: Sharon was my girl, and during weeks of visits by her in the hospital I'd naturally got to wondering what it was going to be like when we were at last alone together and I could function properly. I have to confess that, especially during the last third of my convalescence, I'd been getting pretty horny what with this lovely woman pressing herself against me to kiss me hello and good-bye. I'd already slept with her several times in my imagination, and now that I was about to do it in actual fact, I was excited, and curious, and maybe a little reticent, too.

I took a shower—quite a feat in that tiny metal cubicle— and when I came out with a towel around me, Sharon was wearing pajamas and turning down the bed. With a simple and easy grace she slid her arms around my shoulders and we kissed for the first time for real. Her mouth opened like a soft flower, and her body flowed into mine. We hit the bed naked. There was no foreplay; she seemed to be as hungry as I was, and I was on top of her and driving inside her before I knew it. It was frantic and impassioned, and over very quickly. But that was just for starters. We settled down and made love again slowly, carefully. For me it was a wonderful yet a strange experience. It was a little like making love to a woman I'd picked up at a party because, while I knew Sharon's voice and face and much of her mind, her body was brand-new to me; the jut of her bony hips rising into me, her hot, chunky nipples, the grainy silk of her sex, the clutch of her strong legs—the intimate things I must have known and been well used to were all a first-time experience in my present state, as was fornication itself.

"Forever," Sharon sighed into my ear, "it seems like you were gone from me forever."

Later, with her warm presence curled into me in sleep, it occurred to me that I might very well be gone from her forever; not in spirit maybe, and certainly not in body, but irretrievably in mind.

I woke to see the red hour numeral in a digital clock blink silently in its magical change, a five becoming a six.

Early-morning sounds pressed against the windows in the front room, a truck making an early-morning delivery to the stationery store below. But the truck wasn't what had pulled me out of my slumber. Something was buzzing around my mind; nebulous things that sleep had molded into awkward and disturbing shapes. I can't say I felt that something was wrong, it was more like everything not being quite right, if there's a difference. Part of it was that guy outside the bar. It really had seemed that he'd been speaking to me when he'd called me Jack. Had he known me? If your name was Jerry, did people call you Jack? But then nobody else had used that name; to Tom and Karen and the friends who'd phoned or come to see me I'd been Jerry. So it had to be a case of mistaken identity. But then that big guy had bumped into him, starting an argument and stopping the guy in the striped sweater from crossing the street to talk to me, or so it had seemed.

And Sharon's comment about the bar being full of low-lifes, and yet neither of those men had been coming out of the bar, they'd been moving along the sidewalk.

On the surface the whole thing didn't seem much and yet I couldn't shake the feeling of unease. I put a lot of it down to the fact that today, the one coming up, was my first official day back in society: today was Monday, and I was due to start my old job again. I was more than a touch apprehensive because I didn't see how I could be equipped to do it now. I didn't know the first thing about tracing people; I didn't even know where you started or who you talked to, or any of the steps in between. I just couldn't see how I was going to walk straight back into a job I had no recollection of.

I drifted off to sleep again, dwelling on this, and woke an hour later to an empty bed and the rich aroma of coffee. Sharon brought me a cup, and a doughnut to dunk, then we took turns in the shower cubicle. I'll have to say that the sight of water glistening on Sharon's luscious curves got me all ready to go for a repeat of last night's exertions, and I made unmistakable moves in that direction.

Sharon laughed and flicked her towel at me. "Down, boy. You want to be late your first day back?"

"I'm not sure I'm ready for my first day back."

"Yes, you are. So let's get dressed and get out of here."

She gave me a polite little pep talk, positive, hang-in-there-and-hack-it stuff; dutiful strong support. But very little of her confidence rubbed off on me.

We left the apartment together. The deal was, she'd take me to my job the first day, and from then on I had to find my own way around the city. We walked west to Broadway, and caught a crowded bus uptown to Thirty-fourth Street. We worked fairly close to each other, which was nice. Sharon was an assistant buyer at Lord & Taylor, a department store whose ads I'd seen in the *Times*. My office, the job with the Acis Corporation, was located at Thirty-third

Street, just west of Fifth. Sharon walked me to the corner of Thirty-third, pointed the way, kissed me, wished me luck, and left me to drag myself down the block.

It wasn't a very attractive trip. Thirty-fourth is a wide, busy thoroughfare but Thirty-third is like its back alley, the structures drab and unimpressive except, of course, for the Empire State Building, but that belongs on Thirty-fourth. Office blocks crouched in its gigantic shadow like mushrooms around an oak giving the street a dark and dank look.

I was looking for 135, and was sorry when I found it: a nondescript gray building with a grubby lobby, a cracked marble floor, a couple of tired elevators, and a client board that needed cleaning. I rode up to the fourth floor with a group of silent Monday-morning people, and stopped outside of room 415. Gold lettering on a half-glass door proclaimed the national headquarters of The Acis Corp. Some headquarters! An outer office held a chipped desk and a green metal filing cabinet which had seen better days. The desk contained a typewriter with an unfinished letter in the roller, a box of Kleenex, and an overflowing out tray. The paper-bag brown walls featured a single piece of decoration: a terrible drawing of a tearful clown attached to a calendar.

I knocked on the door of the inner office. An indistinct voice responded with what I took to be an invitation, and I walked into an office that was a duplicate of the one I'd just left. This one, however, was inhabited—by a fat man savaging an overstuffed hamburger. "Jerry!" he said cheerfully. Fifty pounds overweight, he got up with an effort. "Good to see you back, kid." He wiped his right hand on his pants pocket. His handshake was soft and fleshy, like the man himself. He looked like he might have been a wrestler some time in the past. He had a fat round face, a bulbous forehead, and wrinkled flesh under his chin folded around his jaw. He wore some kind of loose, sagging lounge suit that did nothing to shave his bulk. He reminded me of a guy I'd met in Lenox Hill Hospital, an ex-boozer who'd saved his liver but had been left with all the calorific residue hanging from his body.

"Sit down. Listen, I woulda brought you some grapes to the hospital only they woulda taken one look at me and I never woulda made it outa there."

"Thanks for your calls, anyway." I took the chair opposite his green metal desk. It held some papers, two telephones, the half-eaten burger, and a candy-striped milk-shake container. I knew this was my boss, Al Charmain, but I hadn't expected him to look like this.

"How's the old memory box? Any progress?" He picked up the burger and contemplated a good place to go into it. I assumed this was his breakfast.

"I'm afraid not."

He sucked noisily at the milk shake, waved the cup. "You don't remember any of this, in all its glory?"

"Nope. I don't even remember my brother."

"Your brother. Ted, is it?"

"Tom."

He'd regained his chair but reseated himself again. In addition to a cushion he was sitting on a thick wad of sponge rubber. "Well," he said, grinning at me, "I guess I can tell you all my rotten jokes for the first time."

"I guess you can," I said. I hated being there; the place was awful. This was where I worked? This slobby fat man was my boss? I was having a hard time with it.

"You're looking good." The words came out around a mouthful of food. His tiny, flesh-shrouded eyes roamed my head bandage. "I like the chapeau. You look like a biker. No pain? You all mended?"

"Good as new."

"It's a wonder. I saw the car. Looked like a bowling ball. Cops said you hit an oil slick. I always told you to get a piece of Detroit iron. Those little Jap imports got no protection."

It was the first time anybody had mentioned any of the details of my accident, apart from Doc Wein. Sharon and Tom had stayed away from it, and I gathered by their reticence that I might have been negligent. The oil slick was good news; I didn't want to think of myself as some clown driver who'd lost control of an automobile.

"So," Charmain said. "You ready to go to work?" He lifted the top bun of the burger, pinched off a piece of meat or gristle, and tossed it toward a far corner of the office.

"I don't think I'm gonna be much good to you. Whatever I knew about finding people I've forgotten."

"A memory problem's not gonna affect you, not as far as the job goes. I talked with your doctor. He said your instincts are still in place, and that's what you need in this business, instinct."

I was sorry to hear it. I would have been happy to have been fired so I could've said good-bye to this guy and his crummy office.

"And Jerry, my boy," Charmain continued, "you got instinct like Mother used to make. You got a gift."

"What kind of a gift?"

When Charmain shrugged, his whole upper body quivered for a moment.

"You get hunches. Very smart hunches."

"You mean I guess? That's how I find people?"

"It's more than a guess. It's like you get a flash. Like tuning a radio, going down the dial, and all of a sudden there's the ball game you're looking for. I've seen you do it. It's fantastic."

"Have I always had this . . . gift?"

"Far as I know. You told me once your mother was some kind of psychic. Gotta be in the genes."

I pondered this bit of news; I'd had no intimation that I had any talent out of the ordinary. Nobody had mentioned it, and it certainly hadn't manifested itself during my stay in the hospital. But then I hadn't been looking for anybody.

The fat man slurped up the dregs of his milk shake, dropped the cup into a metal wastebasket, and dabbed at his mouth with his fingers. "You got any other questions?"

"I have a statement. It's not gonna work. I'm not even exactly sure what this organization is or what I do in it."

"So I'll tell you. This is the head office of the Acis Corporation, right? We find guys who've run out on alimony payments. Wives who take the Volvo and beat it with the local tennis pro. Kids who bust out for the streets of San Francisco. We find 'em and let the client know where they are, and for that we get a nice fat fee. I got eight guys and two chicks out in the field working for me, so I only need a phone and a desk, which is how come I got this terrific, award-winning office space. So that's what the company does. And what you do is get results for the company. And you are one shit hot person-finder because, like I say, you got the gift."

I watched Charmain half rise in his chair, adjust the foam rubber cushion, and sink back into it with a wince of discomfort. I wasn't sure if he was telling me the truth or merely ladling me with compliments in order to win me over. But why try to win me over if I wasn't any good at my job?

"This gift, as you call it. How long have I had it?"

"Don't ask me. But I know you had it in your last job."

"In insurance? My brother told me I used to be a claims adjuster."

"That you were. And you were damn good at it, too. You have an ability to know when people are jerking you around, to get inside their heads. It's the next best thing to reading minds."

"It doesn't seem to be working now."

Charmain started a throaty chuckle as he got what I meant. "You don't believe me? You will. You'll get a flash soon enough once you start after Frohman again."

"Frohman?"

"The guy you were chasing before you were derailed." Floating amidst the papers on Charmain's desk was a red folder. He pushed it toward me. "Werner Frohman. A Kraut. Came over here about a year back. Took to democracy and the consumer society like a duck to water. Got himself a deck of credit cards and spent a fortune, took a loan from a finance company, paid the bills and stiffed the company. Naturally they want his ass."

"How close did I get to this guy before I ran off the road?"

"Jerry, old man, that is the question. You don't work like the other guys on the payroll. They call in with progress reports like they're supposed to. But not you. You never have. I must've sent you out that door two dozen times, and I never see you again until you come back, sometimes months later, with the address of whoever you're chasing, and a swindle sheet guaranteed to give the client a miscarriage."

"Was it the same this time? Didn't I tell you anything?"

"Oh, sure. You deigned to call in one day, let me know you were getting close. But you didn't elaborate. If you'd kept a written record, like you're supposed to, you could start off where you left off. But now you'll be starting from scratch, so it's entirely possible, probably probable, you'll run over your old tracks."

I took the red folder and checked into it, doing more thinking than reading. Run over my old tracks? I supposed it was a possibility if I was going to start all over again, that is, if Charmain was right about my handicap not holding me back. But he had to be wrong, surely. How could anybody function efficiently at anything if all their training had gone down the tubes? I closed the folder. I didn't want any part of this job. I didn't want this messy guy as my boss. And I wasn't at all interested in some refugee whose sudden freedom had gone to his head. But I knew I had to have a shot at it if only because of Charmain's last remark. If there was a chance the job would take me down the same paths I'd trod before, it could well be the vehicle that would bring my memory back.

"Where do I start?"

The fat man, gulping down the last of his breakfast, spoke through a bolus of bread and beef. "I don't know. I'm not gonna tell you what to do. If I did I wouldn't need you."

"Anything else?"

"Yeah. Call in from time to time for a change. And listen, if you're gonna total a car again, make it an Olds or a Buick, okay? Stay away from those cute little imports."

I left Charmain searching for crumbs in his take-out carton and went down into the dreary confines of Thirty-third Street. I felt ambivalent about the interview, bothered, on one hand, that I worked for a man who threw food around his office, but excited at the prospect of finding my old self.

I wandered into a coffee shop, took a booth, ordered coffee, and studied the report in the red folder. Werner

Frohman, a German Jew, had emigrated to Israel, spent some time in Europe, then moved to the United States. He'd lived in New York and worked in New Jersey as an industrial chemist. According to the report, he'd gone on quite a spending spree: a Chrysler, designer clothes, an eight-thousand-dollar stereo setup. It appeared that I'd at least been in the habit of keeping some kind of records because included in the folder was a report, with my name typed at the bottom, listing the bases covered in my initial search; mainly airline reservations. Frohman had either not flown anywhere or he'd used an alias or driven or taken the train.

A black-and-white photograph was clipped to this sheet, Werner Frohman's name written on the back. He certainly didn't look like the type who'd go in for fancy clothes; he looked thin and frail with a long, consumptive body and large eyes that seemed placed a little ahead of his slim, lugubrious face. I assumed that his personal details, and this photograph, were all I'd had to go on when I'd begun my original quest, and I wondered where I would have started. Perhaps with his last two addresses: his residence and his place of employment.

In spite of my dislike for the project, I was curious to see if I did have an instinct for the work as Charmain had claimed, so I got started. I left the coffee shop and hailed a cab.

"One twenty-seven West Thirteenth."

"Aw, shit," the driver said. "Not the Village. I always get lost. Goddamn streets run every whichway."

And that was my first piece of information from a stranger in my search for Werner Frohman.

There was going to be a lot more; some of it a little more disturbing than a description of a neighborhood street pattern.

The woman who answered the door wore a voluminous paisley shift and too much makeup, her eyebrows penciled semicircles, her mouth lavish with lip gloss. Her hair looked as if it had been dry-cleaned.

"Hi. My name's Parrish. I'm with the Acis Corporation." I held up the photograph. "I understand that this man lived here. Werner Frohman. I'm trying to trace him."

The woman had started nodding her head before I got halfway through.

"Yeah, I know. You told me that the first time around, but he ain't been back."

As simple as that: I'd knocked on a door and a woman with a painted face had given me a glimpse of myself. I felt a surge of excitement, and a realization at the same time: I was on the track of two people—Werner Frohman and Jerry Parrish.

"Was this about nine, ten weeks back?"

" 'Bout that. You must be a busy boy, you can't remember. What happened to your head?"

She was looking at me as if I were some kind of an idiot. It was to be expected; if I was going to be asking people the same questions I'd asked them before, they were going to wonder what was wrong with me.

"Would you mind if I took a look at his room?"

The woman shifted her considerable weight, held the door open just enough to have a conversation. "I told you the first time, it's rerented. It still is. I can't let anybody in without I get the tenant's permission, and I'm not gonna waste time trying to get it."

The rebuff didn't matter; if I hadn't got in before, then it hadn't helped me.

"Did he ever say anything about having any relations in this country?"

"No. You asked me that, too." She peered at me, slitting her eyes and thrusting her head forward. "It *was* you, wasn't it? You look a little different, the bandage and all. And you're not as"—she searched for a suitable word—*"pushy,* either."

I stored that observation and essayed a little grin. "I'm sorry to ask you everything twice, but I lost my notes. Did he ever mention any friends? Do you know what his interests were? Any hobbies?" The questions just popped into my mouth; I didn't have to think about them. It really didn't surprise me because, as Al Charmain had inferred, the main thrust of the job was asking simple common-sense questions.

"I never talked to the guy. He slipped the rent under the door every week till he took off without a word."

"Did he stiff you for the last week's rent?"

"He knew better than to try. I would've slashed the tires of that car of his."

"Did he park it outside?"

"Nah. We got alternate side parking here. It's a real hernia moving your car every night. He kept it in a lot around the corner. I already told you that, remember?"

I gave her the helpless grin again. "Without my notes I'm lost. Where is this parking lot?"

The woman blinked, faking pain. "Between Greenwich and West Fourth. Now you're gonna ask me if he was friendly with the other tenants, right?"

"Right."

"Jesus, I feel like I'm watching a rerun. I told you before, he kept to himself. He didn't speak the lingo that good anyway. He sounded like the foreign psychiatrist in all them

40

dumb jokes." There was a pause. I was wondering what else to question her about, but nothing sprang to mind.

"Look, um"—this was the embarrassing part—"when I was here before, did I ask you anything else?"

The woman sucked at her teeth, annoyed by the interrogation now. "Yeah. You asked me if I'd rather sleep with you or Kevin Costner, and I said Kevin Costner. I also said good-bye."

She backed inside, the door slammed, and I was left looking at its brightly painted woodwork. My first working interview had ended on a sour note, but I was cheered by the experience all the same. I'd apparently asked all the same questions I'd asked the first go-round and, while I'd looked foolish doing it this time, I'd got the info. So maybe I could function at this job after all without benefit of a memory. Buoyed by this tiny triumph I decided to go ahead and do what I'd probably done next: check on Frohman at his workplace.

The red folder told me that his job had been in Jersey City, and I knew from my hospital geography lessons that the state of New Jersey was just across the Hudson. I vaguely recalled that the subway ran underneath the river, but I opted for a rental car so I could see the sights. I found an agency by checking a phone book. Renting was no problem—I had a license and a credit card—and driving was no problem, either; it was one of those learned mechanical functions that Doc Wein told me I wouldn't have any trouble with. The only difficulty was finding my way around, but a road map from the rental agency solved that. I found the Holland Tunnel after a couple of tries and, after emerging in the Garden State, eventually arrived in Jersey City.

I'd better admit right here that not everything a person forgets is going to be missed. Nobody could possibly care that much if they could never recall Jersey City, at least the part I was in. It appeared to be nothing but a succession of grim and smelly factories, and the one Frohman had been employed at—it manufactured agricultural pesticides—was perhaps the grimmest and most aromatic of them all: two stories of blackened brick and murky glass tagged on to a potholed parking lot.

I spoke to a woman who ran the personnel department, and was delighted to find myself still on my trail. Like the colorful landlady in the Village, this woman wondered why I was back asking the same questions about Werner Frohman. I told her something close to the truth: that the trail had gone cold so I was starting over from scratch, hoping to spot something this time I might have missed at our first interview. She was an obliging person and didn't mind reiterating what she'd told me ten weeks back. Frohman didn't owe them anything except a resignation notice; he'd simply called up one morning, said that he was quitting, and given no reason. He hadn't even picked up the half paycheck that had been owed him. He'd been doing theoretical work on a new kind of pesticide. He'd left all his notes behind and they proved that he'd been nowhere near the point where he could have sold anything to a competitor. The woman told me that Frohman had kept to himself and played not the slightest part in the limited social life of the company. She had the same theory as his ex-landlady: that his shyness stemmed from his heavy accent. However, I found this not to be so. I hung around till the lunch break and got to talk with some of his colleagues. One of the chemists was German, and he told me that even with somebody who spoke his own language, Frohman had been guarded about forming friendships. He also said he'd been under the impression that Frohman had been working on something unrelated to his immediate job, but he had no details.

I wasn't allowed into the lab itself because of security, but I was able to get a look at his locker. Naturally there was no old brochure for California, no leftover note about a plane reservation for New Orleans. It was just empty space. Driving back toward Manhattan I thought about what I'd learned so far. Not much, but I'd begun to form a picture of the man I was trying to find, and he just didn't seem to be the type to go on a buying binge and spend a wad of somebody else's money. I knew very little about people and what they might do or not do, but that seemed obvious.

I decided to check on him at the parking lot he'd used mainly because it was the only other place that I knew he'd gone on any regular basis. I retraced my route back under the river wondering where I'd made the breakthrough before, the one that had allowed me to call Charmain and tell him I was getting close to the quarry. Had I been close? So far there was just the merest glimmer of his trail. It was possible I'd been exaggerating my success. I had no real reason to suspect I'd cheated; it was just that, more and more, I was getting the impression that the old me had been different from the new me. Frohman's landlady had spotted the difference, too. Less pushy, she'd said.

There was a huge question building here, and it was simply this: had the brain injury, and subsequent repair, resulted in behavioral change? A personality shift? It was something I didn't feel capable of addressing at that moment because, if the answer was yes, the possible ramifications of such an event were more than I cared to contemplate.

I returned the rental car and got a cab to Greenwich Street, to the place the landlady told me Frohman had kept his automobile. It was a corner lot attached to a row of brownstones whose Victorian elegance had been allowed to fade gently away. I doubted the lot had ever been anything more than it was, a cleared space of broken asphalt with the skeletons of some scrubby bushes struggling against a rusty chain-link fence. It held a dozen cars that were jammed together and in a tight garbage-strewn corner a tiny office constructed from an old packing crate turned on its end and covered with peeling tar paper. The man who ambled out of it was dressed like a farmer for some reason: blue coveralls, a heavy checked shirt, rubber boots, and a tartan wool cap pulled low down on his straggly hair. A tall guy with slow, laconic movements.

"Help you?" he asked.

"I hope so. I'd like a little information about somebody who used to park here."

The man pocketed the twenty-dollar bill I handed him as if it were in settlement of a long-standing debt. He asked me his name.

"Frohman. He's German."

His answer told me I was still doing okay.

"Oh, sure." The tartan hat bobbed up and down. "Thought you looked familiar. Didn't find him, huh?"

"Not yet, so I thought I'd start over, see if I maybe missed something."

The man had a large bunch of keys on a leather thong. He spun the keys in a circle, and the jingling sound accompanied his words.

"Well, I ain't seen him lately. Not since he up and left."

"I've forgotten what kind of car he drove. Something fancy, wasn't it?"

"Fancy? It was an '81 Montego. Nothing cute about it. It was an old car. And with Frohman behind the wheel it got

44

older fast." The parking guy grunted, swung the keys in a reverse direction.

"Sheesus, what a driver that guy was. He shoulda owned a tank."

"Lousy driver, huh?"

"Lousy? He coulda drove in the demo derby. He put about five more years on that car in a coupla months. He'd take it out in the morning, bring it back in the evening with a headlight busted or a fender bent. A rolling calamity, that one."

"Did you tell me this before?"

"Man, you got a memory like a tea strainer. Sure, I told you. You said something about some people should have their license revoked. I go along with that. I have to battle clowns every day on the FDR."

I handed the guy one of my Acis cards, asked him to call if Frohman showed up again, then left. I stored the fact of the German's poor driving in my new memory where it rattled around with the rest of the stuff I'd learned over the last month. With thirty-five years of recall gone, it must have been like storing a grain of sand in a suitcase.

I wondered if that was how I'd got onto Frohman's track, through his lousy driving, although I couldn't for the life of me see how that could have led me anywhere.

I walked back toward Frohman's apartment house. I'd just made his regular daily drive, from Jersey City to the parking lot, and I wanted to complete the trip to see if I could maybe get inside his skin by walking the same ground he had. It was a pleasant stroll. Once I got off Greenwich Avenue, the town houses regained their handsome looks, and there were some interesting people passing by: a lot of young people, young mothers with small children. The Village had a neighborhood feel, although I got the impression that even the good parts had been a lot better once upon a time.

By the time I'd reached the house where Frohman had lived, something was pinging at me, or *in* me. I'd spotted something during the walk which had struck a responsive chord, but I couldn't identify it. I turned around and walked back the way I'd come and, a few minutes later, found the thing that had grabbed at me. It was a little Spanish restaurant that looked like it had been a fixture on the block for a quarter century. Curiously, it shared a side window with a travel agent, which looked to be part of the restaurant. In the window was something I'd glanced at in passing, and it was this item that had reached out and hooked my subconscious: a bright blue-and-white poster for Pan American Airlines. It showed a drawing of a statue in a pretty green park, and a line about low fares to Boston. I'd seen the same billboard driving back from Jersey City, and seeing it again in the window of the little travel agency had sparked something.

Now I can't say what the process was—I can't even get close to explaining how it arrived or where it came from—but I was immediately convinced that Werner Frohman had gone to Boston. He'd driven past that billboard each day on his way home, had been reminded of it walking from the parking lot, and had decided to go north.

I know it sounds absurd, a piece of reasoning as shallow and unfounded as that, and I was loath to accept it myself, yet, at the same time, I knew in my bones that Boston was where he'd fled to.

I wondered, standing there on the sidewalk staring in at that airline poster, if this was what Al Charmain had been talking about when he'd told me about my hunches. Was this one of them? And what was the difference between a

46

hunch and a dumb guess? Flashes, he'd called them. Well, the Boston idea had been like a flash; one second it was just a name on an advertisement, the next it was certain knowledge. I decided to go and see Charmain and put my intuition, if that's what it was, to the test. So I grabbed a cab and, twenty minutes later, I walked into his grubby office.

It was way past lunchtime, but he was eating anyway. A compulsive feeder, I doubted he ever stopped.

"Hey, there." He waved the end of a hero sandwich before it disappeared into his maw. He had two milk-shake containers in front of him, both empty. He chewed and swallowed, and pointed to them. "When I can't decide between chocolate and strawberry, I order both." He supplied his own laugh, then said, "So how goes the chase?"

"I might have something."

"That was quick."

"I said *might.*"

"Okay." His chair squeaked when he leaned his weight back into it. He waited patiently for me to say something more, his flushed cheeks ballooning as he half stifled a burp.

I took a chair myself, but couldn't get comfortable. I didn't particularly care what Charmain thought of me, but I didn't want to be laughed at, either. "I want to try something," I said. "Is it possible to check out traffic accidents? I mean, can you call up whatever department handles that and get info over the phone?"

"Sure, if you got something specific to give 'em." Charmain ran a hand through his wispy hair and examined his fingers for foreign bodies. He was trying to appear casual, but I could tell he was hanging on my answer.

"That car Frohman bought. It was an old one, incidentally. Nothing flashy. An '81 model."

"You sure? That ain't what I heard."

"There's no record of him taking a plane anywhere. So I'm wondering if he maybe drove that car to get where he was headed and had an accident when he got there."

"Entirely possible, but we don't know where he went. And to check traffic accidents from ten weeks back till yesterday, in all the major cities in the country, not to mention the major towns, would take until next New Year's Eve."

"Try Boston."

I thought Charmain was going to ask me what I had that pointed to that particular place, but he didn't. He just went on watching me, his pudgy face pursed and contemplative. Then he picked up a phone and spent the next twenty minutes making calls.

We waited for the replies.

He ate two candy bars.

He was considering unwrapping a third when three calls followed each other in quick succession. He made notes during the last one, then hung up, chuckled, and wagged his bulbous head at me.

"And you wondered if you had any talent for this job."

"He's there?" I knew he had to be, but I was astonished that I'd turned out to be right. How the hell had I known?

"An '81 Montego, registered to Werner Frohman, was involved in two fender benders last month. One in Cambridge, the other in Somerville—both suburbs of Boston. What tipped you off?"

"An airline poster."

"An *air*line poster?" When his mouth stretched, it put several more creases in the fat man's face. "Kid, you are something else. You're worth every penny we pay you." The smile broadened; he was immensely pleased. "You woulda made those calls to the Boston cops yourself, then you

48

called me and told me you had a lead, and you were off to run it down. You were on your way to La Guardia when you piled up. You pay on board the Boston shuttle, that's how come you didn't have an airline ticket."

So there it was: an all-important section of my previously unknown life falling into place. The first little piece in the jigsaw puzzle.

Charmain handed across the note he'd made. "Frohman's address. That was current ten days ago, which don't mean it's current now. Get on your horse and go on up there. If he's still at that address, don't go near the guy, just call me. You got it?"

"I'll go tomorrow. I have a date tonight."

"Hey, c'mon, fella. This is important. Now that we've found the guy, we don't want to lose him again."

"*If* we've found him. You just said he may have moved. How long's it take to fly to Boston?"

"About an hour."

"Okay, I'll catch an early flight, be there by what . . . eleven?"

Charmain's cheeks wobbled when he sighed. "Okay, star, have it your way. But get the first flight, okay? I think it leaves around eight. We want this guy."

I told him I'd do my best, and left the fat man looking a little peeved. I went down to the sidewalk extremely pleased with the way things were shaping up. I was beginning to like my work now that I was having some success at it, and I was growing progressively intrigued about my ability to hunch. I was feeling far more confident about my prospects because I'd proved I could do a job, and the niggling little doubts that had plagued me, the vague worry that something was wrong, seemed to have receded.

But they came roaring back again. And with a vengeance.

Something happened that night that turned me upside down and left me wondering just what in God's name was going on.

And exactly what my part in it was supposed to be.

CHAPTER FOUR

We ran into trouble on our way home, trouble that could have been pretty serious.

We'd gone to Tom's place for dinner, Sharon and I—that was the date I'd referred to in Al Charmain's office. Tom rented a large apartment on the southern verge of Westchester, and we'd taken a train from Grand Central. I told Sharon on the way up about my first day back on the job, about my success in tracing Frohman to Boston, although I didn't tell her how I'd come to pick that particular city; I couldn't explain it to myself, let alone somebody else.

The evening had been relaxed and pleasant. Karen, Tom's wife, was her usual maternal self and was very sympathetic regarding my head problem. She made an attempt to wake things up in there when we were alone in the kitchen. She told me about somebody named Pam whom she said had been my girl before Sharon. She told me that Pam and I had lived in a house Pam's mother had left her in Dongan Hills, a ritzy section of Staten Island, and that I'd hated Pam's country club life and hadn't wanted to share it, so we'd called it quits.

Tom had another try at me, too. He showed me his old high school yearbook and pointed out kids we'd both grown up with. But their combined efforts didn't do any good; it was like punching phone buttons too fast and being told by a recorded voice to please hang up and try the call again.

We left around 11:45 and caught the train, but it threw a shoe or something, and we only made it as far as 138th Street. We were told it would be a while before they could get things moving again, so we decided to go down to the street and get a cab. The problem was half the other passengers had the same idea, so I suggested to Sharon that we start walking and find a cab farther east. She didn't think that would be a wise move, saying that it wasn't the kind of neighborhood you walked around after midnight, if at all. I still didn't know much about New York and so I wasn't impressed by its dangers. Also, being six one, and weighing 190, I hardly looked like a pushover. And there was another also: I had to get an early plane to Boston in the morning, so I wasn't crazy about waiting forever for a taxi. Sharon didn't like it, but we set off through a depressed and run-down area, walking quickly. Many of the streetlights had been vandalized, and the main source of illumination came from the headlights of beat-up automobiles blasting cacophonous rock and roll into the night. Now and then a clenched yellow glow snuck out feebly from a tenement hallway.

I could feel Sharon's nervousness beside me: the quick click of her heels on the sidewalk, the tight pressure of her hand on my arm.

We came to a section that was undergoing some road repairs and had to detour around the sidewalk on a narrow wooden walkway. When we came out at the end of it, and turned its inclined corner, we almost walked into a group of youths, black guys, four of them, arguing over whose turn it was to play which tape in a huge and barely portable cassette radio. When they saw us they fell silent, glanced briefly at each other, then stepped aside to let us pass, as if they'd suddenly remembered their manners.

Sharon's fingers lanced into my forearm, but she was worrying about nothing, or so I thought, because we moved by them without any problem.

It was half a block farther on that they appeared again,

just two of them, one stocky and muscular, the other tall and gangly, both of them wearing the New York street uniform: jeans and sneakers and sweatshirts with hoods hanging down behind. They'd taken some kind of shortcut through the construction work and got ahead of us, and there they were, waiting.

"Tax on you, man," the short one said. He had the wide shoulders and thick neck of a fighter.

I heard Sharon breathe something like, "Oh, God!" and felt her sudden tension. She was very scared, and had a right to be, and I should have been, too, but for some reason I wasn't. Instead I felt an adrenaline rush in my body, and the reverse in my head, a kind of icy computation, although I didn't know what I was figuring. But I knew I wasn't afraid of these kids, even when I saw the gun.

"Death and taxes, big fella," the fighter said. "Only thing certain in this life. Your choice. Which you want?"

The tall kid reached for Sharon's handbag, and she let him take it. But he seemed to have more on his mind than money.

"Lady, you sure got nice hair." He moved closer to her. "Your pussy hair same color?"

"Hey, kid," I said, surprised that my voice was coming out without a wobble. "Get away from her or I'll break your mouth."

The fighter looked around to see what his pal was doing, and the gun that had been pointing at my belt buckle swayed away slightly. I moved then, and it was like being outside of myself. It was as if somebody who knew what to do in a situation like this had borrowed my body. I clasped my left hand on the fighter's wrist, turning it away from me. My right hand chopped him on his bicep, and I stripped the gun from his fingers when they splayed in reaction. My right

53

arm stayed in motion. There was no pause between the hand chop and the forearm I caught him with on the jaw, and no pause between that blow and another chop to the bridge of his nose.

I was amazed by the speed of my defense; it was like one second the muscular fighter was standing up with a gun in his hand and the next second I had his gun, and he was stretched out on the sidewalk with his jaw at a funny angle and blood pumping from his nose.

And the way I then handled the gun was another big surprise. Before I knew I'd done it, I'd dropped the bullet clip from the handle and worked the slide, sending the round in the chamber flying out. I'd unloaded that gun in nothing flat.

The tall kid's eyes had saucered, and his mouth hung. He let go of Sharon as if she'd caught fire and ran, sprinted for all he was worth.

I took Sharon's shaking arm and got her out of there, found a cab at last, and held her to me all the way home. I poured her a shot of something when we got inside, then she went in and showered and let the hot-water soothe away the shakes. While I waited for her I wrapped the gun in a supermarket bag and dropped it into the garbage. Then I made myself a drink and handed Sharon hers when she came back into the room wearing a terry robe.

"Boy, that was scary. You were magnificent, Jerry. Thank God for those karate lessons."

"What's karate?"

"Self-defense. Martial arts. You used to go regularly to a club uptown somewhere. You must have been their star student."

We didn't discuss it anymore; it was just a piece of bad luck, our second street altercation of the week.

I went into the tiny bathroom and washed up. When I came out, Sharon was putting down the phone on a wrong number. I hadn't heard the phone ring, but then I'd been splashing water in my face with a towel over my head.

We finished our drinks and went to bed. Sharon snuggled into me, still needing some comfort, and our embrace led to a kiss, which led to our making love, but with none of the strenuous excesses of our first night together. The street incident was far from my mind as I lost myself in the grip of her thighs, but after we'd finished and Sharon had dropped off to sleep, I wrestled with this new element, this new addition to a mix that had become a real puzzle. I was a skip tracer, right? And before that I'd been an insurance adjuster. So how did an insurance man know enough to strip a gun from a mugger and leave him a crumpled wreck in the time it took to snap your fingers? The karate school? How many lessons did you need to know how to break a person's nose and jaw with an extension of the same light-ning blow? And did karate teach guns? Did it teach you how to locate an automatic's magazine release and work the slide practically at the same time? It was true I had all those gun manuals, but Sharon had told me I didn't own a gun, so how come I was so expert with one? Karate, gun handling, these weren't the talents of an insurance man, surely.

What kind of person would be taught skills like that? What would be his job?

Doubt pecked away at me in the dark, sank its cruel talons into my thoughts.

Had I been lied to? Was I being used? If so, who was using me?

And, more important, who were they using? A guy named Jerry Parrish?

Sure.

But who was Jerry Parrish?

Sharon, remembering that I had an early plane to catch,
was up before I was, got me coffee, packed me a bag, gave
me some instructions, and watched me get into a taxi outside the front door. It was a little like a nine-year-old being
sent off to his first summer camp, and I felt as if I should
have had a card marked "Boston" pinned to my jacket. I
told her I'd be back as soon as I'd located the guy I was
looking for, and I'm sure it sounded like routine stuff. Had I
known that several large men would behave rather violently
toward me I could have made the next couple of days sound
a touch more exciting.

The cab took the Midtown Tunnel to the Queens Ex-
pressway, perhaps approximating the same trip I'd started
out on once before. This time, however, I was being driven,
and by a happy Jamaican bopping along to the beat spilling
out of a cassette player. He was either a better driver than I
was or he knew how to dodge oil slicks, because he got me
to La Guardia in one piece.

I assumed I'd flown many times but, for all intents and
purposes, this was my first experience of the sky, and it
showed. For example, I was the only person who actually
read the safety instructions, and I clutched suddenly at the
arm rests when the landing gear thumped up into the wheel
bays. An avuncular type sitting next to me assured me that
flying was quite safe and that I wasn't to worry. I told him I
was a pilot myself, and that it always bothered me when
somebody else drove.

A cab took me from Logan Airport into some pretty intense downtown traffic. Boston looked historic and interesting once I could see past the steel-and-glass office blocks,

and the house I was driven to—Frohman's address, gleaned from the police traffic accident reports—reminded me of the one he'd lived in in the Village, a four-story row house built about a hundred years ago.

The first apartment on the street floor belonged to a live-in manager who came to the door carrying a box of Kleenex under his arm the way I'd seen motorcyclists carry their helmets. His greeting was interrupted by a snorting intake of breath, a grab for a tissue, and a whooshing sneeze.

"Nothing catching," he assured me. "Pollen allergy. I got a bumper sticker on my car says Impeach Spring." He blew into a Kleenex, mopped up. "I've had all the shots, got an arm like a junkie, but it don't do no good." He glanced down at my overnight bag. "You looking to rent? I don't have a thing."

I told him it was just information I was after, and asked him if Werner Frohman lived there.

"Used to. He moved away."

"He leave a forwarding address?"

"Uh uh."

I sagged mentally; I'd been expecting more positive stuff than this. But then the manager handed me a surprise that was as nice as it was puzzling. He wiped tears from his eyes and took a second look at me.

"You asked me about him, what, a coupla months back. Wasn't that you? Sure it was. Only without the head gear."

So I'd been to Boston, and evidently kept it quiet. That was interesting. And I was back on my old trail again.

"I missed him the first time, right?"

"By a couple of days. You don't remember that?"

I gave him the excuse about rechecking everything, and added a new twist. "I'm not sure I've got the right man. Tall and thin? Wears expensive clothes?"

"Frohman? No way. He looked like he got dressed in a Goodwill box every morning. But he was tall and thin all right. Like he maybe kept a vampire bat in his pocket."

I pulled out Frohman's photograph. After warding off another sneeze attack, the manager identified the German. I asked him if Frohman had driven a Montego.

"Yeah, until he sold it. He rode the subway to his job, so he didn't need a car."

"Where did he—"

"Work? He never told me. Never told me anything, not that I could understand him that good. Had an accent on him thick as a housebrick. Quietest tenant I ever had. I saw him one night walking in with some records under his arm, but he must've played 'em with the sound near zero 'cause I never heard music and he was right next door."

"But I understood he had an expensive stereo setup."

"If he did, he wasted his money."

I asked about friends, if Frohman had had any. The manager said that Frohman had had visitors on several occasions.

"I didn't see 'em, but I heard 'em."

"Men or women?"

"Two guys it sounded like. One American, the other German. I think German. He was talking foreign, and Frohman was German, so I guess German." I gave the manager a card, told him to call collect if Frohman showed, and left him battling another nasal eruption.

I walked for a while. The weather was chillier than it had been in New York; some recent rain had cooled the air. I wandered into a small park built around an old-fashioned verandalike structure which I think was a bandstand. A guy in a wildly painted lunch wagon was doing a brisk business with a bunch of college kids, so I joined the line, bought a sandwich and a can of 7-Up, and took my early lunch to an empty bench.

I thought about what the allergic manager had told me, and added a few more facts to my slim file on Werner Frohman. He liked music although he played it at very low volume. What kind of music would a man like Frohman listen to? A mousy little scientist who kept to himself. German music, probably. I thought back to my tutor and our brief musical studies. The course had been called From Beethoven to the Beatles. Beethoven had been German; I recalled the tutor saying that Germany was well represented in the classics, so maybe it was reasonable to assume that this was the kind of music Frohman liked. But wasn't a lot of classical music played by a symphony orchestra? Or opera with huge casts singing ensemble? Could it be possible to listen to such big productions at almost zero volume?

I ate my sandwich slowly, and went at the puzzle from another angle. The manager had seen Frohman with records but hadn't heard him play any music. But he had heard him in conversation with somebody. So I put those two facts together, juggled them a little, and came up with the possibility that Frohman had been playing, not music, but conversation.

German and English conversation.

English and German.

It made all kinds of sense: I'd been told a couple of times that Frohman had been embarrassed about the way he spoke English, so he'd bought some English lessons on records.

I knew I was facing my first real piece of legwork: tracking down the store where Frohman had bought those records. Why do such a thing? Because I figured I had to talk to anybody who'd had any kind of contact with the guy, because one of those people might be able to tell me where else to look for him.

I left the park, asked some college kids the best way to get to the hotel section. They told me to grab the bus that was coming down so I did. I rode it for several blocks with a question ticking louder than ever in the front of my mind: where had I been going when I'd crashed in that car? Not to Boston, because I'd already been here. So the trail must have led to another city. How close had I got to Frohman the first time around? Whatever the answers, one thing was clear: I was successfully dogging my own heels; slowly but surely overhauling myself.

I left the bus when I spotted a Holiday Inn, corner of Blossom Street and Cambridge. I registered, bought a city map at the newsstand, and followed a bellboy up to my room. The first thing I did was check the phone book. I called about twenty stores in the downtown area, but only six of them sold language records so, checking my map, I cast my net a little wider. It was entirely possible that Frohman had bought the records near where he'd worked, and if he'd worked within, say, a five-mile radius of where he'd lived, that brought in Brookline, Cambridge, Somerville, and Chelsea. I called record stores in those suburbs and added half a dozen names to my list, then I went down to the street and started on my self-appointed rounds.

Covering the downtown was easy. It was small, compact and circular, but it didn't do me any good. I showed Frohman's photograph to every clerk I could find in all of the stores that handled language records but nobody remembered him. Then I rented a car and took on the suburbs, which was a major chore as I had to cover a hell of a lot of territory, most of it in a fine, misting rain.

It took me till eight o'clock that evening, and all I had to show for my efforts was a pair of insulted eardrums courtesy of the inane Top 40 record store music. I had a couple of beers and some lobster claws in a seafood house downtown, then went back to the hotel and hit the sack. I lay with the light off pondering my strategy for the morrow: more foot slogging—Frohman had to have bought those records somewhere.

It was my last thought before I fell asleep and my first thought when I woke up next morning. *Why* did he have to buy them somewhere? My music tutor had brought me some educational tapes and they hadn't been bought, they'd been borrowed. From a library.

That got me out of bed in a hurry. I grabbed up my rain-ruined map; there was a public library on Newbury Street, just west of the Common, and only a five-minute walk from where Frohman had lived. I made it over there not long after the library opened, and right away my luck started on another roll.

The first librarian I spoke to remembered me. And she remembered Frohman. She repeated what she said she'd told me ten weeks back: that she recalled the German not because of the language records he'd borrowed, but because she'd helped him locate a particular scientific treatise. It had been published in a small magazine at Boston University, and was available through the city's library system. I asked her if she could recall what the magazine had been concerned with, but she couldn't tell me. But she was certain that none of the articles had anything to do with something as commercial as an industrial pesticide. Frohman had left town before the magazine had been delivered, and Frohman had given the librarian a mailing address.

He was using a private mail service.

In New York City.

I had to smile when I heard that; what a smart move for somebody who wanted to disappear: he'd fled New York, established himself in Boston, then returned to the last place anybody would expect to find him.

Again I had to wonder what was going on. Contrary to what I'd been told, the man I was looking for didn't wear designer clothes and didn't drive a fancy car. What he did do was live quietly and request scientific papers concerning stuff that was way out of his own field.

Frohman hadn't skipped on any finance company, so either Al Charmain had been sold a bill of goods or he was selling me one.

As short as the flight was back to New York there was plenty of time for me to do a whole lot of thinking.

There were too many things that seemed off center about my new life and the outfit I was working for; too many contradictions. It was true I had no experience against which to match the various inconsistencies and that in itself was something that bothered me. Without experience I had no basis of judgment; my defenses were almost nil. I couldn't honestly decide if something was going on over my head or not, but if that proved to be so, then an unpleasant fact had to be faced. And it was this: if something was happening, Sharon had to be part of it.

I hated the thought of this because she was a warm and lovely person, and I had an idea that my feelings toward her could really blossom into something important given time. I had to wonder if I was reading too much into things, being overly suspicious, but that line of thought proved inconclusive. I decided that the best thing to do was go along with everything for a while, perform as expected, and see what happened.

The first thing I did when I got back home was call Al Charmain.

"Hi. Where you calling from?"

"The apartment. I'm back in town."

"So how was the home of the bean?"

"Rainy."

"Yeah, it ain't all in Seattle."

His voice was indistinct again, almost certainly because he was talking around a chicken leg or a hot dog.

"I had a piece of luck. Frohman's back in town. I don't know where he's living, but I have his private postal address."

"Jerry, babe, you done it again. Let's have it."

For a moment I was tempted to hold back, but I stuck to my game plan and told him.

"Okay, got it. How'd you dig it up?"

"He played his music too low."

"His music too low?" I heard Charmain's throaty chuckle, and could almost see those heavy wattles shaking under his chin. "You know what? I believe you. Okay, buster, I'll have that box staked out. When he comes in for his mail we'll grab him."

That pronouncement blinked a red light. "Hold it a second. You told me that we just call the client. I understood that we don't touch anybody."

"Figure of speech, is all. We won't actually lay hands. We'll put a tail on him, follow him home, then call the client." He chuckled again. "Nice going, buddy boy. Better come and see me about a raise while I'm feeling generous."

I told him I'd check in later, and hung up. Now I had something else to add to my negative list: Charmain had weaseled out of that statement—he'd said, grab him and he'd meant grab him.

# TONY KENRICK

I suddenly couldn't wait for Sharon to get back from her job; I wanted to talk to her now and get some straight answers. I left the apartment and went looking for a cab, but they all seemed to have their off-duty signs on and went sailing by. So I walked it; strode up the traffic-jammed slash of Broadway. I realized I'd got it wrong when I got to Thirty-fourth. It was Macy's I was standing outside, not Lord & Taylor; Lord & Taylor was further east. It was the tail end of the lunch hour, and the crowds on the sidewalk outside the store were formidable. But as thick as they were I caught a piece of movement that didn't belong: a guy in a dark suit shoving his way past people with a tight look on his severe face, a large guy who seemed to be heading straight for me. To the right of him a man who could have been his twin, wearing that same harsh expression, was coming at me in a pincer movement. The first guy was only a few feet away when his right hand dived into his jacket. I had no idea what was going to be coming out, but it wasn't going to be free tickets to a TV show. I made sure it didn't come out with anything.

When I say *I* made sure, it was my instinct that took over, as it had the night I'd stripped the gun from the mugger uptown.

I grabbed the guy's right elbow, pushed it further into his jacket, and smashed the heel of my hand down on to his shoulder where it joined his thick neck. He grunted, wobbled unsteadily, and was brushed roughly aside by his partner, who regretted his haste when my stiffened fingers knifed into his belly button. The people around us released a collective gasp and reared back out of the way of the fight, a fight that would have been all over had it not been for the reinforcements that arrived. Four guys, maybe five, all wear-

64

ing those dark suits, all with the same big builds and closed faces.

I took off. I spun through Macy's revolving doors, and kept going. I didn't know the store, not in this life anyway, so I didn't know where I was going, but an immense place like this would have a dozen exits, a dozen different ways to escape, and it was escape that was foremost on my mind. Just why these guys were chasing me wasn't so pressing a question right then. I was just determined they weren't going to catch me.

The street-level floor was packed with shoppers who, being seasoned New Yorkers, parted for me, making no attempt to interfere with a fleeing man. I charged up an escalator and glanced behind me as I reached the top. Two of the dark suits were on my tail, one of them pretty close. I leaped off the escalator and almost fell over a wide table piled with long bolts of fabric. I grabbed one, swung around, and rammed its six-foot length into the guy's legs. As he stumbled forward he made a dive for me. I straight-armed him and sprinted to a far wall, jumping into a crowded elevator just beating the doors. I was swamped by outraged protests as I barged into people, but they had to do without an apology. I caught a glimpse of the second dark suit running hard, then the elevator bobbed and shot up to the next floor where I hopped out and took off again.

It was a mistake; my thinking was flawed. I figured that guy would head for the escalators, and I thought that if I went back down to the street floor I'd miss him and thereby reduce the odds. So I dashed toward the doorway of the emergency stairs and collided with the guy who'd read my mind and had come up the stairs. He took a better shot than I did, so I was ready first. I aimed a blow at his neck and found out I wasn't perfect at this martial arts stuff. He re-

acted astoundingly fast: he turtled his head, and my hand
landed harmlessly on the beefy part of his shoulder. I
blocked his groin kick and slammed him behind the knee
he'd so thoughtfully presented. He went down swinging—
way off target—but he got me all the same. I didn't see what
kind of weapon he had, some kind of short billy club
maybe, but it caught my upper left arm and stunned the
nerves. As I rushed by him I saw something in his other
hand; not a gun but a small black box which I was pretty
sure was a two-way radio. I should've smashed it, but I
didn't; instead I bolted out through the door and up the
stairs, shelving my plan for an immediate street-level escape.

I burst out onto the fourth floor and ran for daylight, ran
into the wide-open spaces of this cavernous store, its customers, recognizing drama when they saw it, moving
smartly out of my way. But the chase had attracted official
attention by this time, and I spotted a uniform, a security
man, running to head me off.

I beat him to the crossroads of two counters, and
bounded up a couple of steps, a glimpsed sign informing
me that I was now in the Seventh Avenue store. I did something that's probably pretty hard to do in New York, I ran an
entire city block indoors, Broadway to Seventh Avenue, but
I paid for it—eight weeks on my back in hospital had left
me ill prepared for a two hundred yard sprint, and my lungs
were in flames, and there was something sharp and urgent
gouging into my side. I wanted desperately to stop, but I
was in no shape to take on three heavies plus a security
guard, so I kept right on running. I zigzagged between
counters, fled past stacks of sheets and a display of shoes,
caromed off a meaty college kid who reeled into a mountain
of suitcases and started an avalanche of leather and nylon.

Another thirty feet brought me into a section devoted to racquet sports and a woman near a rack trying a slow backhand. I snatched the racquet from her startled grasp as I flew by and heard an outraged salesman yell at me. I needed that racquet more than that woman did; I needed some kind of weapon to make up for my frozen left arm.

I had to get out of the store, get out to the street, so I made a dive for another bank of escalators, shouting people out of my way. I made it almost to the street floor, but two women, too shocked or frightened to move, blocked my escape. I had to go around them, up over the black handrail and down the metal sides. I hit a display mannequin and added her spinning plastic body to the rough and tumble of my flight. I heard the two women cry out and, on top of the sound, the thump of running feet: a couple of the dark suits hot on my heels. I knew why I couldn't shake them: they had communication, they were organized, as were the security people who were another big problem. Before, I'd just been a man traveling too fast through a crowded store, but now, with the racquet in my hand, I was a shoplifter flying for the exits.

And fly I did.

I swung away from two uniforms, vaulted a counter, and gave the girls in the perfumery a real thrill as I cleared out what must have been sixteen hundred dollars worth of Chanel No. 5.

Against the wall, a sign, Thirty-fifth Street Exit, popped into my vision, and I went for it, but one of the dark suits dashed in from the right and beat me to it. He stood there muscularly blocking the way, a radio device in one hand and a short billy club in the other. He didn't get a chance to wield it. I hurled the racquet at his head and, as his hands flew up to protect his face, gave him a shot under the heart which temporarily retired him. I burst out of the doors, scattered pedestrians, and plunged straight into the traffic, which sounds braver than it was because the cars and the trucks were bumper to bumper waiting for a green light.

I made the opposite sidewalk, and ran west, putting in a sprint, knowing that it wouldn't be a long one; my heart was thumping like a gong, my vision was starting to blur, and my legs were beginning to feel like my nerveless left arm. I started to slow, my body refusing orders. I had to get off the street.

The parking lot appeared like a wish in a fairy tale. It was one of those narrow, open, vertical ones that take the cars up in an elevator. I rushed in, raced all the way to the rear, feet clumping behind me. I jumped into my second elevator of the afternoon, leaped on board as it was rising. A guy who could have been Puerto Rican, smoking a cigar and wearing a Mets jacket, stood at the hand control, a shiny white Toyota on deck, its engine running. He removed the cigar and started to say something about the illegality of my presence, but he stifled his comment when he saw the sweat on my face and my exhausted condition. He glanced down at the two dark suits arriving below, their mean, puffing faces watching us rise, then looked at me again and, I think, recognized a fleeing felon. He went back to smoking his cigar and contemplating the grubby wall as we slowly ascended. I leaned against the Toyota and sucked air, and wondered how many more of them were down there. The one I'd hamstringed wouldn't be able to run, and the first guy I'd met out on the sidewalk would be nursing a busted collarbone, so there'd be at least three of them after me.

I knew what I had to do, even though I didn't know how I knew: I had to attack them before they attacked me.

I yelled at the Puerto Rican. "Take it down! Take it down *now*!"

He didn't even think about it; he reversed the control lever.

The elevator moaned to a stop, then began to sink.

I hopped in behind the wheel of the Toyota. I was fully aware that there was no way I was going to roar out of the lot and zip away over the horizon, not in the kind of traffic that was jammed in a honking crawl out on the street, but I figured they'd send two of their number up the stairway and post one as sentry at the exit, so I'd only have to get past him.

That was my thinking anyway.

I realized when the elevator was less than fifteen feet from the ramp that I'd guessed wrong again. Grabbing a car was exactly what they'd expect me to do, and they would've moved to counteract it. But it was too late to rethink anything, I had to make the best I could of it, so as the elevator hit the ramp, I mashed the gas pedal, shot out of the cage, and skewered wildly on the driveway. I muscled the wheel, forced the car under control, and gunned it flat out toward the exit.

What I feared would happen happened: those guys hadn't wasted time coming up for me—when they'd seen me going up with an automobile they'd known I'd be coming down in that automobile. They'd simply grabbed the nearest thing with a key in the ignition, a large and heavy van, and had got ready to use it.

As I pulled out of my skidding turn they came barreling in right alongside me. They belted the Toyota amidship, swung away, crashed into me again, so hard this time that the car was hammered five feet to the left, and was suddenly making a beeline for an interior stanchion. I stood on the brakes, but it was pointless. Burning rubber, shrieking like a tortured thing, the car slammed into the steel support, and the hood mashed in and crumpled.

I'd braced myself, my right arm telescoping the shock, and I was moving a moment later, shoving against the door. But the crash had warped the car's frame, and by the time I'd brought my legs up and kicked the door open, one of the dark suits had bounded out of the van, and was on me. I caught a flash of metal and moved to counter a knife thrust, but it wasn't a blade that came at me, it was a small silver canister no bigger than a cigarette. I started to chop at his wrist, but he beat me by a country mile, and a jet of something horribly noxious tore into my nostrils and snatched at my brain.

The effect was instantaneous. Every muscle I owned turned to sand. I flopped back and to one side and vomited all over the passenger seat.

The Toyota's owner would be in for a nasty surprise when he returned. He'd find that somebody had trashed his shiny new car and, for an encore, had barfed up the interior. But that really wasn't what I was thinking as my senses slid away; I was thinking I'd gone and done it again—Al Charmain had told me to drive an Olds or a Buick next time I totaled a car, told me to stay away from those cute little foreign imports.

I should have listened.

CHAPTER FIVE

Coming out of it.

The white fuzz in front of my eyes became walls and ceiling. I thought I was back in Lenox Hill Hospital until I saw the painting: yellow flowers on a red tablecloth, and a small bowl of sliced oranges in front of a crystal vase. The flowers had been drawn with a liquid clarity that made them look as edible as the oranges. I wanted that fruit, and several aspirins. I had a pounding thirst and a raging head-ache, and vice versa.

The tight constriction I felt around my arms swung me back to the hospital theory again, but when I moved my head, at some cost, I saw that it was a sofa I was lying on, and that what I'd thought were bandages were actually wide strips of plastic tape; somebody had strapped my arms to my sides. My legs were free, so I eased them off the sofa and attempted a sitting position. Needles pierced my skull. I squinched my eyes shut, waited for the pain to blunt.

"How are you feeling?"

A pleasant voice, even, and with a note of concern in it.

I opened my eyes on a guy who seemed to have taken my second thought right out of my mind: he held a tall glass of orange juice and had two white pills in the palm of his other hand.

"Codeine," he said, offering the tablets. "That CS gas dilates the blood vessels."

He looked relaxed in light-colored golf slacks and a red cardigan; a guy in his midforties with a comfortably plump body, a benign expression on his cherubic face, rosy cheeks,

71

and a ring of fine hair on his shiny scalp. He was quite a contrast to one of the dark suits who was standing behind him, lashing me with his hard stare. I looked at the pills and wondered about them. These people, whoever they were, had gassed me once; would they drug me now? The needles inside my skull darted again, so I took a chance and let the cherub pop the pills into my mouth, let him help me with the juice, which I drank to the last drop.

"Well, now," the cherub began, regarding me with something close to melancholy disappointment, "I think you owe us an explanation."

I might have laughed out loud if my head hadn't been throbbing. "Five guys come after me with clubs," I said. "They ram a van into me. I wake up to find myself wrapped up like a post office parcel, and I owe *you* an explanation? Who the hell are you, anyway?"

"Aw, shit," another voice said. "Here we go."

The speaker walked into my vision. He had tall, rangy height, fair hair slicked back, but not too carefully, pale, freckled skin, and a surly line to his mouth. He wasn't as neatly relaxed as the cherub or as severely uptight as the heavy in the dark suit; in a tweed sports jacket, and a tie looped loosely around an unbuttoned collar, he was somewhere in between.

"How much they paying you, Jacko?" he asked. "Big bucks or just serious money?"

"Jacko? Is my name Jack?"

The man took a cigarette from his lips and exhaled smoke as if his tongue were on fire. His mouth slid sideways, and his pale eyes flicked at me in disgust. "What's this, the comedy hour?"

The cherub wasn't quite so ready to sneer at me. He was

examining my head bandage, looking into my face. He seemed uncertain.

"He may not be kidding," he said.

The tall guy turned a grunt into a derisive hiss, ground out his partially smoked cigarette, then broke it in half, perhaps trying for revenge on a habit he couldn't quit.

"You look different, Jack," the cherub said. "You don't look like . . ." His plump shoulders lifted a fraction. "You anymore."

"So I've been told. Do you think you could unwrap me? I don't feel so hot."

"We trussed you up to be on the safe side. You sent two of the guys to the hospital."

"Right now I'd happily join them."

I meant what I'd said; I just wanted to lie down in a quiet room and sleep. I felt an immense fatigue floating through my body, hanging heavy on every part of it. It wasn't the knockout gas I'd inhaled, it was simply a reaction to such a violent expenditure of energy. It had taken weeks to recharge my batteries, and I'd flattened them within fifteen minutes. My exhaustion must have been evident because the cherub picked up a pair of scissors and started on the tape. He wasn't taking much of a risk; I was out of it. When the tape had been cut and peeled away, and I was able to stretch my arms, my left one was still out to lunch, although I could at least get some movement into it now. I leaned gratefully back into the sofa, and took better notice of the room I was in. It was expensive-looking, with some fine, dark-wood furniture standing on heavy broadloom, and more paintings hung from elaborate molding on the walls. I could hear the diesel moan of buses, and the petulant honking of traffic, and I could see, out of a far window, a piece of an apartment house, so I assumed I was in one just like it somewhere in Manhattan.

The cherub captured my attention again; he sat down close to me on the edge of a grained coffee table, took another searching look at my face, and appeared to arrive at some kind of conclusion. He turned away and muttered something to the dark suit, who nodded and left the room. I didn't think he was going for anything; he'd just been dismissed now that the cherub could see I was no longer a physical threat.

"What did you mean when you asked if your name was Jack?"

"I meant I wasn't sure. You seem to know who I am. You tell me."

"Who do you think you are?"

"I'm supposed to be Jerry Parrish."

"Who told you that?"

"A number of people. The first person was a guy named Wein. Doctor Wein."

"Where was this?"

"Lenox Hill."

The lanky guy spoke up. His sour, distrustful demeanor had been chipped into by a wary uncertainty. "Wein. Silver hair, little mustache?"

"That's him."

"He's not a doctor."

"I knew that when you called me Jacko."

"Jesus Christ," the lanky guy said slowly, "the sonofabitch's lost his fucking memory."

There was a moment of silence while the two men stared at me, then the cherub asked me what had happened.

"We'll get to that. First, I have a few questions. For starters, who are you guys?"

"I'm George Trilling," the cherub answered. "You've never heard that name?"

"No." I nodded at pale eyes. "And him?"

"Ray Carmody. Does it mean anything?"

"No."

"It didn't mean much to you before, either," the lanky guy said.

"What am I doing here? What is this place?"

The cherub, Trilling, handled the replies.

"One of our offices. And you're here because you were missing and we found you."

They hadn't found me, they'd kidnapped me, but I let that go and, instead, asked if I worked for them.

"Yes, you do. Ray's your partner."

"And who am I?"

"Jack Penrose."

I looked at both of them in turn, Trilling with his rosy cheeks and accommodating manner, and pale-eyed Carmody, tall and moody.

"What's the name of the firm?"

"You mean the head office?"

"Yes."

Trilling bettered his position on the coffee table and leaned forward a little. "The United States Government."

After a long moment I said, "Oh."

"Your turn to answer. What's your oldest memory?"

"Waking up in hospital."

"When was this?"

"Seven weeks back."

"Wein was the first person you spoke to?"

"I might have spoken to a nurse. But Wein was the first guy I had a conversation with."

"How did he explain your being in a hospital bed?"

"I was in a car crash. Split my head open. They had to operate."

Trilling nodded as if he'd been in the operating room himself. "Well, that's partly true. Your head was split open, and you had surgery, but it wasn't because of a car crash."

"Then how did it happen?"

"You were beaten up."

I closed my eyes. The pills Trilling had fed me had put a lid on my headache, but my Band-Aided brain was struggling to cope with what I was being told. The last sixty seconds had overwhelmed me—the U.S. *Government*? But I wasn't going to try to process anything, not till I had all the facts in, and even then I was planning to wait till the clouds of cerebral dust blown up by these revelations had had a chance to settle.

"Who beat me up?"

"A couple of thugs employed by a guy named Al Charmain. Have you ever heard that name?"

I opened my eyes. "Yeah. Up till a few minutes ago I was working for him."

My answer hung in the air between the two men till at last Carmody growled at me: "How'd you get to meet Fat Al?"

I requested some more juice, which Carmody grudgingly went and fetched, then I told them everything about the hospital stay, about Sharon, and Tom and his wife, about Charmain and his grungy Acis Corporation office on Thirty-third Street, and about my search for Werner Frohman.

"Everybody told me I was a skip tracer. Charmain said that Frohman had stiffed a finance company, and that I'd found him once and should try again."

Carmody snorted, and said to Trilling, "Old Al doesn't miss a trick, does he?"

Trilling was shaking his head; he seemed almost amused.

"Please," I said. "I'd appreciate a little information."

"Sure," Trilling said. "You want it in bits and pieces, or all at once?"

"All at once."

"Okay." Trilling resettled himself on the coffee table. Carmody remained standing, his head bent forward a little in a tall man's stoop. Trilling asked me how much I knew.

"Only that I've been lied to. But I don't know why or by whom."

"Charmain gave you some of the truth. He does run Acis all right, only their office isn't on Thirty-third. And they're not skip tracers. They're a group of . . . well, I guess you could call 'em mercenary spooks. They'll do any kind of dirty work for a fee. Peking hired them to find Frohman."

"Peking?"

"The Chinese. They want him because of what he's working on."

"Which is what?"

"Our masters didn't tell us," Trilling answered, his plump face looking a little chagrined.

"Probably don't know themselves," Carmody said in his sour tone.

"Not for sure, maybe. But if Defense is interested, you can bet it's potentially big. Some kind of weapons application, that's certain. All we know is its code name. Glitzenbak."

"What kind of a name is that?"

"German. A made-up word, so I'm told. *Glitzen* means glitter, and *bak* is short for bakterium, which means germ or microorganism. The closest English translation would be Glitterbug, although what kind of bug it is, and why it should glitter, is anybody's guess."

I thought that was interesting—Glitzenbak, Glitterbug— but not as interesting as another name Trilling had mentioned: Defense. He still hadn't explained which part of the U.S. Government I worked for. When I asked him to elaborate, he came back with a question of his own.

"Do you know anything about any government departments, the ones that handle security?"

"A little. I had some tutoring while I was healing. We touched on a whole bunch of subjects."

"Then you've heard of the CIA? And the NSA?"

I didn't answer right away; I'd jumped to an obvious conclusion: my gun knowledge, my karate prowess, naturally I'd know stuff like that if I was an operative for the National Security Agency, or for the CIA.

"Sure I've heard of them. Which are we?"

"Neither. Your tutor wouldn't know about us," Trilling said with a half smile. "Very few people do. We're a section of the Defense Intelligence College, which has a big building in Fairfax, Virginia, and is listed in the phone book. But the investigative arm is something that doesn't officially exist, has no official operating budget, and, like one or two other clandestine outfits, remains only an unsubstantiated rumor. You've heard of the Pentagon?"

"Of course."

"They run us."

"Defense Intelligence College." I tried the name in my mouth to see if it fit. My tongue didn't know it, my brain didn't, either.

"We call ourselves College boys. We call the firm Richard because of the initials, D-I-C."

"Some of us call it Dick, as in schlong," Carmody volunteered, "because every now and then they try to fuck you over."

"Come on, Ray," Trilling said quietly.

Carmody was obviously unenthused about his employers, but I doubted he was the type to be happy about anything. I noticed that the left side of his jaw was lumpy as if it might once have been broken. I got the impression that this guy had taken some other kinds of lumps, perhaps a bum call somewhere in his career. I found him a bore, and not worth thinking about. I needed all the brain time I could get to fit together everything I was learning. And I still didn't have near enough pieces.

"Let's get back to the car accident I didn't have. Why was I beaten up?"

"Because you wouldn't tell Al Charmain what he wanted to know."

"Which was what?"

"Where Werner Frohman was."

"So I did find him . . ."

"Yes, you did."

"Where is he?"

Trilling and Carmody traded looks, a little amusement in Trilling's, a tired sourness in Carmody's.

"That's the jackpot question," Trilling said.

"I don't understand. If I found him, why didn't I tell you?"

"Because Acis got to you first. Snatched you, and tried to beat the information out of you. And you wouldn't talk. One of their goons got a little frustrated, belted you with a length of pipe, and damned near killed you."

"How do you know all this?"

"Go ahead and tell him," Carmody urged, a note of disgust there.

I got the impression the subject was a contentious one between them.

"We have a contact inside Acis," Trilling explained, a touch defensively.

"And they have a contact inside the College," Carmody said. "It's the same guy."

Trilling shrugged at me. "Ray doesn't agree with the arrangement."

"I hate stoolies," Carmody said.

"It's just a term. He's a stoolie to you, but a valuable informant to me."

"The guy's a fucking menace."

"Not if he's controlled," Trilling replied with a hint of asperity. "We only let him find out what we want him to find out."

I wasn't listening to their squabble, I was stringing all this new information together and matching it up with what I already had. The beating certainly accounted for my condition when I'd woken up in the hospital—my busted face, my broken ribs, my swollen testicles—and, of course, a stoved-in head accounted for the brain surgery and memory loss. But how did they react so fast to that loss? I got the answer to that question as soon as I asked it of myself: I'd talked to somebody before I'd talked to Wein; I had a dim recollection of the hard-faced nurse asking me questions. It must have been obvious to her that my memory had gone, so they'd quickly changed gears and made my amnesia work for them. That had to be what had happened, yet it was a struggle to assimilate it. The thought that anybody would go to such lengths . . . hiring a woman to play my soft-eyed lover, a guy to be my brother, another woman to be his wife, and the friends who dropped in to visit me in the hospital, the people who'd called—all actors in the same production with me, the dummy, as the star of the show. It was going to take me a while to come to terms with the scale of it.

I told much of this to Trilling, and he agreed on what Charmain had done.

"He's a smart cookie, and ruthless, too. He figured that what you'd found once you could find again, so he scrambled together a former life for you, then sat back and waited for you to get results. Only he had a piece of bad luck. The guy you told us about, the one who recognized you in the street, called you Jack. Plus you found out you were lethal with your hands. Charmain didn't count on either of those things. Like I say, he just got unlucky."

"I was also told I'd been an insurance man. But I knew I was more than that when a guy tried to mug me and I damn near killed him. Sharon tried to explain my talent away and made a bad job of it. She knew it, too."

"Charmain's too fat and too cocky," Carmody said. He raised his chin at me. "How close did you get to Frohman this time?"

"I traced him to Boston, then back here."

"He doubled back, huh?" Trilling said. "What led you to Boston?"

"Just a hunch."

Trilling nodded and looked pleased. "So they haven't been affected by the head shot. . . . You're still getting them . . ."

"Whatever they are."

"Nobody's ever been able to find out."

"They're guesses, that's all," Carmody said in his dismissive way. "It's like what a horseplayer gets. You win some, you lose some."

"Except that Jack keeps on winning," Trilling replied, quietly taking my side.

I told him about Frohman requesting the college magazine, about the forwarding address he'd left with the Boston
librarian, the private mailbox here in the city. I dug out my
wallet, found the note I'd made, handed it over. Trilling was
delighted. He passed it to Carmody, who went over to a
phone and started making calls.

"We'll stake it out, the mailbox," Trilling said. "Pick him
up when he walks in."

"Then what?"

"Whisk him away to where the Chinese can't get to him,
and see if he'd like to go to work for the good guys."

"I thought we were pals with the Chinese."

"We are," Trilling said. "Today. But tomorrow, who
knows?"

When I looked at him blankly he gave me two minutes
on geopolitics.

"We're talking about future alliances here. The boys in
the Washington think tanks figure it's gonna be Asia versus
everybody else one of these days. China and Japan, two
ancient enemies, teaming up against two recent enemies
. . . the U.S. and the Soviets."

"You think that's what's gonna happen?"

Trilling raised his pudgy pink hands. "It's already happening."

It was going to take me a while to think about that one. I
got back to more immediate concerns. "You may have competition at that mailbox," I said. "I told Charmain about it
when I got back from Boston."

Trilling shook his head. "It's too late for Charmain. He's
lost this one. He'll know by now that we found you, so he'll
know his little game's all over."

I asked Trilling how he'd known where to find me. "Your
contact tell you?"

"No, Acis kept you a secret. He couldn't find out where you were. We had to rely on luck and good surveillance."

He told me that ever since I'd disappeared they'd been watching the airports. I'd been spotted at La Guardia coming off the Boston flight. They'd tailed me to see where I was going, then moved in on me.

"Sorry we were so heavy-handed," Trilling said, "but we didn't know what was going on. When you were spotted at the airport, and you were obviously okay, we had to wonder why you hadn't called in. We had to wonder if you hadn't been coerced into playing ball with Charmain. I'll have to ask you to forgive me on both counts."

I waved the apology away; Trilling's poor judgment was a minuscule thing compared with what Acis had done to me.

Carmody came back from the phone. I asked him about the man he'd commented on before: Wein.

"You said he's not a doctor? He sure sounded like one."

"He's Charmain's lieutenant. Smooth-talking sonofabitch. He would've got the info from the real doctor. The real surgeon."

"But I saw him every day for weeks in that hospital. Why didn't somebody spot him for a fake?"

"Because you weren't in a hospital," Carmody answered, looking at me as if I'd been born yesterday, which wasn't far from the truth. At first I thought he had to be wildly wrong, but then I saw that it wouldn't have been that hard to fake a hospital room. What did they need? A couple of nurses, some equipment, a tape machine outside the door playing recorded pages . . . I'd definitely spent two days in Lenox Hill Hospital, but hadn't they knocked me out for those final tests they'd claimed they had to run on me? Sure. And while I was unconscious they'd taken me from wherever they'd had me stashed and checked me into Lenox Hill for

83

those last couple of days. But that didn't explain the surgery. Where had that been done? When I asked Trilling, he answered with a kind patience.

"In this town you can get any kind of service, day or night, if you've got the cash. There are all kinds of private clinics with full facilities. And a surgeon's no problem. Twenty-five grand left in a suitcase in his car will buy you a good man."

"Twenty-five thousand? They'd spend that much?"

"Peanuts. You have an entire government picking up the tab. The Chinese want Frohman. And when a government wants something they'll spend whatever it takes." Trilling rose from his coffee-table perch, picked up a large, zippered plastic envelope, and handed it to me. "This is your life," he said, and cut short the accompanying chuckle because my mixed feelings must have been plain to see. On one hand I was relieved and delighted to at last have an identity free of the gray doubts that had surrounded my first one. But I was also dismayed by what that would mean: I'd have a whole new person to get used to all over again. It was flawed thinking, of course; did I want to go on forever believing I was somebody I wasn't? Absolutely not. But the readjustments I was going to have to make the second time around were bound to be more than a little confusing.

I unzipped the envelope, then zipped it closed again. I wasn't yet ready to learn all about Jack Penrose; I'd do that later when I was alone. I looked up at Trilling.

"Where do I go from here?" I asked.

"Ease into your new life. Get the personal side started. The pro side's over for a while. Take some time off, get a little sun. There's a credit card in that envelope, take a week's vacation. We'll call it medical leave."

When I was uncertain how to reply, Carmody said, "Give

me the credit card, I'll take the vacation. I'll also take your girl with me."

"I have a girl?" I don't know why I asked the question; why shouldn't I have one?"

"Does he have a girl?" Carmody asked the ceiling. "I've had to pull you out of the sack at least a dozen mornings when we've had a job to do. Couple of minks, you and Jenny."

I was sorry I'd got into it. I wasn't ready to think about a new love, a new domestic arrangement; it was exactly the kind of thing I was going to need time to get my mind around.

Trilling spoke with me for another thirty minutes, filling me in on the basics of my job. Unlike Carmody he was a pleasant guy, and although he would have had little idea of how it felt to be in my weird position, he treated me with care and some sensitivity. He urged me to see a specialist about my condition, but I sidestepped that. I knew it would have been a futile visit; my memory was gone, and there was no way anybody in a white coat was going to be able to entice it out of hiding. It would either come home one day, perhaps without the slightest announcement, or it would stay away forever.

I had stacks more questions I could have asked Trilling, but I'd had enough information for one day so I got out of there. Trilling saw me to the door—Carmody gave me a tired salute—and told me to rest up and that he'd be in touch. Meantime, there was a number in the envelope where he could always be reached. So I went down in an elevator by myself, refusing his offer to have one of the dark suits drive me someplace.

The apartment house, I found, was on Fifty-first just east of Third Avenue. I wondered how they'd got my unconscious body upstairs without attracting attention, but that wasn't foremost in my mind. It would be fair to say that, right then, my mind was in something of a turmoil. I'd barely got to know Jerry Parrish and now, after the roughest and toughest of introductions, I'd just met Jack Penrose and knew hardly anything about him.

I started walking, needing the fresh air even if it was laced with auto emissions. Physically I felt better than I had any right to expect. Feeling had returned to my left arm, which didn't seem any the worse for the blow it had taken, my legs no longer wobbled, and my headache had contracted into a quietly pulsating spot behind my right ear. I guess the thing that was contributing most to my headache, part of the staggering revelations of the past ninety minutes, was a simple question with an unfathomable answer: what in God's name could Werner Frohman be working on that was so desperately important? What was this Glitterbug that was worth the awesome amount of time and effort and money that had gone into fooling me? And boy, had they fooled me! They'd played me like a hooked fish, faked me stupid. And I well knew, with a surge of shame at my naked gullibility, that if they hadn't had a couple of pieces of bad luck they'd still be doing it.

Thoroughly depressed, and with a low-degree anger building inside me, I reached Park Avenue and turned south, navigating by the street signs. A woman spinning through the revolving doors of a fancy hotel bumped into me, and I dropped the plastic envelope. I stooped to pick it up, incurious as to its contents for the present; before I officially began my real life I wanted to see the end of my ersatz one. I decided to go to the Acis office, then back to the apartment on Twenty-ninth.

I walked south till Park Avenue was abruptly interrupted

by a multiarched edifice spanning the street. I followed the crowds through an arcaded walkway and through the doors of a huge building. I arrived at a high bank of escalators and descended into the vast echoing cavern of Grand Central. The last time I'd been here, I remembered, was the night Sharon and I had gone up to my brother's place for dinner.

What was I talking about, my brother? What was I talking about, Sharon? That probably wasn't even her name. A couple of damn actors, the pair of them.

My pace quickened. I felt myself getting madder. I crossed the concourse and went out into the yammering snarl of Forty-second Street. That gave me my bearings and, ten minutes later, I was walking into the shoddy building which Al Charmain had claimed was the New York headquarters of the Acis Corporation. Well, it wasn't then, according to George Trilling, and it wasn't now, according to me. The name was still in place on the filthy client board, and it was still on the door when I got upstairs, but when I went inside, I entered an office that had been abandoned. The tired furniture was still in place, including Al Charmain's foam rubber cushion, but the desktop held nothing but an empty Burger King carton and a candy bar wrapper, an eloquent reminder of the former occupant's compulsion.

I didn't poke around. I didn't want to find the rejected parts of burgers or of substandard french fries; I just left. I hadn't really expected to find Charmain there, even though he couldn't have been long gone, but I was pretty sure what his reaction would have been had I caught him there and told him that I knew which end was up now; he would have given me a merry wave, with whatever he'd been eating at the time, and said something like, "That's show biz, kid." And had I taken a step toward him with retribution in mind

I'm equally sure he would have produced a gun, and smilingly offered to blow away my gonads unless I backed off.

I quit that dreary office, went downstairs, and plunged into the people-jammed sidewalks. The road traffic was barely moving so I hiked it back to the rental on Twenty-ninth, and let myself in with my key.

It was a lot like Charmain's office: that same, untenanted atmosphere, like a feeling of yesterday; something that's been and gone. Everything was in place except Sharon's clothes, her makeup and toiletries, anything she owned that she could carry. It looked like we'd had a spat and decided to separate for a while. I picked up the phone, but it was dead; disconnected. A touch of symbolism there? Apart from the empty closet, and the cleared dressing table, the place looked much the same as it had when I'd left it several hours back: coffee mugs in the dishwasher, a wet towel hanging in the shower stall, the bed hastily made up, the same bed in which I'd spent two warm and sexy nights with Sharon.

I felt very different about the two people who'd fooled me so badly. Al Charmain had had me beaten close to death, and yet his cruelty didn't bother me as much as Sharon's deception did. That really stung. She'd induced my emotion, had given me what, in my naïveté, I'd understood to be love, and I'd responded to it in kind, or something close to it. So the woman had wounded me far more than the fat man had, although his damage would, in all likelihood, last a hell of a lot longer.

I stripped off my clothes—wait, that's not strictly true; they weren't my clothes—and went in and showered in the tiny cubicle, washed the dried sweat off my body and let the hot water soothe tired muscles. I chose jeans and a comfortable shirt from the wardrobe, and some track shoes—I should have been wearing them earlier for my run through Macy's—got a beer from the kitchen, sat down at a table, and unzipped the plastic envelope.

First off was a sheet of paper detailing my immediate personal stuff: Jackson Stephen Penrose, born May 16, 1956. Current address, 337 East 38th Street. I shared an apartment with one Jennifer Halpern whom, I saw, had been security cleared. The next sheet contained some personal history. I had to wonder why Acis had given me a rural background. Maybe they'd felt that growing up on a fruit farm, and splitting wood for a potbellied stove, would be more embraceable than the actual prosaic fact. It seems I'd grown up in Astoria, Queens, the only child of James and Eileen Penrose who were currently living in Coral Springs, Florida. There was a run-down on my education: local high school then liberal arts at Rutgers, a student year in Europe, then back home and—here was a surprise—I'd gone into the Army and been a career officer, at various bases around the country till 1982 when I'd moved into Army Intelligence based in Washington, DC. I'd spent a couple of years there then quit the Army and been employed as a civilian instructor at the Defense Intelligence College in Fairfax, Virginia, later being transferred to New York and something called Recruitment Liaison. I assumed that this was as close as a government document would come to admitting what I did for a living. Included in the package was a copy of my birth certificate, social security number, a medical report—I'd been in excellent health once upon a time—and a duplicate Pentagon ID card with a photograph of me taken maybe five years back when my hair had been lighter and uncovered by a bandage. It was the same shot that was on the ID issued to Jerry Parrish. Acis had simply taken the original and faked it with a name

change. I took my wallet from my jacket, pulled out the stuff
Charmain had supplied me with, and replaced it, thus saying good-bye to Jerry Parrish and hello to Jackson Penrose.
I went to the wardrobe and chose a down vest against the
cool of the spring evening, then walked out of the place. I
was starting from scratch with a whole new clean slate and
was determined to forget the miserable way in which I'd
been used.

However, there was one little piece of unfinished business that was nagging at me, so I did something about it: I
walked around to Lexington Avenue and found the little
Lebanese restaurant Sharon had taken me to the first night.

It was about six-thirty by this time, and there were only a
few tables occupied. The owner, the thick-bodied man with
the filmy eyes, was fussing with something when I walked
in. He turned to greet a customer and couldn't keep the
reaction off his face. He tried to hide it with a display of
professional indifference.

"Good evening, sir. You like table for one?"

"Sure, if I can have the one I had on Sunday night."

"Which was that, sir?"

"Your best one. You told me I'd been away too long.
Don't you remember me?"

He slid a bland little smile onto his face and glued it into
position.

"Forgeeve me. I get so manny customers."

"I'm sure you do. But how many do you get paid to
remember?"

The glued-on smile slipped a little. I left him trying to
salvage it and walked north wondering what I'd accomplished by going in there. I'd spent two minutes with a man
who'd been bought. I couldn't see my little visit helping
either of us become better human beings.

I managed to snare a cab, gave the driver the Thirty-eighth Street address, and took another stab at assimilating the recent revelations. I was thinking that before, when I'd been told I was a skip tracer, I'd been a little disappointed to find that I wasn't something with a touch more class, but now, learning that I was an undercover agent employed by the Pentagon, a guy who could be at such risk that they taught him guns and bone-breaking moves with his hands, well, that put a different complexion on it. It was a hurdle I just couldn't take in my stride. I was going to have to climb over it slowly.

As we got closer to midtown, another thought drove the previous one away: I was about to meet my girl, a woman I'd been living with, and I was a little leery after the last episode. I'd seen Sharon almost every day for six weeks before we'd started playing house, but with Jennifer—or Jenny, as Carmody had called her—the relationship was going to emerge full blown from the beginning; it would start off where it had left off for her, but be totally brand-new for me, and I wasn't sure how to handle it.

The taxi dropped me on the corner of Second Avenue outside of an apartment house much like a zillion others I'd seen around the city: fourteen stories of red brick with a sidewalk awning, and a deli and a dry cleaner and a liquor store opposite. I was beginning to get the impression that New Yorkers liked to eat and drink but were messy at it. I checked the mailboxes inside the street door and found, opposite 6D, the names Halpern/Penrose. There were no keys in the envelope George Trilling had given me—taken, no doubt, by Acis along with my real identification—and I was loath to press the button and announce myself. According to my file Jenny and I had been living together for fourteen months, so there had to be a strong relationship. I must have loved this woman, and so I didn't want to hear her voice for the "first" time through the murky amplification of a squawk box.

However, I got a break: somebody was coming out of the apartment house, which gave me an easy entry.

I rode up to the sixth floor, found apartment D, and knocked on the door knowing it would all be a touch anticlimactic if she wasn't home.

But she was.

The door opened on a safety chain. I got a glimpse of a pink ear, the corner of a mouth, an eye that widened quickly.

"Jack!" The voice was a breathy gasp. The door banged closed, the chain rattled, then the door was flung open and she was in my arms hugging me. "Where have you *been*?"

So far all I knew was that she was perhaps eight inches shorter than me, felt slim, and had sweet-smelling dark-brown hair. She clutched at me, raised her face, kissed me hard. I still didn't know what she looked like, but she tasted great: a warm, sweet breath. Sharon had been a smoker, and her breath was something I'd had to overlook. I mentally kicked myself for already indulging in comparisons, but maybe it was understandable: I was swapping one loved one for another in the space of a few days, and without any preliminaries.

She pulled back from me, tugging me into the apartment, her moist eyes roaming my face and sweeping anxiously over my bandana bandage as she shelled me with questions.

"Why didn't you call me? Couldn't you do it? I've been worried sick. You were never away this long before. What's that on your head?"

"I got held up."

"But why didn't you call? Did you hurt yourself?"

She was a pretty girl, not lovely like Sharon; she didn't have Sharon's soft, rounded features. Jenny's face was made up of angles and contours. Her dark hair was caught back in a pony tail and showed off delicate ears that petaled to a point. With her large, dark eyes and finely delineated nose, it lent her a gamin quality that went nicely with her diminutive size.

"I had a bit of a car accident," I said. The idea came to me out of the blue: to borrow the original explanation and see if I could fake it; see if it were possible to pick up my life and live it as if I were a normal person. I didn't stop to consider any possible ramifications that might result from my trying to fool Jenny, I just snatched at the plan and went with it.

Fright danced across her face, and the corners of her generous mouth turned down. "When? Where was this? Why wasn't I told?"

"Near Boston. I ran into a tree that was driving on the wrong side of the road. They shot the tree and took me to the hospital."

The attempt at keeping it light fell flat. Jenny looked shocked. "You were in the hospital and nobody called me?"

"I just wanted to get back on my feet. If I'd had visitors hanging around I'd—"

She spoke through me. "Visitors?" Her eyes glistened and her lower lip didn't look strong. "We're getting married in August. I think I qualify as a little more than a visitor." She looked hurt and mad at the same time, and her words came out in a rush. "Trilling ordered it, didn't he? No contact with the operatives when they're on official business. God, I hate your job. Look at that bandage! You must have been half dead."

She crushed herself to me as if the grim reaper was going

93

to have to take her, too, if he changed his mind and decided
to come back for me. Between hugs she upbraided me, and
railed against the College. Trilling had told me that Jenny
knew the basic details of my job, but had only a hazy idea of
exactly what it was I did. He'd also told me that I was
bound by military law to keep her, and everybody else, in
the dark. What he hadn't told me, no doubt because he
didn't know, was anything about my impending marriage.
The news was something of a surprise.

For the next five minutes I invented a story, sticking close
to my hospital experience but checking myself into Massa-
chusetts General, a sign for which I recalled seeing during
my trek around Boston. It wasn't hard to be convincing,
drawing as I was, for once, on experience, and Jenny didn't
question any of it. I told her that I'd busted my crown, that
there had been no complications, and that I was now well
and truly back on the road to virile manhood. She simmered
for quite a while, then eventually traded in her anger in
favor of relief that I was okay and back home. My initial
success buoyed me for the moment, although I suspected
things could get rocky once we started talking about events
or people I had no memory of.

And I was right.

I cut short what must have been her twentieth question
by pleading hunger. It was the truth: thanks to the incident
in the parking lot, and the CS gas, I had nothing in my
stomach.

"I don't have a thing. I've just been shopping for one,"
Jenny said, getting in a subtle dig at me. "We can hop
around to Guido's if you want."

I said Yes to whatever Guido's was. When Jenny sped off
to get ready I took a look at the place I'd called home for the
last year and a bit. I assumed that Jenny had been the

decorator; the walls were hung with framed graphic-art posters and the sanded floors bore bright, primitive-print rugs. The chairs were chrome and a leatherlike fabric; they didn't look very comfortable. I checked the closet and found that Al Charmain had done a pretty good job in approximating my clothes, although the gear back at Twenty-ninth Street was a little more conservative than my actual stuff. There was a bunch of his-and-her sports equipment in the sun-yellow, vivid-print bedroom, similar to what I'd seen at the other place, and I'd have to say that Jenny, with her slim, boyish figure, looked far more the tennis player and runner than Sharon, who was a little on the zoftig side. I completed my tour of the apartment noting, stacked beneath a music system, many of the same gun books and tape titles that I'd seen at the Twenty-ninth Street apartment. I was pretty sure the Acis people had got in here when Jenny had been at work. They'd clearly tried for a little authenticity, perhaps on the theory that the closer something was to the actual truth, the greater were its chances of being accepted.

I was just finishing a beer in the efficient little kitchen when Jenny joined me, and we left.

Guido's proved to be not an intimate little candlelit room as I'd somehow imagined, but a noisy and vibrant eatery where the ebullient waiters gave you a snatch of song as they seated you. Jenny fit right into the atmosphere; she was bright and sparkling and enjoyed the quick repartee with our waiter when she asked him what was good tonight. When he switched from the banter and asked for our order, I chose the grilled chicken.

"One of these days you're going to choose something else," Jenny chided me. Her comment boosted my confidence. So far I hadn't made any mistakes or raised her suspicions, although I knew I had a long, long way to go yet.

We snapped breadsticks, raised our drinks to being together again, Jenny back to layering me with questions about my hospital stay. I fielded those easily enough, but when she asked me the name of the surgeon, saying she'd check him out with Robbie, whom I assumed was a doctor pal of ours, I quickly killed the subject. "Enough about me and my wounds. How about you? What have you been doing?"

She started to tell me as the food arrived. There was plenty of it, and it was delicious. We split a bottle of wine, and the evening took off. I found myself warming to her, and it wasn't just the alcohol. She was wearing a stiffly pressed man's dress shirt, black pants, black pumps, a symphony of jangly bracelets, and very little makeup—just a touch of pencil to accent the slight slant of her eyes. She'd given up the pony tail in favor of a fuller hairstyle that curtained the fine bones of her face. When she talked, telling me about her job at a place she called the agency, she was constantly animated, and her hands flew when she told a couple of funny anecdotes. She was such a different type from Sharon: extroverted, out front with her opinions. Slobby Al Charmain had got close on my clothes, close on my books and music, but he'd missed by a mile on my girl.

We didn't order dessert or coffee; we got the check and left. Walking back to the apartment, Jenny wound down a little, and I caught her once or twice darting fast looks at me as if—and I could have been reading something into this— she was wondering if it was really me walking beside her. But I assumed she realized that, having barely recovered from head surgery, I could hardly be expected to be my old self. I saw that as being a major problem if I hoped to carry off this pose: how was I going to perform like me if I didn't know what me was like?

By the time we'd got upstairs Jenny had snapped out of her brief downer and had appeared to have come to some kind of equable decision about what she probably regarded as the change in my behavior. She made coffee, we had a cognac, and then I found myself facing what I'd faced with Sharon that first night: intimacy. I hadn't really expected my homecoming with my real girl to be much different from what it had been with a woman who'd merely been playing the part.

And it wasn't.

Two people who are supposed to be in love, who haven't seen each other for a long time, they go to bed at the first good opportunity—I didn't need to know much about life to know that—and that's exactly what we did.

To say that I was a relative virgin when it came to women is quite true—I'd only been to the starting gate twice, but I got a strong feeling that Jenny hadn't had sex for a long time. It was too early to make a judgment about her character, but she impressed me as the one-man type, and I think, although I had no real benchmark to measure against, that it showed in her lovemaking. She was extremely ardent, again in a different way from Sharon, and again maybe it's not very sporting of me to make comparisons, but seeing Sharon was being paid to sleep with me, I don't feel too much constraint in this area.

Jenny's technique was a match for her personality: she made love with excitement, humor, and total enthusiasm. If Sharon had been luscious in her softness and warmth, Jenny was innovative and demonstrative. Whereas Sharon had assumed what I took to be the classic passive feminine role, Jenny was much more the new woman, often taking the dominant position.

I'll have to admit it was hard for me to keep up with her exertions; after the kind of day I'd had, I was ready for sleep. It didn't arrive, however, not for a long time. Jenny, on the other hand, after a second strenuous session, curled herself into me, locked a leg on to mine, murmured something about only being able to sleep properly when I wasn't around, then promptly demonstrated her ability when I was around.

I lay awake listening to the siren sound of late-night New York and wondering if anybody had ever had two deep relationships with two women as quickly as I'd had them. I could see myself falling easily for Jenny. Probably. But what if I didn't? I was due to marry her in twelve weeks. Could I do it? She had an infectious personality, was fun to be with, and was great in bed, but I didn't know her. Could I walk down the aisle with her and honor a commitment made in a former life? Should I break off the relationship now or let it ride and see what developed? Right then three months seemed like a long time, and I knew I should be far more concerned with the immediate future, like tomorrow and the next day.

The thought of the future brought up another question: what my next job would be, and whether or not I could function as well as I seemed to have in finding Werner Frohman's trail. I was assuming that the hunt for this elusive scientist, and his mysterious Glitterbug, was all over, that he'd emerge to pick up his mail and that would be that; we would have found him.

But, as I was shortly to discover, it wasn't going to be that simple. It was going to be a real killer.

CHAPTER SIX

I ran into my first potential stumbling block at eight-thirty the next morning.

I came out of the bedroom to find Jenny picking up her handbag and making for the door. She gave me a fast hug, told me to call her at the shop, and fled.

The shop. I assumed that was her name for the agency where she worked. Fine, but where the hell did she work? I poked through a desk and found her passport—Jennifer Bryant Halpern; was Bryant a name inherited from a previous marriage or were girls being called that twenty-eight years ago? None of my business, really. I found some other odds and ends: financial stuff, bank statements, expired credit cards, and a letter addressed to her from the Art Directors Club of New York, so I at least knew she was an art director even if I didn't know what kind of art she directed. There was nothing to tell me where her office was.

I was prying into more of her business when somebody rang the doorbell. I opened the door on Ray Carmody.

"Hi there, partner," he said.

He sauntered in past me. I say sauntered, although I'm not sure that's the right word. He had an insolent way of moving, a challenge in his body as if he expected the air in front of him to give him an argument. He dropped his lanky frame onto the sofa. The gray suit he was wearing hung on him as if it had been made for an even bigger man. The back of the jacket, I'd noted, was badly wrinkled. It looked like it had been slept in.

"Trilling told me to swing on by and talk you into taking

a vacation." He ran his pale eyes over my pajamas, my bare feet, my sleep-tossed hair. "Looks like you're already on one."

It was Carmody who needed the vacation. His skin was pasty, and his mouth dragged down at one corner of his lumpy jaw.

"Wouldn't have a cup of coffee for an old soldier, would you? I'm a trifle fatigued."

"You been up all night?"

"And then some. When the friendly folk at Acis clobbered you, it didn't make my life any easier. They gave me a young kid to break in. He has delusions about the job. I don't know what they tell 'em when they recruit these days. I think they must run a fucking James Bond movie." He stuck a cigarette in his mouth, lit it, and squinted at the smoke through bleary eyes. "How about that coffee?"

I went out into the kitchen, made coffee for both of us—I had to read the instructions on the label—and brought two mugs back into the living room. Carmody was just crushing his quarter-smoked cigarette into a painted saucer. "Goddamn nail," he muttered, and broke the cigarette in half as I'd seen him do before. He reached for his coffee, took a long swallow.

"So how's the memory?" He nodded toward the bedroom. "Did unwedded bliss bring it back? That'd be something, wouldn't it? Have everything come back to you right in the middle of a hump?"

When I'd met Carmody the day before I'd thought he was just this side of obnoxious, and his remark didn't do much to change my mind.

"Can I ask you a question?"

"Why not?" He waved limply. "You gonna be asking a thousand of 'em anyway."

"What kind of team did we make, you and I? How did we get on?"

"Better than some. Not as good as most."

"Were we effective?"

"Hell, yes. Coupla bear cats on the job. I'm good at detail, and you kept guessing right." He pointed to himself, then to me. "Legwork Lennie and Madam Lazonga and her crystal ball." He drank some more coffee and frowned as if I'd got the proportions wrong. "Whether you and me are still gonna be able to hit the long ball is highly debatable. Trilling thinks so."

"But you don't, huh?"

Without the slightest attempt at diplomacy Carmody said, "No, I don't. How a guy who couldn't even remember his name is supposed to go back to being a star is beyond me."

"I seem to have done okay so far."

"Yeah, I give you that. You traced Frohman, and maybe I couldn't have done it half as quick. But it was a simple job, and, okay, maybe you made it simple, but the thing is, you did it all on hunch. You didn't have to use any of your training. Your experience. Your tradecraft. And maybe you're gonna need all that next job. And you won't have it. You got nothing to draw on, same as this wetpants rookie I got hanging on my sleeve. And that's gonna make my end tougher."

I couldn't argue against any of this; it was exactly what I'd been wondering about myself.

"And there's something else different than before." Carmody put down his coffee mug, climbed wearily out of the sofa. "You. You're different. I don't mean because you couldn't remember the name of the chick you're banging, I mean different otherwise. Listening to you talking to Trilling yesterday, I swear I wasn't sure if Acis hadn't maybe sent over a ringer in your place."

I didn't like hearing that; it chilled me. It was too close to what had been lurking around the fringes of my thoughts: had my injury changed what was essentially me and put a stranger in my place? I wasn't really interested in the opinion of a churl like Carmody, but as my partner he'd know me as well as anybody, so what he said would have to carry some weight.

"What do you mean, different?"

"You used to be hungry, Jacko. I don't think you're hungry anymore."

"Hungry for what?"

Carmody ran his tongue around his long teeth and picked out a piece of tobacco from his brief cigarette. "Anything. Everything. I mean, I walk in here, I been up all night, I'm tired, right? And maybe I said a few things I could've said softer. About Jenny and that. And you didn't say shit. The old Jack Penrose would've cussed me out and threatened bodily harm."

"I'd do that? Threaten you?"

"You were always threatening people. It was your trademark. You were a competitive sonofabitch, Jacko. It made you a pain in the ass to work with, but, who knows, maybe it gave the drive that made you a good operator." Carmody waved a dismissive hand at me. "I don't see the drive anymore." I listened to him. He'd admitted he was tired; maybe it was just the fatigue talking.

"I'm sorry to hear we didn't get on, Ray. What was my problem?"

Carmody clearly didn't want to field this question. He looked uncomfortable. "We'll talk about it another day."

"We'll talk about it now. What was wrong with me?"

Carmody worked at a crick in his neck and said, without looking at me, "You couldn't handle what happened to Malinda."

I didn't know any Malinda, of course, and I wasn't looking forward to finding out who she was or what had happened to her. I had a lousy feeling in the pit of my stomach. But I steeled myself and nodded at him to continue.

"She was your kid."

"*Was?* I had a family?" I was stunned.

"Your wife's name is Sarah. Ex-wife now. You two split up and she got custody. Coupla years back you took Malinda out for the day. Took her to the park. She fell off the carousel. They couldn't save her."

I couldn't speak. I was horrified.

Carmody shrugged his hands and tried for a little indifference.

"You blamed yourself, but it could've happened to anybody. It wasn't your fault. She just slipped."

"How old was she?"

"Seven."

I stared at Carmody. I got the impression he was playing it a little too cool.

"You're holding something back."

He shrugged as if it wasn't important.

"Better tell me, Ray."

He waved his hand and tried to toss the line away.

"Hell, you'd had a few pops."

I turned away. I felt ill. It wasn't exactly hard to read between the lines—if I hadn't been drinking, my daughter would probably still have been alive. It was a tremendous blow, more than I could handle right then. Don't think about it I told myself. Get your mind back to things you can do something about. So, I took emotional refuge in that small part of myself I seemingly had some control over.

"Let's get back to my job. Did I ever have any other partners?"

"Bet your ass you did. Do you remember a guy named Demchuk?" Carmody grunted, tapped a finger against his freckled forehead. "What am I talking about? You don't remember anything. Harry Demchuk was your partner before me. You two didn't get on for the same reason we don't, because you bring something to the job that the other guy can't understand. The carny bit, the hunches. So it sets up friction. Only the friction got outta hand between you and Demchuk so you invited him out into the alley one night. Take a look in the mirror."

"What?"

"Go ahead."

I didn't know what he was getting at, but I walked over to the front door. A gilt-framed mirror hung to one side of it.

"Look at your right eye."

I knew what he was referring to now: a small scar that slit the hairs of my eyebrow. I'd noticed it when the primary head bandages had first come off. It was an old scar and I'd wondered about it.

"Demchuk did that to you. Five stitches, so I heard."

I ran my finger down the thin, raised edge. "Demchuk clobbered me, huh?"

"You got up. You left him lying in the alley for the medics."

Carmody couldn't have failed to see the effect his earlier news had on me. He was watching me watching myself in the mirror. I was examining more than my scar. I was looking at a guy who'd been responsible for his daughter's death.

"What happened to Demchuk? Was he okay?"

"After a while, sure. He quit the College and went over to ATF."

"What's that?"

Carmody blinked heavily. His expression said, "See what I mean? I'm going to have to teach you everything."

"Tobacco and Firearms." He reached for the door handle. "Go get some sun."

"Wait. Where does Jenny work?"

"You didn't ask her?" Carmody waited for an answer, then understanding flattened his bored expression. His mouth took on a derisive list. "You won't fool her for long. She's a smart kid." He opened the door, said, "Holden and Somebody" and left.

I went back to looking at the stranger in the mirror. Ex-husband, ex-father.

And ex what else?

I called Jenny at her agency, an advertising agency I found in the phone book—Holden, Irwin, and Kapell—and told her I was being urged to take a paid vacation and I thought I might just go down to Florida and see my parents. She said she wasn't about to be widowed again, that she had some time coming, and would be free to come along if I wanted some company. It was fine with me although it meant I'd have to fake a normal memory with my parents, but I'd already decided to do that anyway. I was holding on to a small hope that I wouldn't have to fake anything at all, that the sight of my folks would be the catalyst that would bust my memory loose. I'd done quite a bit of reading up on my condition, and the textbooks said that the more familiar a person was to an amnesiac—the longer the relationship—

the greater the likelihood of a sluggish memory being stimulated.

I left all the arrangements to Jenny who didn't get back till ten that evening. She'd had to finish up some work so she could get free. She brought home some Chinese food and some Mexican beer. We dined while we watched part of a movie on TV, then went to bed and enjoyed some athletic and enthusiastic sex. On the verge of sleep she curled herself into me, kissed my neck, and told me she loved me. I told her I loved her, too. It was a fib, but I figured I must have loved her before and no doubt would again. I was happy being with her, sharing her bed and her life, happy with her sunny personality and pretty pixie looks, so I rationalized my fib that way.

We left the next day; caught a morning flight from La Guardia. Jenny was excited by the trip and talked about taking my folks down to the reef again, so I learned from that that she'd made the trip with me in the past, although I wondered what she meant by the reef. I think she was glad to be going to Florida more for my benefit than her own. She wanted me to get some sunshine because, as she'd told me more than once, I was looking a little peaked. But I was apparently looking a little more than that because I caught her twice during the flight peeking at me with an expression on her face I couldn't read: puzzlement maybe, or uncertainty. Whatever it was, she instantly switched to a smile and looked away. We landed at a place called Fort Lauderdale. Jenny had a rental car reserved, and I asked her would she mind driving, telling her I had a headache from the flight. I had to come up with some excuse because, while I knew my parents lived in Coral Springs, I didn't know how to get there.

It was a fast drive; we zipped the Interstate with the air

conditioner humming and some rock gospel on the radio. We turned off at a town called Pompano Beach and headed west.

"By the way," Jenny said. "We have an invite to John and Nancy's next Saturday."

"Great," I replied.

Jenny didn't answer immediately, and I assumed she was concentrating on picking up the right route. The road she chose traveled through pretty country spread out under a vast blue sky. High white clouds in the brilliant distance were being slowly towed around by invisible winds that stayed up in the stratosphere. Florida looked placid, flat, pleasant. I think the state flag should have been green and blue: green for the Bermuda grass that grew everywhere, and blue for that never-ending sky. I liked the look of the place. Florida had a relaxed, welcoming feel to it, and I was glad to be there.

"We can get a ride with Pete and Mary Carlson," Jenny said. "You want to do that?"

"Fine with me."

And then she went very quiet, listening to the music, or so I supposed. She slowed the car and pulled in to a rest area. I thought she was going to ask me to take the wheel, and I was getting an excuse ready, but I needn't have bothered. Jenny got out, walked off aways, and sat down at a redwood picnic table. I figured she just wanted a break so I got out, too, crunched over a white crushed-shell path and onto grass that was like stiff broadloom underfoot. The temperature was way up, and humidity lay like a wet sheet in the air, but it didn't seem to bother Jenny; in a cream skirt and blouse that embraced her trim little figure, she looked cool and composed. But when I saw her large, serious eyes and the firm set to her mouth, I knew something had gone wrong. She didn't pussyfoot into it; that wouldn't have been her way.

"What's going on, Jack?" Her pretty face squinched a little as she looked up at me, the sun over my shoulder.

"What do you mean?"

"I knew you'd changed somehow, I knew the minute I saw you. But I put it down to what you'd been through. But there's more to it than that."

"What makes you think so?"

"A couple of little things, and one not so little thing."

"Like what couple of little things?" I knew I was dead. I was just stonewalling, curious to hear where I'd fallen down.

"When I told you about John and Nancy's party, you said great like you meant it. But you've never been able to stand John Ellis. I had to drag you to the last party they had, and you stayed about ten minutes."

"I'm trying to be a little more tolerant, I guess."

Jenny dismissed my lame excuse with a quick shake of her head. "I also said we could get a ride with Pete and Mary Carlson, and you said fine. I don't know anybody by that name."

And that was that. I suppose I could have claimed I hadn't heard her properly, but that would only have set up a quiz on how many of our friends I could name, so I threw in the towel and fessed up about my amnesia. But I told her it was the result of a car accident; I said nothing about the Acis Corporation, or my brief life as Jerry Parrish, and certainly nothing about Sharon. I lied my head off and told her that the accident had occurred on the way to the airport, and that I'd woken up in Lenox Hill with no recollection of anything or anybody. George Trilling hadn't informed her, or my parents, because technically I was still on an assignment and College policy forbade any contact with anybody but the brass until I'd been debriefed. I'd be kept incommunicado until the brass had been satisfied they'd got all they could from me which, because of my problem, was zero. It was a convoluted excuse, but Jenny appeared to accept it, what she'd heard of it anyway. As soon as I'd said my memory was gone, I don't think she listened to anything else. She looked floored.

"My God! I knew something was—but I never—Jack! . . ."

"I should have leveled with you, I know. But I wanted to see if I could pass for normal."

"Of course you're normal." She reached for my hand and held it fiercely. "You have a memory problem, not a mental problem." She burbled a string of questions, and my considered answers helped assuage some of her fright. Then the hurt surfaced.

"Then, you didn't know me. When you got back yesterday. As far as you knew you'd never seen me before. Never spoken to me . . ."

I had no reply except a confessional shrug.

"You only knew I was your girl because you were told I was. So you've been making love to a stranger." Jenny's eyes blinked tears. "You told me last night you loved me. You lied. Everything's been a lie."

"Jenny, listen to me. It was awful being nobody. I wanted to be who I am even if I didn't know the guy. What he thought, what he believed in, how he behaved, what he liked, what he hated. I wanted to be Jack Penrose, and Jack Penrose turned out to be living with a terrific girl, and that was a wonderful thing. I thought that if I could pick up my old life without anybody noticing, then it'd be like I never left it. So I didn't tell you. I tried to fool you because I didn't want to be a freak."

She squeezed my hand again, clinging on tight, her head shaking away my thinking. "That's a dreadful word to use, and totally wrong. You're simply a man who could use a little help from time to time. You should have confided in me, Jack. What you did was wrong."

"I know. And you're right, I could use a little help. Especially on this trip. I want to try to get by my parents."

"That's why you asked me to drive, isn't it? Because you don't remember where you're going. You don't remember your parents, or where they live, or anything about them."

"Maybe it won't matter. I want to give it a shot, anyway. My folks, our friends . . . I think I can do it if you're there to fill in the blanks. How about it?"

Jenny rubbed a finger along her cheekbone, brushed moisture away, took a breath, recovered. "Well . . ." She gave me half a smile. "I'm in the advertising business, I've had a lot of experience at fooling people."

I pulled her to her feet and hugged her. But whereas before she would have entwined her arms around me and brought her body into mine, she kept her arms at her sides, her body stiff. She said, "You're going to have to get to know me all over again."

"I already know you a little."

"But you're not in love with me. How could you be?"

"It'll come. I'm the same person I was before. What happened before will happen again."

There was no response from her. It would have been totally quiet but for the sound of cars whipping by, and a high insect buzz coming from a covered litter bin. It looked like I'd hit a nerve with that last remark. I got the impression that Jenny had a reply all ready to go but was holding it back.

"Come on," she said, taking my hand. "Let's get going."

We got in the car, and Jenny took it away.

"What do the doctors say?"

"Only what they read in the manuals. It could come back in bits and pieces or not. Depends on the amount of cell damage. I wake up in the morning expecting it to be all better—like a fever that's run its course. I try to reach back beyond that first day I came to in the hospital, but it's just figures moving in smoke." The air-conditioning leaned its cool breeze against us. The radio had been switched off, and silence separated driver and passenger. I could tell there was something Jenny was leaving unsaid, and I was pretty sure what it was.

"Back there I said I hadn't changed, but I get the feeling you don't agree."

That brought her head around. "How did you know?"

"A couple of people have told me I'm different now. Ray Carmody for one. And I see it when I look at photographs of myself. Especially in the eyes."

"There was something clenched about you before," Jenny said to the windshield.

"Because of Malinda?"

That swung her head again.

"Carmody told me all about it."

Jenny nodded sadly, let out some breath. "You could never get over it. Never forgive yourself. Even though it could've happened—"

When she broke off, I finished the sentence for her. "Even if I hadn't been drinking?" I gave it a beat, then asked her how the tragedy had affected my behavior.

Jenny changed her grip on the steering wheel. She clearly didn't like talking about it, but she was into it now.

"You got physical."

"You mean I shoved people around?"

"I'm afraid so."

"Did you ever meet somebody named Harry Demchuk?"

Jenny nodded with great care. "You came home one night with plaster over your eye. You told me you'd made a wrong move in some kind of refresher course. Next day Ray Carmody came around, and you introduced him as your new partner. I wondered what was wrong with your old partner, Harry. Sometime later, when I'd got to know Ray better, he told me you'd had a fight with Harry, put him in the hospital."

"He told me that, too. Yesterday I wasn't sure it was true. There's something about that guy that doesn't inspire my confidence."

"Ray's an upfront guy who's not crazy about his job. You can believe what he says, he just doesn't know how to put it nicely."

"Did you ever witness any of this? Ever see me take on anybody?"

"Yes, I did. Twice at football games you got into arguments you could have walked away from. You're a big man, Jack, but you always managed to find somebody bigger so you could cut them down."

I didn't like what I was hearing. And it didn't get any better.

Jenny took her eyes off the road long enough to give me a plain look.

"You became belligerent toward me, too. Not physically, but you did an awful lot of yelling."

That surprised me. I couldn't imagine, even in a wild rage, yelling at somebody as lovable as Jenny.

"Give me a for instance . . ."

She did. She told me we'd been discussing Ray Carmody one day and she'd said she thought he was good-looking in a surly kind of way. I'd blown up her remark into an accusation that she was sleeping with Carmody.

The information disturbed me. The person I was hearing about didn't sound like me, and yet it had to be. Jenny had known him, Carmody had known him. And I hadn't. But that person was no longer me, or I was no longer that person. I'd taken zero pleasure in belting that guy with the gun uptown, the mugger, and the two dark suits I'd taken out in Macy's had been a straight case of personal survival, or so I'd thought. I'd felt nothing but relief at getting past them. I certainly hadn't got any jollies from slugging anybody. However, that thought didn't stop me from feeling ashamed of myself and suddenly uncomfortable with my big and muscular body.

We stopped talking for a while, then resumed again a few miles farther on when we turned off at a crossroads. Our speed dropped as we came to the edge of an urbanized area, a sign welcoming us to Coral Springs. Jenny, wanting to get back to some kind of normalcy, began to chat about the town, telling me a developer had reclaimed some acres from the Everglades and built pretty houses on the lots. Then two guys from Madison Avenue had come down, put some TV spots together, and sold the lots as the Last Piece of Gold on the Gold Coast. The place had taken off and just gone on growing.

We drove into a downtown area, and I got my first good look at Florida retirement folk. Everybody was dressed as if they were on their way to a carnival: floral shirts, pastel-

113

colored shorts, and a weird assortment of caps and hats, although, when it came to strange head gear, nobody beat what I was wearing.

Jenny said she wanted to pick up a little present for my parents, some chocolate mints they both loved, so we pulled into the parking lot of a shopping mall. Jenny disappeared into a candy store, and I wandered over to check out a display in the picture framer's opposite. I was trying to work out a bizarre-looking painting when I heard a voice, full of astonishment, say, *"Jack!"* I turned around. A tan-faced, gray-haired woman holding a garden rake and a shopping bag, was gaping at me, a big, surprised smile beginning to expand her face.

"What in the world . . ." She came to me, dropped the shopping bag, hugged me, kissed my cheek. "Why didn't you call? Is Jenny with you? Why didn't you let us know you were coming?"

I knew it was my mother because it had to be, but I had trouble keeping a smile on my mouth because I didn't recognize her. She could have been just anybody. It zonked me; I'd really been hoping that the sight of somebody who'd raised me would burn off the fog inside my head.

"We wanted to surprise you," I said, doing the best I could.

She held a hand to her heart and pretended to sag. "You certainly did that. I got such a shock. What happened to your head?"

"It looks a lot worse than it is. A car accident."

"Jack . . . !"

"It's no big deal. I'm fine. The medic was getting paid by the stitch so he worked overtime, that's all."

"Eileen . . ."

It was Jenny coming out of the candy store looking surprised and a little concerned. As the two women embraced, Jenny shot me an inquiring look. I mouthed an "Okay," and Jenny relaxed. They chatted together for a minute, mutual greetings and long-time-no-see remarks, then my mother said, "Come on, let's get home. I want to hear about this accident. When was it? No wonder we haven't heard from you."

It was a pleasant few days; I enjoyed it. I liked my parents and felt surprisingly close to them. My mother was a warm person, a little scatty, with lots of personality and a ready laugh. My father, maybe five years younger than my mother, a big, bluff guy—I could see where I'd got my size from—seemed relaxed and comfortable with me, and we got on well. But I noticed he was very much the boss, inside the house and out of it, too. He liked to organize people, liked his own way. Being as big as he was, I guess he was used to getting it.

I was able to cover my memory problem largely because I had Jenny backing me up. Whenever the conversation got around to something that had happened on a previous visit, or mention was made of somebody I was supposed to know, Jenny nudged my answers in the right direction.

We drove to the reef Jenny had been talking about, which turned out to be in a place called Key Largo, the John Pennekamp reef. We took the ferry over. My folks sat on the beach and relaxed while Jenny and I went diving with masks and snorkels. I loved being surrounded by all the incredibly colorful marine life, dropping into a world where there was no gravity, no sound, where I didn't have to pretend to anything, and where no conversation could remind me that I didn't know a damn thing about the world. The following day my parents went out for a couple of hours after lunch to see some old-time tennis stars at a tournament in Boca Raton. I opted out, telling them I was expecting a call from the office, an excuse which, to my surprise, I was able to support. I wanted some time to myself in the house. It wasn't the house of my boyhood, of course, but there were things in it I wanted to get close to. I found a real prize in a chest in my parents' bedroom: a photo album. It was old and well used; the shots had been pasted in, and somebody, almost certainly my mother, had written in details beneath each shot. As I turned the pages I watched myself growing up: as a baby, held by my mother, a good-looking woman in her midtwenties; as a fair-haired toddler, straddling my father's broad shoulders; aged about nine, in a too-bright interior shot, a festooned Christmas tree in the background; another of me perhaps a year later, sitting proudly behind the wheel of a pickup truck pointing to the legend on the door: Penrose Building Supply. In the high school and college shots, shared with simpering cheerleaders in sweaters and skirts, my hair had darkened and I'd begun to fill out. The last couple of pages had more recent photos, with the bright Florida sun replacing the seasons of New York. "Jack and Marlee, May '87" was written under one of me and a blond woman—Marlee, cute and diminutive like Jenny, was obviously an earlier girlfriend. There was a good one of Jenny, her hair worn longer then, clowning in a barbecue apron, brandishing a spatula at the camera. An unknown photographer had taken a shot of Jenny and me and my folks standing beneath the palm tree on the front lawn.

I found what I was really looking for on the last two pages of the album: photographs of my ex-wife and Malinda. The shots had been relegated to the back, probably because my folks hadn't wanted to be reminded of their dead grandchild every time they opened the album. She was a pensive-looking kid with a serious expression and lots of straight blond hair. She'd clearly got that hair from her mother, my ex-wife Sarah. Sarah was tall and angular with an amused slant to her mouth. Pleasant-looking. But it was the shots of Malinda I stared at. There were several with me. One in particular brought a lumpy feeling to my gut. I was holding Malinda, who looked to be about five years old then, on my shoulders, and she was looking down at me in trepidation as if she were afraid I'd let her go. The thought that, a few years later, I had let her go, was a crusher.

I put the album away. I felt ambivalent about finding it. On one hand, it furnished painful evidence of a child whom I'd failed. On the other hand, the album supplied vivid evidence of my own childhood, clearly a happy one, and it was wonderful to discover that, instead of being a Mr. Nobody from Nowhere, I had good strong roots.

The phone call I mentioned, the one from the office, came through about an hour after everybody got back from the tennis tourney.

It was Ray Carmody, complete with his usual blunt manner. There were no preliminaries; I answered the phone and he said, "Trilling wants you back."

"I thought he wanted me down here."

"That was then, this is now. We lost contact with Frohman. We gotta find him again."

"What happened?"

"Tell you tomorrow. There's a flight leaving Lauderdale at noon. They're holding two seats for you. I'll meet the plane."

"No need to do that."

"Bet your ass there's a need. Charmain and his merry men know the Kraut's loose. They may try to grab you again. They'd try now if they knew where you were."

"How did they find out? About Frohman?"

"You ask a lot of questions for a genius."

"I need a lot of answers."

"You'll get 'em. Just be on that plane."

CHAPTER SEVEN

There looked to be only three people meeting the plane who weren't Hispanics; one was Ray Carmody, and the other two wore the uniform of the New York City police.

For a minute I didn't realize that the two cops were with Carmody. He'd got some sleep since the last time I'd seen him, but he still managed a rumpled look. I don't think he chose his clothes with much care. His large, freckled hands dangled from the sleeves of his off-the-peg suit, and the collar of the jacket was having a hard time accommodating his wide, sloping shoulders. The slightly scruffy look was a perfect match for his hardness; he had an internal toughness that shone through. I couldn't imagine him smiling, or telling a joke, or even getting one.

As we came up he ignored me and greeted Jenny.

"Hi, Jen. You bring me some key lime pie?"

Jenny was polite, but that's all. She seemed itchy in his presence, and I wondered if they'd had words in the past. Whatever it was she certainly wasn't crazy about him, which made two of us. She nodded at the patrolmen. "How come we rate an escort?"

"C'mon, I'll tell you."

Carmody ferried us over to a less populated section, the two cops, young guys already bored with their day, lumbering along behind. "Me and the genius," Carmody explained to Jenny, stopping our little group in a far corner, "have got to find a guy. But there's another outfit looking for him, too. And they know your boyfriend's good at finding people. So

119

we got a cop escort in case they have ideas of applying pressure.''

Jenny's face had picked up quite a bit of sun, but she lost a little of her color then.

"What kind of pressure?"

"They may try to get to him through you or his folks—or both.''

That was news. It was a shock hearing it.

"My folks? Why the hell didn't you tell me on the phone? I just left—"

Carmody waved me to a halt. "We got it all covered. A couple of Florida State troopers are camped on their door.'' He swung his pale eyes to Jenny. "Same thing's gonna happen with you. You'll have one of New York's finest sitting outside your apartment. And he'll walk you to work and hang around there, too. Tell your boss you're a protected witness or something. It'll give you a touch of glamour.''

Jenny took my arm. She wasn't worried for herself, it was more a gesture of protection for me. She knew there'd be no uniformed cop following me around.

"How about Jack? Who looks after him?''

"I do. What are partners for?''

I was wrong about Carmody, he did have a sense of humor, warped as it was, and that was his idea of a little joke.

"You don't have to worry about him," he told Jenny, as if he were talking to a nervous bride, "he's gonna vanish for a few days. Him and me together.''

He led the way through the terminal, the silent patrolmen swinging their nightsticks, herding us along.

I told Jenny there was nothing to be concerned about; nobody could touch me if they couldn't find me, and if the US Government couldn't hide somebody, nobody could. She appeared somewhat mollified but didn't like the idea of being separated again. I didn't, either, especially if I was going to be swapping roommates—Jenny for Carmody.

We retrieved our baggage and went outside where two cars waited for us, nondescript vehicles, a Chevy and a Plymouth. I kissed Jenny good-bye, told her it would only be for a few days. From the look on her face I gathered I'd told her the same thing last time when she hadn't seen me again for weeks.

She hugged me, then got into the Chevy. The driver was one of the dark suits, one of the guys who'd chased me. He looked at me as if I'd already vanished. One of the cops got in next to him, then the car pulled away.

Carmody and I got into the Plymouth, which had a similar arrangement: a dark suit behind the wheel, the second cop riding shotgun. I didn't understand why we needed a patrolman assuming, as I did, that Carmody was armed. But he soon set me straight about that. "Because," he said, rolling down the window on the pleasant afternoon, "as bad as Acis would like to get their hands on Jack Penrose, ace person-finder, they're not about to shoot a uniformed flatfoot to do it. They'd kill one or two of us without even thinking about it. Why not? I mean, who are we? Some government agency with initials nobody's even heard of. But you kill a duty cop, you can't buy any deeper shit. And to snatch you or Jenny or your folks, that's what they're gonna have to do, because the cops have orders to hang tough."

"They'd kill to get Frohman? Why do they want him so badly? Who is this guy?"

"A brain is who he is. I told you, or Trilling did, whatever he's come up with has got to have a military application. The Chinks want it, and we want it."

"A germ weapon, that right?"

Carmody pulled his lips back on his teeth as if a migraine

121

had struck. He wasn't in pain, he was just uncomfortable with the conversation, and not crazy about being with me.

The feeling was more than mutual. I didn't want to be in New York with my dyspeptic partner, I wanted to be in Florida with Jenny and my parents. I wanted to be back where I felt I was wanted, where I could get a little sympathy and affection.

"I don't know," Carmody said, "maybe he's finally come up with the O bomb."

I had to ask him what that was.

"The orgasm bomb. You drop it on the other side and their whole fucking army comes in their pants. They lie down and go to sleep, and you capture 'em."

More of Carmody's humor. He sure didn't like being my teacher, but I wasn't going to stop asking questions. I needed to know things: like, for example, how they'd come to lose Frohman.

"Frohman called the mail service and canceled his box. Told them he wouldn't be needing it anymore."

"Did you check with that library in Boston? Maybe he gave—"

"Sure, we checked with them. First thing we did. He called the library and canceled that Boston U magazine. Said he didn't need it after all. They'd sent it anyway."

"Were you able to get hold of it?"

Carmody had it on the seat beside him, a copy, as he explained.

He handed it to me, an innocuous-looking thing: sixty-five pages bound by a blue paper cover with the university's crest on the front.

"I don't know if he smelled a rat or what," Carmody said, "but we've lost the fucker again. He's in town somewhere, but so are eight million other bastards."

"We don't even know that," I said. "He could have called the library from anywhere."

Carmody recognized that as an unfortunate truth, and a morose silence settled in.

The traffic squinched and slowed as we hit some backed-up stuff.

It seemed to reflect our position in the hunt for Werner Frohman. I asked my moody partner about this disappearing trick we were supposed to do. He told me, in his usual grudging manner, that because of the informant Trilling insisted on keeping around, Acis knew as much as we did and would be following him, Carmody, in the sure knowledge that we'd be getting together to try to pick up Frohman's trail.

I swiveled round to check the rear window.

"Forget it. You wouldn't know what to look for anymore."

A real charmer, my partner. He regarded my memory loss as something I'd brought on myself, like a bad hangover.

"Why aren't you looking?"

"What's the point? They're back there somewhere, let 'em follow us. We both have to lose them. It makes sense to do it at the same time."

The conversation evaporated. I flicked through the magazine, a scholarly, dry-looking thing. I ran my eye down the index page, which listed the names of contributors and the subjects covered. They were all way too esoteric for my limited knowledge. I gave myself up to the scenery, which was a little weird: we were passing some kind of huge globe set in a lake, an abandoned-looking scene that reminded me of an illustration in a science fiction book my tutor had shown me. Looking at it, although I don't think there was any connection, something popped into my head, something I couldn't identify, although I was certain it had to do with a word or a phrase or a name in the magazine. I couldn't pin it down, so I decided to let it cook and thought no more about it. The traffic unblocked, and we made good time into Manhattan. The driver took us to Lexington Avenue, to a subway entrance on Twenty-eighth and Park.

I fetched my suitcase from the trunk. Carmody had one, too. I didn't know what was happening, but I followed him down the stairs and got my first look, in my new life, at a New York City subway station. I knew right away it wasn't one of the things I'd been missing. The cop had a word with the token seller, then led the way through a gate where we joined maybe a dozen people waiting on the platform. The patrolman took up a position near the turnstiles heading off some people coming down the stairs.

"Short holdup, folks," the cop said.

The announcement was greeted with obscenities and moans of complaint. Another group clattered down the stairs and they, too, were repelled. Looking over the angry crowd I knew that any one of those people could be an Acis person: the guy with the briefcase, the woman with the Gristedes bag, the kid who looked like he was on a delivery. The crowd stirred and pressed forward at an approaching rumble up the tracks. A rush of hot metallic air preceded the thunderous arrival of a train. As the car doors slammed back, the cop called out loudly: "Anybody tries to board gets a busted head. This is poleece bidness."

About a dozen people got off the train, but Carmody and I were the only ones to board, plus the cop at the last moment.

"Not bad," I said to Carmody.

"It gets better," he answered as the train began to roll.

The cop hurried into the next car and kept going. Several

passengers glanced curiously at us, but when they met Carmody's hard stare they lost interest.

The tunnel walls darkened for a fast few minutes, then we burst into light at Twenty-third Street and went right on by some astonished people waiting on the platform. The cop had clearly got to the driver, and I understood what Carmody had done: if Acis had raced from Thirty-third to Twenty-eighth, thinking to pick up the train there, they'd been neatly foiled.

We changed to the express at Union Square, where the cop left us. He jerked his chin at Carmody in a kind of salute as we swept by him and plunged into the tunnel again.

"That's all it takes," Carmody said, close to bragging. "A little cooperation from a certain section of the NYPD, plus a hundred bucks for the flatfoot's back pocket, and it's bye-bye Acis."

We rocketed along for maybe five minutes, hemmed in by bodies swaying from handgrips, not stopping till we reached a station called Borough Hall. I followed Carmody off the train and up the steps to the street. The towers of lower Manhattan reared up a couple of miles away across a river. It had to be the East River, which meant we were either in Brooklyn or Queens. Carrying our cases, we walked into an area that reminded me a little of Greenwich Village. The buildings were of the same period: fine propor-tioned, red brick structures with long sash windows. I caught a street sign: Montague Street. We stopped outside number 66 and went up the stairs to an apartment on the third floor. It was a handsome place: solid oak floorboards glossed with polish, oil paintings on exposed brick walls, small, leafy trees in ceramic tubs. The apartment clearly belonged to a family; there were framed photographs of a man and a woman and two young girls, pretty like their mother. A custom bookshelf held hundreds of books and records, and a large brass object, all tubes and knobs, shaped like a giant fat flower. Next to it was a thin metal stand holding an opened double page. Strange-looking marks, black and squiggly, marched across the paper on a series of horizontal lines. I thought it was maybe Hebrew— I'd seen the Jewish newspapers around town—but when I read the heading on the pages, Exercises for the Tuba, I was no better off because I didn't know what a tuba was.

I explored the rest of the place. There were two bedrooms. Carmody had already grabbed the best one. I put my stuff into the other one, and took the Boston U magazine with me out into the living room. Carmody had a beer going and was sitting on the sofa waiting for me.

"Okay, genius, what d'you say we get right to it? The sooner we find Frohman, the sooner we're both outta here —me on vacation, and you back with Jenny's warm bod."

"Hey, Ray. I'd like you to do me a favor. Why don't you just leave Jenny out of it. She's not part of finding Frohman, so let's not get personal, okay?"

"That's more like your old self," Carmody said. "Your memory coming back?"

I didn't answer him. He'd made a few tasteless remarks about me and Jenny since I'd known him, and I knew he wasn't making them in an effort to spark my memory. He was just flat out jealous. I was convinced he wanted Jenny, which was another reason he didn't like me, because Jenny was mine. And his habit of calling me genius was another tipoff. I think I'd maybe shown him up in the past with my hunches; I think he might have been just a wee bit jealous of my ability to guess right. All in all I was very definitely

126

working with a guy who had two big reasons to want to see me fall on my face.

"Let's rehash what we know," Carmody suggested, sliding the conversation out of harm's way. "Frohman quits Germany, spends some time in Israel and Europe, gets tired of that and moves to New York by way of Israel. He gets a job in Jersey, then vanishes. You track him to Boston, but you're too late because it looks like the guy's come back here. He wants a scientific magazine and gives a Boston library a mailing address here in town. Then he calls up and cancels the box. He calls the library and cancels the magazine. But they've already sent it and we've got it. Now . . ." Carmody spread his tall frame a little wider, his gaze leaning on me like a weight. "The experts took a look through that magazine you got there and couldn't find word one about any potential superweapon. And there's no reference to the name Glitzenbak or Glitterbug, either. So we have to ask ourselves why the fuck did Frohman want the thing? The obvious answer is because there's something in there that the experts are missing. Maybe it's so new they never heard of it or can't even guess at it. But the bottom line is it ain't gonna help you and me find Frohman. So the question is what *will* help us find the bastard? It still comes down to that magazine, and that magazine don't tell us shit unless you and your crystal ball got something out of it."

"I haven't had a chance to take a proper look at it yet."

"Now's the time, ace. Meantime, I'm gonna burn a little daytime oil." Carmody got off the sofa and took his beer to the dining-room table. He laid out a notebook, clamped sponge rubber headphones over his ears, and clicked on one of those walk things, the little tape players. He started writing. I left him to it and opened the magazine. The first article was concerned with something called molecular vi-

rology. The rest of the articles covered subjects equally ob-
scure.

I was a little confused. When I checked the index in the
car, something in it had rung a bell, although the clear peel
of a bell is not an accurate analogy. The intuition had been
shadowy and vague, out of reach. And it was staying out of
reach.

I rose and went for a walk around the room, examined
the books in the shelves. A lot of works on movies, I noticed, and many titles by Dickens, Faulkner, and somebody
named Graham Greene. My travels took me past Carmody
at the table. He spoke to me without looking up.

"You cracked it yet?"

"It's up to me, huh?"

"You're the wonder boy."

I saw what he was working on: a language course. Japanese. That was a surprise, I didn't see Carmody as a scholar.

I returned to my chair, and a minute later, out of nowhere, I got a flash.

I think I can backtrack it—I think it was seeing the Japanese lesson, and my thoughts about a foreign language. Foreign language, foreign people, Frohman's time in Europe
. . . it went something like that. Anyway, I knew what had
grabbed at me in the car. I jumped up, crossed the floor,
thrust the opened magazine under Carmody's nose. "Right
there. What kind of name's that?"

Carmody read it out. "Doctor Gerard Peliac. French,
probably, Gerard. Why?"

"This article, Peliac's article. I think it's the reason why
Frohman wanted this magazine."

Carmody eased the headpiece off his ears, and regarded
me as if I were trying some desperate joke. "You ever heard
of this guy before? Peliac?" he asked.

"No."

"Then for God's sake, why should he be part of this?"

"Because he sounds like he's from Europe. And we know Frohman spent some time in Europe before he came here."

"So what?" Carmody's long fingers thumped the printed pages. "He's been in the States over a year or something. All the other names look American. So how come you latch on to the French one?"

I couldn't tell him because I didn't really know. I didn't know where the certitude had come from, or what made it unquestionable in my mind.

"I can't explain it, Ray. I just know I'm right."

Carmody beseeched the ceiling. "Did you hear that? In his heart he knows he's right." He brought his head down and snorted a laugh. "This another one of your terrific guesses?"

I was starting to get a little angry at the guy, at his boorish behavior, and I wanted very much to see that jeering grin congeal. "Check the phone book. I'll bet you a hundred bucks Doctor Gerard Peliac's living in New York."

"You're on." Carmody reached out a long arm, grabbed a phone off a side table, punched in three digits. "Manhattan," he said into the phone. "Name's Peliac." He spelled it out. "Initial Gee."

After a beat I heard the tape computer cut in giving the number. Carmody scribbled it down, hung up, and said to me, "Maybe that Gee Peliac is a George or a Gordon or something."

"Why don't you try him."

"Goddamn right I'll try him." Angry, looking at defeat, Carmody punched in the number he'd written down. I only heard one side of the conversation; he turned away as if to keep it secret.

"Yeah, is this Mr. Peliac . . . ? I'm not sure I got the right guy. Is your first name George?. . . . Gerard, huh. Are you a surgeon? . . . Doctor of science. Okay. Sorry to trouble you."

Carmody replaced the phone and slashed his eyes toward me. "What are you, a fucking Martian or something?"

"What's a Martian?"

I wasn't trying to bait him, but apparently he considered my question a little too cute. The table jumped as he slammed his hand down.

"How the fuck did you know that a guy writes an article for a Boston college magazine lives in New York?"

"I didn't know it; I figured out the sequence. Frohman canceled the magazine. Why? Because he no longer needed it. Why? Because he only wanted it for one of the articles, and maybe he found out the author was living right here in town. Maybe he did what we just did, checked Peliac in the phone book on the off chance the guy was local. And he found him. And if he could talk to Peliac, and ask him exactly what he wanted to know, he didn't need his article."

"Fucking genius." Carmody turned his sourness away from me and reached once again for the phone. He hit buttons, spoke. "Doctor Peliac? I called before. Name's Mc-Nulty. You turn out to be the guy I'm looking for after all. Do you know a guy named Frohman, Werner Frohman? I'm making inquiries on behalf of the German Consulate. . . . Uh huh. Well, thanks anyway." Carmody hung up and rose from his chair, found a Manhattan phone book, checked an address.

"What did he say?"

"He said no. But he said it way too fast." Carmody snatched up his jacket. "Let's go."

We left the apartment in a hurry. I was excited. Peliac would know where Frohman was, I was sure of that. All we had to do was persuade him to tell us.

We hit the sidewalk and hadn't gone ten feet before Carmody slowed. He was looking down the block, his face tight with suspicion.

"What's up?" I asked.

"That green Buick. I don't like it."

I could see the car he was talking about. Two figures sat in the front seat, but they were too far away for any detail.

"It can't be Acis," I said. "Nobody could've tailed us on the subway."

"That doesn't mean they didn't find a way. I'm gonna check 'em out. If they make a move, get upstairs in a hurry."

He was gone for a few minutes, then rejoined me. We started off toward the subway, toward the green car. Carmody was walking on the outside of me, his jacket unbuttoned, his right hand hovering near his belt.

"I called in," he said. "As of yesterday Acis people weren't driving a green Buick. But they change cars like some people change their socks."

"If it's them, do you think they'll try anything?"

"If they do they'll be wearing a lot of little holes."

We got closer to the parked car. We shared the immediate street with about a dozen people: some kids, some women coming back from the supermarket, some office workers getting home a little early. I wondered if they were about to have their ordinary day violently interrupted.

Twenty feet away I made out the Buick's occupants: a man and a woman. Closer still I saw them clearly—teenagers, the boy with a clamped expression, the girl in tears.

Carmody relaxed.

We went down into the subway and caught a train back

to Manhattan. Peliac lived on the West Side, on West End
Avenue, a wide street which, in the section we were in, was
lined with old-fashioned and forbidding-looking apartment
buildings. The one we entered featured the usual tenant call
board. Dr. G. Peliac lived on the top floor, but there was no
answer when we buzzed him, so Carmody pressed another
button and spoke to the super. A gravelly voice told us that
Doctor Peliac went out for a walk at this time of day, usually
getting back around five. We went around the block to a
little park, sat on a bench, and killed half an hour watching
some old ladies feed pigeons. It gave me a chance to bring
up a subject I'd been wondering about: namely, how come
Carmody had a gun and I didn't.

"We're ghosts, is why," Carmody explained. "We don't
exist. The name of the game is low profile, and guns are
high profile. If we get into trouble and the cops come into it
and they pinch us, we'll get out of it okay, but if we're both
heavy it gets sticky."

"It could get stickier if I suddenly need a gun and don't
have one."

"You don't need one if I got one. I'm your nursemaid.
You were never that good on the range anyway. You were
always better with your hands."

The rationale didn't make me feel any safer, but I knew
the right man had the gun. I was certain Carmody wouldn't
hesitate to use it, and I might have. And something told me
that indecision was not what you needed when it came to
gunplay.

We got a break when we got back to Peliac's apartment
house; a janitor had the inner door open as he mopped out
the lobby, so we went on through and up to the top floor.
The place needed some work; the paneling in the elevator
needed replacing, as did the broadloom we stepped out on

to, and a smell of cooking milled around the corridor, evidence, perhaps, of a broken extractor fan. Carmody rang the bell of apartment H, then rang it again when nobody came to the door.

"Shit," Carmody muttered. "He's not back yet."

I could hear the low sound of music coming from inside, and I wondered why somebody would leave their radio on if they were going out.

For a reason I couldn't have explained, I tried the door handle. It turned.

Carmody pushed the door open, stepped inside, called out, "Doctor Peliac?"

The radio played back at us. It was tuned to a classical station. The music filled the silence, seemed to bounce off emptiness. I knew something was wrong because something hummed at the back of my neck. I spoke softly to Carmody. "Better get your gun out."

"What?" he said. But there must have been something in my voice because the gun came into his hand.

We moved in tandem across a tiny foyer that elbowed into a living room. The place had been furnished without a lot of thought—the only good piece looked to be an untidy rolltop desk. The walls were undecorated, and cheap rattan matting layered the floor. The L shape at the bottom of the room led into a small kitchen just wide enough to take a counter and two stools. Laid out on the sink were the remains of a meal, water slowly dribbling down onto a greasy dish. Opposite the L, on the other side of the main room, was an armchair, an old TV set, and several small rubber plants sitting in a copper box. I crossed this space and entered the bedroom. Light streamed in from the unshaded front windows. They overlooked the busy avenue down below and a cement playground full of kids leaping up at a suspended hoop. A long bookshelf ran down one wall, at least fifty books stacked in it, leatherbound and bulky. The bed was neatly made up.

The only place left to check was the bathroom.

The door was partly closed. I knocked on it.

"Doctor Peliac?"

I moved the door open. Toiletries on the basin surface, a magazine on the tank of the john. The tub had a white shower curtain drawn across it. The metal rings squealed on their aluminum support as I pulled back the curtain.

The tub was as empty as the rest of the apartment.

Behind me Carmody exhaled noisily. "Jesus, you had me spooked. What was all this get-your-gun-out shit?"

I couldn't relax. The zinging was still dancing on my neck.

"C'mon," Carmody said. "He's gone next door or something. Let's beat it before he does us for trespassing."

We went back into the living room, but I continued into the kitchen because there was something I wanted another look at. The door in the unit beneath the sink was open, and an empty plastic bucket stood in front of it.

I knew where Peliac had gone now: he'd put the front door on the latch and taken the trash to the garbage chute. I'd done the same thing myself at Jenny's apartment. I suggested this to Carmody, who agreed with me for once.

"So what's keeping him? You figure he's a scavenger? Found some good junk in there?"

I volunteered to take a look.

I walked the length of the corridor, my footsteps barely muffled by the faded broadloom. I heard sounds coming from several apartments, and there was a fat lady with a fat dog getting into the elevator, but I saw nobody else.

The door of the garbage room seemed stuck. It had one of

those gadgets at the top that kept it closed. I pulled the door open. There was nothing in the little room except a piece of used carpet padding rolled up and tied with string and a busted trash bag split open on the floor. It was absurd but I felt an impulse to open the actual chute cover, and I gave in to it. I gripped the handle, and pulled it down.

A man's face stared back at me, gaunt and colorless, the sparse gray hair above the scalp line all mussed up. The top half of a blue cardigan was all I could see of the rest of him. He'd been stuffed into the chute but his body hadn't dropped. His shoulders, as thin as they were, had caught on something, and he hung suspended in that metal tube, dangling over a basement dumpster two hundred feet below.

I let the chute cover slowly close and left the room.

Down at the end of the corridor Carmody was standing outside Peliac's apartment waiting to see if I'd found him. I didn't doubt that I had.

I waved to my partner, gesturing for him to get down here. He came in a hurry, brushed by me, strode into the garbage room, then angrily swung around on me starting to say something. I cut him off.

"He's in the chute."

Carmody jerked open the metal door and froze. "Jesus Christ!" He let the chute handle go as if it were electrified, produced a handkerchief, and gave the handle a quick polish. He spoke so fast his words ran together. "What-else-you-touch?"

"Just the doorknob."

Carmody wiped it, then sprinted back down the corridor. I was right behind him. He worked quickly in the apartment, wiping down anything we may have touched. He finished as the sound of sirens climbed the outside of the building.

"Shit! C'mon!" My partner rushed past me. I cast a covetous glance at that rolltop desk, then ran. We banged through a door to our right, clattered down the stairs, taking them three at a time, raced down to the next floor, and kept going to the one below that. We fled together down the corridor to the elevators. Carmody was reaching for the call button when the doors popped back. As soon as I glimpsed the blue uniforms I sucked in breath so I wouldn't appear to be panting. A woman got out of the elevator leaving three impatient patrolmen and a fourth man in a brown suit.

"Going down?" Carmody asked, matter-of-factly.

"Up! Up!" the suited guy said, jabbing angrily at the control panel. The doors closed.

I let out the breath I'd been holding. I had to admire Carmody's cool, and his acting ability; he'd bluffed those cops so effortlessly. The elevator arrived on its way down. We jumped in. Carmody hit the bottom button then slammed the edge of his fist against the aged paneling.

"That fucking *bastard*!"

"Who?"

"*Jantzen!*"

Carmody must have known I didn't know who he was talking about, but I don't think he cared; he seemed to be in a private fury of his own.

"I'm gonna kick that shithead's butt. Trilling's, too, the dumb-ass cretin!"

Why I didn't know, but it was clear that Carmody was blaming Trilling and this Jantzen person for Peliac's murder. I was still trying to understand what I'd just seen: a dead man stuffed into a garbage chute. Who'd killed Gerard Peliac? Acis? Had to be. But for what reason?

"Listen up." Carmody's anger was tamped down under his words. "We gotta get past the cops, and we gotta get past fucking Acis. They'll be waiting out there to tail us, so we can't walk outta here, we have to drive out."

The doors slid back at the basement level. We hurried past a laundry room, two women in there folding clothes. We pushed through a door marked Garage. It opened on to a poorly lit stretch of water-pooled concrete, cars close-parked in orderly rows, fat ceiling supports squeezing the spaces tight.

Moving at a trot, Carmody threw his hand to his left, spoke fast.

"Take that side. Check under the rear bumpers. You're looking for a little tin box about two inches long."

I did as I was told. I hadn't the slightest idea what kind of box he was talking about or what could be in it, but, amazingly, I found one after I'd examined about twenty cars. Carmody came running in response to my call, snatched the little box from me, flipped it open, took out the two spare keys it contained. He shoved one into the driver's door, but left the door closed. I knew why when I spotted a decal on the side window. It said: "Not this one. This one's REMCO alarmed." Carmody moved to the front of the hood, issuing instructions. "There's a trigger under the dash to the left of the wheel. Get in there and pull it fast." I opened the door, found the trigger handle, jerked on it, heard the hood pop. Carmody wrenched it wide, studied the engine for maybe a second and a half—I could almost feel the alarm gathering itself to scream—then pounced and pulled out an oblong item no bigger than a matchbook, then let the hood slam. He jumped for the driver's door, popped the trunk, and ordered me into it. It was his party. I was getting a vivid demonstration of just how out of it I was, so I obeyed without question.

I climbed in, sharing the space with some sports gear and

some towels. Carmody slammed the lid and I was compressed in a sweaty-smelling darkness. I felt the driver's door slam, heard the engine kick over, rocked as the car backed and filled. Beneath me tires screeched. I felt the kick of acceleration. I braced myself as the car inclined steeply, and imagined a ramp from the acute angle and the tight turn.

The car leveled, dipped, stopped. I heard a deep voice, which had to belong to a cop, say, "Name?"

Carmody answered him. "Woods. Seven oh two."

I heard the cop repeat it, then the answering squawk of a radio, and the cop say okay.

We got going again, and for the second time I had to admire Carmody for his smarts. It had to be less suspicious for one guy to leave the apartment house than two, that's how come I was riding on a bed of sweat socks. And that name and apartment number he'd come up with had to be something he'd noted on the way into the building in case he needed it.

All the tricks of the trade, and I'd forgotten every one of them. Carmody had been right when he'd said he'd have to carry me. He was literally doing it.

It was a quick trip; less than five minutes later light speared into my cave as the trunk popped while the car was still slowing. I scrambled out the moment it stopped. Carmody was flagging down an empty cab he must have spotted from behind the wheel. We climbed in.

"Columbus Circle. Now!" he told the driver.

"Good luck" was the lethargic reply.

"There's twenty bucks in it."

"That's different," the driver said, and took the cab away fast.

I looked back. Our escape car was skewered across two

lanes of horn-crazy traffic. If Al Charmain's men had spotted Carmody driving out of the garage, and had reacted fast
enough to tail us, they were going to lose us now. But just to
make absolutely certain of that we piled out of the cab at a
corner of a gigantic park, went into a building, exited
through the back entrance, and were lucky enough to step
right into a waiting bus. We stayed on it for a dozen blocks,
buried in the anonymous rush-hour traffic, till our progress
was choked off by twin streams of converging automobiles.
When we quit the bus I followed Carmody through the
doors of a large touristy-looking hotel. He was still seething
—he looked like a man who wanted to wring somebody's
neck—and several people in the crowded lobby moved
smartly out of his way.

"Two doubles. High floor," he snapped at a desk clerk.

"You have a reservation, sir?"

"What do I look like, a fucking squaw? Just get me the
rooms."

"I'm sorry, but all our—"

Carmody slapped down a hundred-dollar bill. "Check
again!"

The clerk found something after all: two connecting sin-
gles.

Upstairs Carmody thrust money at a bellboy, got rid of
him, grabbed up a phone, and savagely punched out a number. He demanded to speak to Trilling, waited a moment,
then launched into a scathing tirade.

"Listen, George, and listen good. The genius found somebody who knew Frohman and maybe knew where he is. He
wasn't in when we got there so we cooled our heels for half
an hour. He was there when we went back, only he was in
no condition to talk. Acis got to him. How'd they do it?
They tailed us from the Heights apartment. How'd they

know about that place? Because that fucking stoolie of yours got into the files, that's how. So now they know more than we do because we don't know shit. So how about them apples?" Carmody listened for a bit. I could imagine George Trilling offering arguments to calm him down. If that indeed was what he was doing, he wasn't having any success.

"Fuck the long run! What long run? There ain't gonna be a long run, not on this job. Jantzen's no longer tame, George, face it! I got enough to contend with what with a partner I got to wipe his ass every ten minutes and fucking Acis breathing down my neck. I don't need any more handicaps. So either Jantzen gets sent to Uganda or some-where or I'm off the Frohman job, hear?" Carmody slammed down the phone. "Jerkoff!" He pulled open the door to the other room, then whirled around on me. "You wanna know why I study Japanese? 'Cause I've had it up to here with the fucking College. I want the Agency, the CIA. And, these days, if you can speak Jap you're in. They got their share of idiots, too, but none of 'em's as big a putz as that dumb ass Trilling. Fuck the College." He stomped through the door, banged it behind him, and left me think-ing about dissension in the ranks. And a few other things.

I went into the bathroom and splashed cold water on my face. I wasn't feeling that hot; I was having a late reaction to the grisly sight of Peliac jammed into that garbage chute. It was my first dead man that I could remember, although, in this charming line of work I'd found myself in, I'd probably seen a few others before. Carmody had warned me that this game could get tough, but I'd discounted it because I hon-estly hadn't thought anybody would go that far. Again I had to wonder what Werner Frohman was working on that was worth this kind of mayhem.

It began to dawn on me that to Al Charmain's clients a

man's murder might be seen as a cheap and insignificant price to pay for the whereabouts of the German—and that Glitterbug might well be worth a dozen such killings. Certainly mine and Carmody's.

After all, we were the immediate competition.

CHAPTER EIGHT

A couple of hours later a cooled-down Carmody walked in and informed me that we were going back to Peliac's apartment.

I'd been thinking we'd maybe try to get in there in a few days' time, but my cynical partner told me the apartment would be free now; the cops would have got what they wanted and moved on to the next homicide in this exciting city.

We arrived there around ten P.M., and once again I was treated to Carmody's artful ability to lie and bluff. Out in the building's lobby he hit the super's call button. "Police," he said. We were buzzed in. He was right about everything being over—there had to have been an ambulance, a gawking crowd, police cruisers with their lights flashing, but there was no sign of any of that now. The super was a short, tired-looking man with a crick in his spine. He was chewing on something; I think we'd interrupted a late dinner.

Carmody metronomed a finger between himself and me. "Carrol and Schenley. Rosetti say we were coming?"

"Rosetti?"

"Lieutenant Rosetti. He ran the homicide today. I got the wrong block? You didn't have a homicide today?"

"Yeah, we had one."

"Take us up, huh? We got chores."

The super bought it. Why not? Carmody was big and brusque; he looked and sounded like authority. The super fetched his keys, rode with us up to the top floor. A fat piece of yellow tape stretched across the door of 14H, a police notice pinned to the wood. Carmody peeled the tape as if it were barring the way to his own apartment, then nodded to the super who unlocked the door. The place looked much the same as it had earlier, except it was a lot more untidy. Things had been poked into, pulled out, examined, and a fine layer of black powder lay on many of the surfaces.

We made straight for the rolltop desk. The police had already gone through it, but they wouldn't have been looking for what we were looking for: something that linked Peliac to Frohman.

"You looking for clues?" the super asked.

"Yeah, you got any?" Carmody answered.

The short man took himself off into a corner and sulked.

It was an easy search; Peliac had been an orderly person; all his personal stuff was in neatly labeled folders. We found something interesting in a lower tier: his passport. He'd been Swiss, not French, and had lived in a place called Thun before emigrating to the States. In back of one of the many pigeonholes I discovered a small hook whose purpose, I believed, was to hold a key. The police had found it because a key was protruding from a bottom drawer. Carmody had spotted it, too, but we finished with the top part of the desk before taking a look.

We hit the jackpot straight away.

Lying on top of some scholarly-looking magazines was a pink folder with a blue-and-white mailing label gummed to it. Written on the label, in a tight and cramped hand, was the word Glitzenbak.

"O-*kay*!" Carmody breathed. He opened the folder on several lined pages full of the same crabbed handwriting. "German," he said. Attached to the back of the folder, caught by a paper clip, was a color photograph of two men.

I recognized both of them, although I'd never seen Peliac alive and I'd never seen Frohman at all.

They were standing together on a wooden dock, a perfect stretch of blue water behind them ringed by snowy mountains. On the reverse side of the shot was some more German, just six words: *Werner und ich wahrend einer arbeitspause.* The photo looked like a vacation snapshot. Carmody went to the phone, called Trilling, and told him we needed to see him now.

He was almost smiling.

We went midtown to a late-night cafeteria.

George Trilling was sitting at a lonely table dunking a tea bag into a steaming mug. In a red shirt and a white sweater he looked more than ever like a cherub, his pink, smiling face glowing with benign good cheer. He seemed like the last person to be running an undercover Pentagon agency; he was the antithesis of the stern-visaged, hawk-featured military man, and I had to wonder if he wasn't a round peg in a square hole. Carmody certainly thought he was a calamity and, as much as I disliked my partner, I'd seen how good he was at his job, so I was inclined to accept his opinion.

"Jack," Trilling said, offering his hand. "Sorry we had to pull you off vacation."

"No problem. It was too humid down there anyway."

"How's the memory?"

"Still among the missing."

"You really should let somebody look at you."

"Later, maybe."

Trilling eyed Carmody as the big man slid into a chair beside me.

"Still mad at me, Ray?"

"Depends what you've done about Jantzen."

Trilling's smile lost its oomph. "Jantzen's been transferred."

Carmody pointed to the ground. "South?"

Trilling gave the barest of nods.

" 'Bout time," Carmody said.

He filled Trilling in on the day's events, giving me credit for locating Peliac. When he told his boss that Acis had killed the Swiss and had tried literally to dispose of his body, the cherub went on placidly drinking his tea as if murders were an everyday occurrence—which they may well have been if I understood correctly about Jantzen's fate. Trilling leafed through the pink folder Carmody handed him. He was delighted with our find.

"It's a great shame losing that man," Trilling said, "but we may have everything we need right here."

I was wondering why Acis hadn't found the folder, and I asked Trilling, but it was Carmody who replied.

"Because they got what they came for. They leaned on Peliac till he told them where to find Frohman. Then they aced him so he couldn't tell us."

"It's possible he gave them a false address," Trilling suggested. "Protected his friend. We'll have to assume that anyway. Assume they haven't got to Frohman, and go on trying to find him." He dumped more sugar into his tea, stirred it, and regarded me a little sadly. "If only you'd been able to speak to Peliac he might have recognized you. He's probably the way you found Frohman."

I agreed with that. It seemed a pretty safe bet.

Trilling examined the snapshot we'd found, peering at it back and front. "This looks like your only lead now, unless the experts find something in these notes."

"Where do you think it was taken?"

"Europe, I'd say. The mountains, the lake."

"Peliac was Swiss. Maybe that's Switzerland."

Carmody had fished out a cigarette. He blew smoke, and took the shot. "Could be anywhere. Italy's got lakes. And Scandinavia's got a ton of 'em. We'll have to use a private firm to get this around. Pull a hundred prints, get them to airlines, travel agents, consulates, and play Name That Lake."

I asked Trilling about the inscription on the back of the photo.

He took it from Carmody and frowned over it.

"Werner und ich has got to be Werner and me. But I'll need help with the rest of it."

"Probably not gonna matter," Carmody said. He crushed out his cigarette and wreaked his usual vengeance on it. "Frohman's probably drugged out of his skull and on his way to Peking."

"That's what I like about you, Ray," Trilling said, pleasantly casual. "You never quit."

Carmody pointed a finger at him. "Believe me, I'm close to it."

Still with a smile on his face Trilling said, "I'd hate to lose you, Ray. But please, next time you have a beef with me, a complaint to make, try to keep your voice down, would you? We'll get on better."

Carmody grunted through his nose. "Anything for a happy ship." He yawned, blinked. "I'm gonna grab some sack time." He rose and ambled toward the doors, leaving his boss a little less composed than I'd seen him.

"He's a good man, your partner," Trilling said to me. "I just wish he had better manners."

We got up from the table, followed Carmody out to the sidewalk. I told Trilling where we were staying, and he promised to send over a copy of the snapshot and whatever he could find out about the contents of the folder. Then he said good night and walked away. I joined Carmody, who was standing at the curb pointedly ignoring Trilling's exit.

"Okay, buddy," he said. "It'll be a few days before Georgie Porgie comes up with anything, but one of us better stick around the hotel. Like you, for instance."

"Where are you going?"

"I'll be around. I got a chick I haven't thrown a leg over in a while. You know how it is, love 'em or lose 'em."

He stepped out into the street, waving at a taxi.

It surprised me, Carmody having a girl. Not that he didn't qualify—as Jenny had remarked, he was good-looking in a surly kind of way—but I couldn't imagine him giving any of himself in a relationship. Still, the fact that he had some romance in his life made him more human, so maybe there was something in his makeup I was missing.

I grabbed a cab myself, rode back to the hotel, and went straight to bed. In the space of a little over twelve hours I'd flown up from Florida, shaken some pursuers via the New York subway system, found a dead body in horrific circumstances, gained illegal entry into a police-sealed apartment, and stolen something from it.

For me that was a heavy day.

I got up around ten the next morning and called Jenny first thing.

"Hi, it's me."

"Jack. I was hoping you'd call last night."

"I was kind of busy. Everything okay?"

"Fine. Except I miss you and I worry about you."

"You don't have to. The hotel I'm in I can hide behind the tourists. How about you?"

"I have a cop parked outside my office. I'm telling everybody it's to ward off my groupies."

"Does he camp outside the apartment, too?"

"All night long as far as I know. I think there are three of them working shifts."

"I sincerely hope they all have pot bellies and snap gum."

"I can vouch for the gum snapping. They kept me awake all night. How long do you think it'll be?"

"I don't know, but I'll tell you one thing; I'm gonna do all I can to speed it up."

"Call me tonight. Round about eleven when I'm in bed."

"I may not be able to stay put if I do that."

Jenny blew a kiss into the phone. I hung up feeling a little blue. I wanted Jenny, wanted to be with her; and I was tired of this hotel room already. I resolved to do what I just said I'd do: bear down and get the job done.

I went downstairs and was delighted to find, in an envelope left for me, a print of the Frohman/Peliac photograph. Trilling wasn't wasting any time, and neither would I. The desk clerk told me where I could find a bookstore. It was a big one with books stacked waist high. I located the section I was after, and found the same kind of atlas I'd studied in hospital with my tutor. When I say studied, it had been basic stuff: we never concentrated on the lakes and mountains of Europe.

I started on a page headed The Alps. It included parts of France, Switzerland, Austria, northern Italy, and most of Germany. There were lakes everywhere, big ones, small ones, long ones; some running between countries. It didn't get any easier when I started turning pages. Spain had mountains and lakes, Norway and Sweden, too. Scotland had them, as did Turkey, and those two countries were something like two thousand miles apart. I had my hopes pinned on Switzerland—it made sense, Peliac being Swiss. And, as the atlas showed, there was no shortage of alpine lakes in that country. But if Switzerland turned out to be a dead end, and there was nothing in Peliac's notes to indicate where the shot had been taken, Trilling had a huge task in front of him. Perhaps an impossible one.

I flicked through the colored maps. The sight of all that territory was depressing me. Right then would have been a good time for one of my hunches, but I'd never felt flatter. The maps were saying nothing to me. I was seeing them as a child would see them, with the country borders in green and yellow and pink, and rivers and roads crisscrossing. I was wasting my time trying to conjure up something; the atlas was like a flaccid weight in my hands.

I put it back and moved on, wondering if my hunches came in some kind of cyclical pattern and, if so, how long the cycle lasted and how long before it returned.

I wandered morosely through the store, heading for the street, moving through a part that, in a way, was related to the section I'd just been in. It was the cooking department: hundreds of large-format books on display, some of them open to glossy four-color spreads. Several of the world's cuisines were on show: glistening Chinese ducks, a haunch of beef roasting on a spit, garlicky mounds of shiny pasta. It was a bad place for a hungry man to be in and, having missed dinner the night before and having had only a cup of coffee for breakfast, I was starving. I was considering taking an early lunch when one of the cookbooks caught my eye. Its title was *The Pastry Cooking of France.*

It was opened to a mouth-watering photograph of an apple tart in which the fruit slices rose up out of the pastry in a small, juicy hillock. The summit had been lightly dusted with a fine white powdery substance, a fine kind of sugar perhaps, and the whole thing looked very much like a snow-covered alp. The dessert carried the heading Les Montagnes des Pommes. I didn't know what Pommes meant, but Montagnes had to be mountains and, looking at the luscious picture, something zinged inside me and I knew, with unquestionable certainty, that the snapshot of Frohman and Peliac had been taken in the French Alps.

There was no rhyme or reason for it; like the flash I'd got about Peliac, it was like an instant wave of information, of knowledge, as if I'd always known it. But there was an addition this time as well—I knew the location of that photograph had something to do with cooking.

I know that must sound ridiculous, seeing I'd been looking at pictures of French pastry but, nevertheless, that was the message that appeared in my mind.

I left the store with my pulses fluttering. I think I was more relieved than excited, relieved that this weird talent of mine was still with me. I found a phone booth and called the number Trilling had given me. It took a minute to be put through.

"George? Jack Penrose."

"Hello, there. You get that print I sent over?"

"Yeah. Listen, George, you wanted a hunch, I have one for you."

"Let's hear it."

"I think that shot was taken in France."

"Could be."

"And it has something to do with cooking."

"What does?"

"Where they are in that shot."

"That doesn't help much. France is famous for its cooking."

"Well, that's the message. Something tied in with cooking."

"You can't get any closer than that?"

"I don't get details, George. Just the big picture."

"Okay, France it is. And cooking. We'll try to run it down."

"Sorry it's so hazy."

"Look, it's something to go on, and we really need something because Peliac's notes turn out to be a variation of the article he wrote for the Boston U magazine. Only in German."

"What's the article about?"

"It's a highly technical treatise on the effect of heat on liquids."

"Then that's what it is, Glitterbug? Some kind of liquid?"

"Who knows? I had three science whizzes working all night and they're still scratching their heads. They say there's nothing in the article that would even point to a weapons application. That say it's just a meticulous piece of lab research."

"But Frohman wanted it, so it has to be important."

Trilling proposed that the German may not have wanted the magazine for its content but as a means of reaching Peliac. "Maybe he lost contact with him and didn't know he was living in New York." I allowed that that was possible, but I didn't really buy it.

"Did you find out what's written on the back of the snapshot?"

"It says, Werner and me take a break. A work break is the literal translation."

"I was hoping for more than that."

"So was I. Still, we're moving. This hunch of yours, was it a strong one or a weak one?"

"Like a neon sign."

"Then we've practically got it kicked."

"Thanks for the confidence, but was I always right?"

"Almost always. Check with you later."

"You bet."

I hung up thinking about that line on the back of the photograph. A work break. It proved that the two scientists had collaborated sometime in the past. It hadn't been a vacation they'd been on. And it was a good bet they'd been working on Glitterbug, seeing the shot had been pinned to the Glitterbug file.

I had to find out where that lake was. I had to go there and try to pick up Frohman's trail, however cold it would be. I went back to the bookstore and bought the atlas, two books on the French Alps, and a couple of standard travel publications, and took everything back to the hotel. I ordered up a sandwich then sat down and pored over the books, trying to spark a memory. Had I been to any of these places? Had I gone to France, found where the two men had worked, and somehow traced Frohman from there?

I had my passport in my pocket; I'd taken it with me to Florida because Jenny had mentioned the possibility of hopping over to Nassau. I pulled it out and checked it. There were quite a few stamps; my job had evidently got me around Mexico and Central America and the Bahamas, but there were no stamps from any European countries. But did they always stamp passports? I called the French Consulate and asked them. I was told that passports were rarely stamped these days: too many travelers. There was nothing to prove I'd been to France, and yet something told me I had. It wasn't a flash, just a gut feeling.

I called Trilling again, but had to wait a couple of hours before he got back to me. I asked him if, as a College boy, I might have traveled on another passport. He told me that we all had travel documents issued in another name for security reasons. He took a minute to check his files, then informed me that the name in my fake passport was Jack Peck. When I explained why I wanted to know, he told me I might have hit on something. He gave me three airlines I might have used, big ones that flew nonstop to Paris. I called them all but ran into a wall: they only kept a passenger's name in their computers for twenty-four hours.

It occurred to me that Al Charmain would probably know if I'd flown to Europe because he had to have my Jack Peck passport, taken from me when I'd been picked up and worked over. Too bad nobody knew where he was, I could have asked him.

The phone calls, the book study, the waiting around ate up most of the afternoon, and I was growing tired of the four walls again. I took a shower, and shaved with the razor I'd bought downstairs at the news stand, then went out and bought pajamas and a change of clothes. I had dinner around six at an Argentine grill, then strolled. The evening had come on although it was still pleasant out, the temperature having dropped only slightly. I walked east to the yellow metal road of cabs streaming into Times Square and joined the crowds gawking at the gigantic signs, was swept up by them as they cruised the garish movie houses, the blaring record stores, the million-lightbulb theater fronts. I appeared to be about the only solo person; everybody else was either with a pal or in a group or a family, or part of a boy/girl couple. It made me feel lonely. I missed Jenny. I missed her bright sparkle, and I missed her sexy little body, too. I was due to call her at eleven, but that was at least three hours away. I wanted to hear her voice now, but not over a hotel phone; I wanted to hear her voice against my face, feel her warm breath on my neck, her tongue in my mouth.

I stopped walking and considered something: the only reason I wasn't heading for the apartment now was because Acis would be watching the place, waiting for me to drop by and see my girl, waiting to snatch me or tail me. But to do that they first had to recognize me, didn't they?

I doubled back to one of the novelty stores I'd passed, its wares a wild assortment of the clever and the crude. I bought two items: a wig and a yachting cap. The wig was little more than a skull cap onto which thick strands of teased nylon had been sewn, and yet it looked like hair. It covered my scalp bandage, which was a dead giveaway for anybody watching for me, and fluffed out around my ears. The yachting cap, extra large to accommodate the wig, further changed my features by virtue of the bill that hooded my eyes. I felt like a bit of a fool, and I no doubt looked like one, but Broadway accepted me without comment, and I joined that weird and wonderful mix of humanity and seemed to fit in better than I had before.

I added one more item at a clothing store a block south, something a salesman told me was called a jock jacket, a baggy, two-tone affair with big bold letters on it. Checking the whole effect in a long mirror I didn't know who I looked like, but that definitely wasn't Jack Penrose gazing back at me.

I stuck my regular jacket in with the clothes I'd bought earlier, then cabbed it to within a block of Jenny's place.

I didn't want to appear to be checking, so I couldn't tell if any of the cars parked nearby were occupied or not. But to be on the safe side I breezed into the apartment-house entrance and faked pressing a bell on the call panel, making out I was a visitor. Then, with my body hiding my key, I let myself in the front door. The lobby was empty, as was the elevator that took me up. I thought briefly of leaving on the wig and the yachting cap and giving Jenny a laugh, but then I knew I'd first have to get past the cop who was guarding her, so I thought I'd better play it straight. I took off my disguise and added the wig and cap to the bag I was carrying and stepped out on to the sixth floor. The first thing I noticed was an absence of something: the cop I was expecting to find lolling in a chair.

The corridor was empty.

I thought this was a little strange at first, but then I wondered if Jenny hadn't maybe invited him in for a cup of coffee. Or her. It might have been a woman cop tonight. Jenny would have liked that. She was an ardent feminist, and would have welcomed the idea of being guarded by a woman instead of a man.

I slid the key into the lock, opened the door quietly, planning to surprise her. I thought at first she wasn't home. There was no music, and Jenny always played a tape or the radio. I figured she'd been held up at the office, and I was disappointed; I'd been expecting to find her working at her easel, or washing her hair, or doing some little household chore, and I'd been looking forward to seeing her face when I came out of nowhere.

I crossed the broadloom and flopped on to the sofa, and then realized something I should have seen before: If Jenny wasn't home yet, how come the living-room light was on?

I revised my thinking. She'd come home and gone out again; maybe hadn't felt like cooking so had gone up the block for some Chinese take-out. I remembered her saying they took forever to deliver, so it was faster to fetch it yourself. Cheered by that thought—I wouldn't have to wait long for her—I was on my way to the kitchen to get a beer when I heard what sounded like a whimper.

Jenny's voice.

It had come from the bedroom.

I went cold. I froze. I felt real fear for her even as I was explaining the sound away in my mind: the victim of a sudden headache, Jenny had gone into the darkened room to lie down. I fought away the other thoughts, terrible things that came complete with ghastly visuals.

I didn't run, I walked very slowly, scared of what I'd find.

I pushed open the door.

Light spilled into the room. Jenny was lying on the bed. She was naked. And Ray Carmody was naked, too.

He was fucking her.

It wasn't a rape—no torn clothes lay anywhere, no bedside table was tumbled on its side—Jenny had her legs locked around him, her hands clutching his flanks, pulling him into her hip thrusts, rising to his drive.

I don't think I felt anything at that moment. I think all my emotions had been shortcircuited. I was so absolutely flabbergasted I didn't know what to say or do; I just stood there like a voyeur. The light I'd let in finally registered on Carmody. He turned his head, saw me, and stopped his plunging. His face squeezed in on itself.

"Aw, shit," he said.

Jenny opened her eyes. The little moans and cries she'd been emitting, the same kind of yips she'd made when we'd made love, choked in her throat as she saw me, too. I forced myself to back off, to spin around and get out of that room; otherwise I think I would have started hitting Carmody and not stopped.

I made it to the front door, fumbled it open, but Jenny

came running behind me, slammed the door closed. She spoke fast, breathlessly gabbling at me.

"It happened while you were gone, Ray and me. Tonight was supposed to be the end of it, but one thing led to another and I just . . ." Her body was flushed and sweaty, and jism glistened in her pubic hair. Her musky scent came to me as I watched her kiss-bruised mouth trying to find words.

I pulled open the door and left her calling after me.

Coming out on to the street I think I would have been happy for Acis to have spotted me, and to have tried to do something about it. I would have welcomed a fight. But nobody got out of a car, nobody came down the block toward me, and nobody fell into step behind me.

I hit the first bar I came to, a White Rose on Third, had a couple of quick belts, and waited for the flutters to recede. Partly because of the fast alcohol, and partly because I'd had a little time to think about it, my anger was slowly replaced by an immense gloom. The sadness was much stronger than the swift rage because it was so much more longer lasting, and so much more the correct sentiment. I found, after my third drink, the booze bringing me down, that I no longer wanted to belt Carmody's teeth in. What was he—a guy who'd taken advantage of my long absence and moved on my girl. So what? He was that type anyway; it was exactly the kind of thing he'd do. Especially as he was jealous as hell of my ability to hunch the right solutions; he'd certainly demonstrated that with his sneering references. Another thing he'd always made clear was his envy at my having Jenny, which went a long way toward explaining why the guy disliked me so much: officially I belonged in Jenny's bed while he had to sneak around the back way. No, Carmody didn't upset me, it was Jenny that was the crusher.

That first day when she'd met me at the door and thrown her arms around me, told me all those warm and wonderful things, that was when she should have leveled with me, told me that she'd been seeing Carmody. But she'd chosen to keep it quiet. She'd fooled me and gone on fooling me, and that hurt, doubly so because I'd just come off being fooled by a woman.

I knew what the basic problem was—the same one it had been since I'd woken up in that ersatz hospital room: without a memory I had no experience to draw on. I was right off the boat, a rube, a naive hick down for a day to gape at the skyscrapers. If I'd been burned a few times, maybe my receptors would have been out and working, and I might have picked up on the sexual tension that I now realized had been stretching between Jenny and Carmody when he'd met us at the airport.

Jesus. Of all people, Ray Carmody. The guy had even warned me in an oblique way. He'd told me, the last time I'd spoken to him, that he was going over to see his girl. And I'd even felt a little better about him for having one!

I stopped drinking and just sat there staring at the back bar lights shimmering through the bottles. I didn't want to go back to the hotel; I didn't want to run the risk of seeing Carmody quite so soon. I had to work with the guy, but I wasn't going to be able to do that until I got the right mindset. I knew where I wanted to go: to Florida, to my parents' place. I wanted to be with somebody with no lies to hand me, no deceit behind the hugs and embraces.

I cabbed it out to La Guardia, checked into an airport hotel, slept fitfully till around six, then went over to the terminal and had breakfast. Somebody had left a *Daily News* on the counter. Peliac's killing had been given quite a play, complete with lurid photographs. I skimmed the piece: the police had found a car stolen from the "murder" apartment abandoned on Central Park West. There was a poor composite drawing of the driver whom the police were interested in talking to. I could have told them that the driver was probably too busy to talk to anybody at that moment.

I bought a ticket, found the departure gate, and boarded a plane. It wasn't a Lauderdale flight, but a nonstop to Miami would do just as well. I brooded every mile of the way, was first off the aircraft, first in line at the Budget counter. I picked up an automobile, found my way to the Interstate, and drove north for forty minutes. In the blue mood I was in, I couldn't help but think that, only a few days previously, Jenny had driven me up this same stretch of highway, under the same gorgeous sky promising to help me fool my parents. Well, I wasn't going to fool my parents anymore; I was going to tell them about Jenny and get their advice.

I made the turn at Pompano Beach, and headed west through Margate to Coral Springs. I was cheered by the sight of the busy little town. I had no real concept of the word Home, yet I felt a pleasant warmth, a surge of security, when I skirted the golf course and my parents' house came into view. A police cruiser was parked outside which reminded me of a question I hadn't yet considered: where had the cop gone who was supposed to have been guarding Jenny? It wasn't hard to figure: Carmody had simply told him to come back in the morning, that he'd look after the lady that night. And look after her he had.

I belayed that line of thinking and pulled up next to the cruiser. I got out of the car and walked in the smell of sunshine and fresh-cut grass. I skirted the screened pool— the water looked inviting; I was looking forward to a swim

—and went around to the side door. My route took me past the living room, and I could see into the house. My father was sitting in an armchair with his feet up watching TV. He hadn't heard me drive up, nor had he seen me. He was intent on the show, a fishing show I think it was. I can't really say because I wasn't paying much attention to the entertainment, I was more interested in the way my father looked, the way he was dressed.

He was all in blue.

He was wearing a cop's uniform.

I walked back to the rental car and drove away.

CHAPTER NINE

I don't recall much about the drive back to Miami, or the flight back to New York—I was locked in the iron grip of bewildered shock.

An explanation occurred to me regarding my father's clothes: the cop who'd been assigned to guard him had had something better to do, had left his cruiser outside to act as a deterrent, and loaned my father a uniform. The idea was absurd, of course. Ridiculous. I knew what had happened, I was just trying to hold off admitting it to myself. The plain and inescapable fact was they'd done it to me again.

Acis.

Al Charmain.

They'd realized their original scam had collapsed so they'd gone to plan B. They'd faked me out a second time.

It was a devastating blow. I felt like the dumbest guy in the world, and maybe I was. God, I'd been such an easy mark for them. I'd been candy. They'd fooled me like a magician tricking a five-year-old at a kids' party. And they'd had the hide to practically tell me what they were doing, confident that I'd never tumble. They'd told me that Acis had bungled it once. They'd neglected to mention that they were going to take another shot at it. Same game, different game plan. They'd got Ray Carmody, or whoever he was, to be my partner, and thus ride herd on me. Jenny had been the new Sharon, the new set of warm arms and thrilling thighs. And George Trilling, if that was his name, was the smiling, avuncular good guy to Carmody's rude, scowling

163

bad guy—somebody I was supposed to have confidence in, somebody who was on my side.

Oh, what a pushover for them. I had the moves of a pro but the mind of an amateur, so they'd done all the things an amateur might expect of a clandestine government department. About the only thing that hadn't been in the script, as far as I could see, was the wild scene in Macy's. I think the idea had been just to grab me off the sidewalk, which in itself would have been a nice piece of dramatics, but I'd made it even better for them by bolting and setting up a chase. But everything else had been carefully and callously laid on for me. That subway production, shaking the Acis tag—what a laugh; I'd had Acis right next to me. And I'd fallen for it, been impressed with the scheme, blocking off that small subway stop for a few minutes. The cop who'd held the crowds back? Probably a real one doing it for a lot more than the hundred dollars Carmody had said he'd paid him.

Going back over the sequence of events it was clear how they'd skillfully maneuvered me around. The advice to take a vacation, for instance, and my "parents" just happening to live in Florida. They'd wanted me to go down for a visit, had banked on it. It was a good way of further cementing my new identity just in case I had any suspicions after their failure with Tom, my "brother." They'd even faked a photo album that had been left for me to find. They'd got hold of some shots of me as a teenager and a young man and patched me into family shots with my "parents."

Pretty good actors, those two, the ones who'd played loving Mom and dear old Dad. The woman so warm and charming, concerned about me. The guy, now that I could see him as a big and bossy cop, no longer seemed much like a retired building supply man, but he certainly had then.

GLITTERBUG

Carmody I knew was a good actor because I'd watched him bluff people, had admired his performance, not realizing it was *all* a performance and that he was bluffing me all the time he was fooling those other people, talking his way in and out of Peliac's apartment house. And that show he'd put on reaming out Trilling on the phone. Trilling must have been chortling on the other end of that line, slapping his thigh with laughter, knowing that numbskull Jack Penrose would be standing right beside Carmody taking it all in. And being taken in.

But Jenny was the one who made me cringe. Now there was an actress for you! The performance she'd put on, stopping the car by the side of the road at that picnic area and telling me she felt something was wrong . . . getting me to confess about my amnesia then acting so shocked and hurt that I'd been making love to a stranger. God! Reliving that scene crushed me. She'd been laughing at me all that time, the dummy boyfriend, the puppet with sawdust for brains that she moved right or left, up or down with a jerk of a string. But then they'd all had their fingers on the string: Jenny, Carmody, and Trilling, with Al Charmain at the top of the heap pulling the master cord.

All this time and trouble, this huge production, for one reason only: they wanted Werner Frohman. And I was the boy to find him for them as long as I thought they were the good guys.

A colossal charade, and yet not everything had been faked. Certainly not Peliac's murder. If you wanted to fake a dead man, surely you'd simply give him a fake bullet hole and some fake blood. You wouldn't have to shove him into a garbage chute.

I thought hard about the Peliac sequence and figured I knew what had happened: when we'd been leaving the

165

Brooklyn apartment to see Peliac, and Carmody had spotted that green Buick, he'd gone back upstairs and checked on the car, so he'd said. But the call he'd made had been to Al Charmain. He'd given him Peliac's address and Charmain had sent his goons, the dark suits, over to Peliac's apartment. They'd got Frohman from Peliac, or thought they had, then they'd killed him to stop him giving the information to somebody else. Just who I didn't know. But I knew there was another player in the game. And maybe they were tailing me and Carmody.

I wasn't that fascinated at that moment. I didn't need another puzzle, another deception, I had my hands full trying to recover from the one I'd found myself starring in.

Coming out of the terminal at La Guardia all these realizations had hammered me close to the cliff of depression. But by the time I'd reached town I was pumped up again, because there was a wonderful silver lining to the deception, and it was simply this: if my brother and my parents were all lies, then having an ex-wife and a dead daughter were lies, too.

For the first time I realized just how clever Acis was. I almost had to admire their cunning. By inventing a daughter whose death I'd been "responsible" for, they'd fed me a heavy dose of guilt. And I'd opened my mouth wide and swallowed every drop. Why had they done that? To get to my mind on another level. To chip away at my confidence and make me that much more malleable; that much more grateful for love and affection. They'd wanted me open and vulnerable, the bastards—a piece of silly putty they could shape any which way.

I can't describe the feeling that surged through me when I realized that no child of mine had died through my negligence. I practically burst into song. It was as if a two-hundred-pound boulder I'd been carting around on my shoulders had been vaporized. What a reprieve!

And there was another thing that made my heart jump. Not with relief but with an extremely satisfying sense of anticipation: this time I knew something Acis didn't. They thought they were still getting away with it, still had the dummy with the head injury believing everything he was told. But they didn't know I'd been to Florida and seen what I'd seen.

Now it was my turn to do a little fooling. My turn for a little revenge.

I was going to act as if everything was normal, as if I was still the know-nothing kid. I'd go along with them until I got close to Frohman, then snatch him right out from under their mendacious noses.

What I'd do with him after I had him I'd have to think about. But if Acis, who were very definitely the bad guys, wanted him, then it followed that the good guys must want him, too. All I had to do was figure out who the good guys were and how to recognize them. For the first time since I'd woken up in that all white room I felt excited. Not only was I on the verge of a very welcome payback, but I was also on the verge, I felt sure, of getting an answer to a couple of important questions. Number one, what was Glitterbug?

And number two, who was I?

I got a chance to play my new part a couple of hours after I got back to the hotel. Ray Carmody came through the connecting door wearing that same granite expression I'd got to know pretty well.

"We got some talking to do, you and me," he said. "About Jenny."

"No, we don't. There's nothing to be said. She was mine,

then while I wasn't around, she became yours. Okay, she's still yours. I'm out of it."

"Boy, have you changed. The old Jack Penrose would've told me to stay the fuck away from her, then tried to dump me on my ass."

"The new one might just have a shot at doing that, too." I didn't care one whit about Carmody and Jenny now, but I was into my role of betrayed lover, and I figured some angry threats would be appropriate. Carmody rolled his head, eased his sloping shoulders, the actions of a man getting loose. I was regretting having challenged him, I wasn't afraid of him—I'd seen what I could do with my hands—but he was a big guy and had to know stuff, too, and if we came to blows one of us would have got hurt, and that could have seriously crimped my plan. Fortunately, I think something like the same thing occurred to him apropos his own plan, so he unsquared his stance and backed off.

"Jacko, if you and me duke it, I'll trash you. No question. I'll be happy to prove it one of these days. But right now I need you relatively healthy because the job comes first, even this crummy one, and we got to find Frohman."

"What's the matter, Ray?"—I couldn't resist it—"You can't find him yourself?"

Some concrete poured into Carmody's backbone. Regardless of the part he was playing, I don't think he liked being teased. "I could find him the best day you ever saw. But who knows, maybe you'll get one of your lucky fucking gypsy hunches and save us time."

"I already had a hunch. I told Trilling about it."

"I know that. And you got lucky again. Trilling came up with a lead."

That was a surprise, Trilling getting a lead so soon, but I wasn't complaining.

Carmody sauntered toward the door. "Let's go, genius." I figured a little revolt would be in order at this point, considering I'd caught the guy cheating with my girl, so I chilled my eyes and thrust my jaw out at him. "Uh uh. Not with a sleazebag like you. I'm calling Trilling. I want a new partner."

Carmody sniggered. "Won't do you much good. I'm your partner. He won't break up the set. You're stuck with the sleazebag, champ."

I huffed and puffed a little more, then settled for a resentful acceptance of the situation.

We left the hotel and cabbed crosstown heading west. I was busting to know what kind of lead Trilling had unearthed, but I stayed silent. But Carmody didn't; he seemed to want to shift our relationship to something a little less dog and cat, and he uncharacteristically tried for some casual conversation.

"Where you been all this time?"

"Out and around."

"I hear that's a nice place." He waited a beat. "What did you do about Acis when you went to Jenny's last night?"

"Wore a disguise."

"Same here."

Oh, sure, I said to myself.

Our taxi got stuck at a light, a horn chorus starting up behind us. On the sidewalk I watched a young woman dressed in a skimpy halter and tight pink shorts being harangued by a black guy in a silver suit. The woman was vehemently denying a forceful accusation.

Carmody had another stab at social contact.

"That service came through, the one Trilling's using. They got fifty guys schlepping that print around the streets and they came up with a frog says it's his hometown."

169

"A frog?"

"A Frenchie. Runs a bakery in the Market."

"He's definite about it?"

"We'll know in a minute."

The traffic unblocked. We made the turn into Ninth Avenue, then a couple of well-timed green lights brought us into an area devoted to food: meat, fish, fruit, and vegetables, numerous delis. Most of the stores—they seemed to be either Greek or Italian—had people in them standing two or three deep at the counters, or shopping from bins set up on the sidewalk.

We quit the cab and I followed Carmody to a bakeshop which, unlike the other stores, looked deserted. Some peeling gold lettering on the window announced to the world that this was La Tour Cakes and Pastries, a claim that was poorly supported by the window display: a small wicker basket containing three shiny rolls shaped like horseshoes. A much smaller sign, this one hanging inside the door, said Closed, but apparently it didn't apply to us because we went in, went by a short counter, and through another door into the bakery itself. The aroma was wonderful: warm and sweet and evocative of creamy butter and fruit-filled jelly. It was a large, square room dominated by a long metal white-dusted table and several large steel box-shaped affairs running down the right-hand side wall. When I peeped inside one of these I realized it was an oven; it was full of trays covered with those curved rolls I'd seen in the window. Several giant silver bowls were set underneath long mixing spindles, and another impressive machine, this one working, shimmered back and forth depositing a fine layer of flour on a tray beneath it. The man running this contraption wore a floor-length apron and a hat fashioned from a sheet of newspaper. When he flashed his eyes at us I sensed that he recognized Carmody and was made nervous by his presence. He killed the machine, came toward us, told us he'd be with us in a minute, then went out into his deserted store, closing the inner door behind him.

It was hot in the room, close too, the ovens cooling, their chores just finished.

"Is that him?" I asked. "The guy we came to see?"

"Probably locking the front door," Carmody said. He took one of the little rolls from an oven, bit the end off it, and chewed as if he expected rancidity. His question came out of the blue. "So how do you like being a College boy, Jacko? You learning anything?"

I practically choked at the irony of that question. Yes, Mr. Carmody, as a matter of fact I was learning a whole raft of things, chief among which was how it felt to be emotionally ripped off and how it feels to be in the driver's seat for a change.

"Bits and pieces."

"You got a hell of a lot to learn yet. You ever heard the expression wet work?"

I don't know if it was the peculiar conjunction of those two words, or the way Carmody was eating the bread roll, or whether the Frenchman was taking way too long to lock that front door, but I knew something was happening here, or was about to happen, and I realized, with a huge sense of dismay, that I wasn't in the driver's seat at all. I'd lost control of the situation. I felt a chilling tension begin to stretch the nape of my neck, and a quick adrenaline surge beneath my skin.

"Wet work," I repeated. "No, I never have."

I was standing left side on to Carmody and about twenty feet away from him. We were separated by the long metal rolling table, a flour sack squatting on it. The sack, opened at the neck, was the size of a small refrigerator.

My right hand closed around a heavy metal flour scoop, my body obscuring the movement. I wasn't consciously aware of doing it, of any straight-line thinking process—brain ordering fingers, fingers obeying—it just seemed to happen naturally.

"We have to do it in this business from time to time, put somebody down," Carmody said, conversationally. "So I'll learn you a little. Never do it in a hotel room. Too many people around. The fucking maid can walk in. Do it some-place quiet."

"Somewhere like this, for instance?" I asked.

Carmody finished his roll, brushed a flaky piece of crust from his sleeve. "Yeah, this wouldn't be bad." His mouth slit into an imitation smile. He was watching me closely. By my reply, and perhaps by my absolute stillness, he knew that I knew something was up. "I didn't think you had any perception, Jacko. You must've picked up a little. But what you definitely don't got is observation. The guy who played your poppa spotted you leaving this morning."

"Leaving the hotel? What do you mean, played my poppa?"

Keep him talking, wait for the moment—that was my first thought.

My second thought, that this was a setup, seemed too obvious to even give head room.

"What happened? You get all hurtsie catching me and Jen-Jen in the sack? Went down to Mom and Pop for a little apple pie, a shoulder to cry on?" Carmody chuckled, his pale, freckled face gone flat. "You should've stayed away from your girlfriend, kiddo. You weren't supposed to see me

172

and her in action. You went and screwed up everything going down to Florida. You weren't expected."

I was waiting for Carmody to casually reach under his jacket, but he kept me on the hook, just standing there moving his neck and his shoulders in that way he had. He was enjoying this, taking his time. He wanted to squeeze me right up to the last moment because he really did hate me. Why, I didn't know or care but, in this situation, I was glad of it. I was hoping his emotions would betray him into being sloppy.

He shook his head at me as if I were beyond pathetic. "Thought you'd try a little reverse scam, huh? Try to shit the shitters? You don't learn much, do you, fella? You should know by now that no matter how hard you hit the ball, I'll always throw you out by half a step."

"Did you find Frohman?" I really wanted to know that. I wanted to know where he was.

"Naw. That bastard Peliac stiffed us. Gave us a bum steer."

"You'll never find him without me, Carmody."

"Well, we sure as hell won't be finding him with you. We blew it. Made a mistake. And there's a cardinal rule in this business—you always erase a mistake."

He'd decided that was going to be his exit line, or rather his line for my exit. He was all through playing God. He turned marginally to his left to get a better draw, but I'd turned to my right to get a better throw.

I beat him to it.

I whipped my right arm over and hurled the metal scoop at his face. His left hand flew up at astounding speed and bounced the scoop off his open palm. He had his gun out and got off a shot, but I'd jumped behind an oven, and the slug hit that instead of me.

173

"Fuckhead!" Carmody yelled. I think his pride was hurt more than his hand. "No neat little hole in the head for you, scumbag. You're goin' out gutshot."

He went on cussing me out, calling obscenities at me. I'd surprised him with the scoop and he had no way of knowing what else I might have found behind that oven. I could have relieved his fears. There was nothing; just spilled flour and dustballs and pipes going into the wall. I leaped the pipes and scampered behind the next oven in line, but there was no heavy projectile here, no weighty bread shovel lying conveniently on the floor. I checked the windows at the other end of the room, now just fifty feet from me. They were there only for a little light and ventilation, too narrow and too high for me to scramble through. And the rear door, I saw, had two heavy flour sacks leaning against it, placed there, no doubt, by Carmody when he'd been setting up the trap.

"You ever heard of the Pine Barrens, putzo?" Carmody's voice sounded closer. "It's over in Jersey. Conservation area. It's the Mob's unofficial burial ground. You'll be in fine company."

I had a strange scent in my nostrils, a combination of fresh-baked bread and my own sour sweat. I didn't kid myself, my chances were extremely poor. Sooner or later maybe everybody wonders about the circumstances of their death, and I'm sure I had in the past. And I was equally sure I hadn't figured a French bakery as the locale. I'd formed a plan, but it wasn't much: keep Carmody off balance, keep him mad, and try to suck him in close.

I risked a peek around the oven, gave him a swift view of one eye. He promptly tried to shoot it out.

The bullet spanged off metal and gouged out a piece of the wooden wall.

"Last one you get for free, Penrose. I got me a Model Twenty-nine here. Nice little piece, but it's only a five shot." Carmody had reached the end of the long table where he stopped to take stock of things and twist the knife a little deeper. "You probably don't remember what a thirty-eight cup point can do to a meat-and-bone target. You get one of these babies in the belly button, it'll take your lunch out through your kidneys."

A five shot. Then he had three left before he had to reload, and he couldn't afford the time it would take to do that because he respected my hands. The way he'd fired from the hip told me he was a little spooked by the situation in spite of his huge advantage and his bravura talk. I had to keep him firing to get him to run that gun down. I badly needed another metal scoop or one of those big silver bowls, something he'd have to defend himself against if it came flying at his face.

I made do with what was at hand.

It certainly wasn't much; almost laughable: an unbaked loaf of bread. It sat on the floor at my heel, squishy and moldy-looking, and slightly flattened by its fall from one of the trays. I scooped up some spilled flour, layered it thickly on my hands, then picked up the still-sticky loaf.

"Carmody," I called, trying for a little distraction, a little time. "Can I ask you a question?"

"You already did."

I could tell that he was staying put. I figured he didn't want to risk getting too close to me, he was too smart to do that.

I stood close to my metal shield, hot and cold at the same time; hot because of the heat radiating from the cooling trays, cold because of the icy trickle beading my flanks. I molded the dough into a ball.

"You still hungry after that roll?"

"What?"

I cocked my arm and lunged, hurled the moist lump of dough around the edge of the oven at approximately where Carmody's single-word question had come from.

The gun roared. The oven deflected the thirty-eight cup point I'd been threatened with.

"Oh, you're cute, Jacko. What is this, a high-school lunchroom?"

I knew from Carmody's comment that the dough had missed him. If I'd hit him he would have been furious. But I'd got what I'd wanted: another wasted bullet. Problem was, I was fresh out of projectiles, or so I thought till I realized I was wearing a couple. I slipped them off. My shoes.

I crouched behind my barricade in my stocking feet and tried some psychology. Carmody fancied himself as a fighter, he'd made that clear during our conversation back in the hotel. I had a shot at tattooing his vanity.

"Ray, you better get me with that gun, 'cause if I get my hands on you I'll lay you right out."

"You? Who'd you ever beat? Trilling's goon squad? Bunch of saloon fighters."

"You're too big and you're too clumsy, Ray."

"Bullshit. Dead drunk in a rainstorm I could whip your ass."

"You sure about that? Put up the gun and we'll go at it right now. How about it?"

"Sister, you got a deal."

I heard the clunk of metal on metal.

I moved fast, jumped around the end of the oven, hurled my shoe at him, sprang back. He had the gun in his hand as I knew he would, but fired too late and too high.

He tried for a laugh. "It's like a fucking wedding round here. You gonna throw rice next?"

"What happened to our deal, Ray?"

"Wake up, schmucko. I got a hobby. Lying to you."

He had one more bullet left, but he sounded confident. Why not? A bullet versus a shoe? I doubted he'd try another potshot, yet it was what I had to try to get him to do again. I had to make him doubt the outcome.

"Ray? I have a confession to make."

"So go see a priest."

"I lied to you, too. I mean, I didn't tell you the whole truth."

"About what?"

The retained heat of the oven pulsated against my cheek. "When you asked me where I'd been today? I went shopping." I got ready to move. "I bought a gun."

There was a moment of leaden uncertainty.

"You're fulla shit. You got nothing in your hand except a fucking Florsheim."

"Here I come, Ray. I'm gonna shoot your ears off. I'm coming out from the other side of this thing. Or maybe the same side. You'll know in a second."

I chose the other side, darted out, fired a left-handed throw. It wasn't very accurate, but it served its purpose. The gun banged, a bullet punched into heavy steel. It happened in a tenth of a second—the throw, the duck back, the simultaneous gunshot and richochet—and then I was out of there, charging around the oven and going for him.

I pulled up in my tracks.

I had good reason to: I was rushing toward my own death. Carmody wasn't frantically trying to reload, nor was he shaping to go at it hand to hand. He was grinning and holding the gun pointed at my belt.

"I was lying again, Jacko. This isn't a Twenty-nine, it's a Brownie Hi Power. Thirteen rounds in the clip and one up the curtain rod. I got nine shots left. We'll start with two in the gut, then maybe—"

"Jack! Geddown!!"

The yell came from up the room. I got a glimpse of a man in a topcoat, a short-barreled rifle swinging up.

Carmody spun around.

I threw myself backward.

The crack of the pistol and the boom of the rifle folded into one concussive sound. Carmody rocked on his heels, made an ungainly turn, slumped against the long metal table, clutched hold of the big flour sack, and brought it tumbling over as he collapsed. I picked myself up—I'd tripped and fallen down—and watched the rifleman walking down the room. He was backed up by another guy, similarly dressed in a gray suit and a topcoat, also carrying a rifle.

I looked down at the floor. I was trying to make connective thought. It should have been me crumpled down there, bleeding my life away. Instead it was Carmody. The big flour sack, tipped on its side, was still emptying on him, pouring flour down onto his back. His torso was covered in the stuff; he looked like a body found half buried on a perfect beach. The white hillocks surrounding him were beginning to lump up and turn a dark red.

Wet work.

An apt expression.

The guys in the topcoats? They had to be the other players in the game, the third group that I figured had to exist in this serpentine venture I was embroiled in. I hadn't a clue who they represented, but they sure as hell looked like the good guys.

The rifleman stopped in front of me, the other guy covering Carmody. He knelt beside him, put a hand to his neck, then straightened up, no longer interested in my partner. Or, more correctly, I was sure, my ex-partner.

"Hell of a way to run a railroad," the rifleman said to me.

I nodded. "Right."

He had blue eyes and a tan, close-cropped gray hair, a face full of hard features, and a body like a neat fireplug. He struck me as the stern, no-nonsense type. He certainly was cool. He sounded as if I'd just had a lucky escape crossing the street.

"I have several questions for you," he said. I told him I had a few for him, too, and went and fetched my shoes.

"I'll hold off till we see the Colonel. Then you can brief us both."

"Fine with me," I answered, wondering who the Colonel was and not really caring. I was zonked by how close I'd come to a floury death. My nerves were trying to handle the aftereffects of another massive adrenaline rush, and my emotions were flying in about six different directions. I was holding my stomach partly because I felt like I was going to throw up, and partly because no bullet holes gaped in it, no punched little mouths ran red, and I may have unconsciously wanted to be convinced of that.

"You got a car outside?" I asked.

"Of course."

"Can we go?"

All I wanted to do was sit down.

CHAPTER TEN

Out on the street two white cars were double-parked, a tall man standing beside each of them.

These guys had to be muscle, but they looked nothing like Trilling's goons. They were both slim and athletic-looking with neat clothes and correct hairstyles, and they gave the impression of polite but tough efficiency.

We got into the automobiles and took off, the rifleman's partner staying behind presumably to do something about the body in the bakery. We got only a couple of blocks when we pulled over outside of a bar. My rescuer went inside and reappeared a minute later carrying a shot glass of amber liquid.

"Curbside service," he said, handing it to me.

I tossed it back. I didn't like it, but it gave me the lift I badly needed.

"Where have you been, Jack?" he asked me when we got going again.

I tried to put it as simply as possible. It was easy. "I have to tell you something. I don't know who you are."

He took a long moment with that; his reaction was tiny. His blue eyes strayed up to my scalp bandage then back to my face.

"What did they do to you?"

"Lost my memory for me."

It was hard to tell if he believed me or not, but he moved his head in understanding, sat back in his seat, and said no more. Eventually we pulled up downtown on Centre Street, an area, I saw, of state and government buildings. We got out and walked by a hinged wooden sign set up on the sidewalk. It said, US Army Recruiting Office. We went into a building, waited for an elevator. In an office to one side a man in a crisp khaki uniform with chevrons on his sleeve was in earnest conversation with an uncertain-looking youth.

We rode up to the fourth floor, made a turn, and stopped at a closed door which bore the number 404 on its frosted glass panel. My escort slipped an electronic access card from his wallet and inserted it into a slot at the side of the door. A bolt clicked back and I followed him into a small lobby area. A uniformed man, a two-striper, sat behind a desk. He nodded at the rifleman, said, "Major," and switched his gaze to me.

"Good to see you again, sir," he said, allowing himself the briefest glance at my head bandage.

My savior had taken a plastic ID from a pocket and was clipping it to his lapel. I saw that his name was Dawkins. When I failed to produce an ID of my own, the corporal handed me a tag that said Visitor. Dawkins wrote something in a large book, then guided me past the desk and along a busy corridor. I got glimpses of khaki uniforms in the side offices, a lot of computer work going on. We stopped at the end of the corridor for Dawkins to have a quick word with somebody. I ran an eye over a cork notice board fixed to the green wall. There was a cost-cutting directive printed on plain computer paper, a handwritten note from somebody trying to sell an '88 Mustang with only twenty-four thousand miles on it, a peeling decal that said Beat Navy, and an appeal for the return of some softball gear. It was a touch of normality that I found very welcome in the middle of this overexciting day I was having.

Dawkins let me into an empty office, sat me down, then

excused himself. A woman came in a moment later—she wasn't in uniform—fortyish, well groomed, horn-rimmed glasses on her nose, and asked me could she get me anything. I plumped for some water, which she brought, with apologies, in a coffee mug. I drained it off as a late chaser to the curbside whiskey, and went on waiting.

There was little to look at: a desk, two chairs, a small, polished table, a furled US flag in a corner, and on the wall behind the desk, a framed photograph of President Bush. The desk held several bound folders, and a triangular brass nameplate. It said: Col. E. McAlister.

"Hello there, Jack."

It was a big man who came into the room, white hair cut short enough to show skin above the ears, a nose that looked strong enough to chop wood, and cross-hatching at the eyes as if he'd done a lot of gazing into sunny distances. He was a commanding figure. He was maybe a few pounds overweight—his striped gray suit had been tailored to keep them a secret—but the extra bulk only made him look more impressive.

"Dawk tells me you have a bit of a problem."

He took the chair behind the desk, sat with a back as straight as a door. He carried himself like a man peering over heads in a crowd. Dawkins drifted into the room and sat down next to me.

"You might say that," I said. "May I ask you a couple of strange questions?"

"Go ahead."

"Firstly, who are you?"

The big man had affected a casual demeanor, but he'd been observing me closely. He glanced at Dawkins and said, as if he were about to make a fool of himself, "My name is

183

Early McAlister. I run this place. You do have a bit of a
problem, don't you?"

"Secondly," I went on, "is this the US Army Defense
Intelligence College?"

"The New York section, yes."

"Thirdly, can you prove it?"

McAlister reached back to smooth his hair. The tiniest
smile flickered across his mouth. "You've managed to ask
me a question nobody's ever asked me before." He checked
with Dawkins. *"Can* we prove it?"

Dawkins looked a touch bemused. It was clear he'd never
been asked that question before, either. "Well," he said, "I
guess he could ask my mother. Except she thinks I'm just a
supply officer."

"Jack," McAlister said, leaning toward me, "what the
hell happened to you?"

I told them everything, starting from when I'd woken up
knowing nothing. I told them about the head injury, why
and how I'd been injured, who had done it, and the ridiculous result. I told them about the meeting with Al Charmain
in the crummy office on Thirty-third Street, and how he'd
set me up with the first lot of players—Tom, his wife, and
Sharon—and how Charmain had got me looking for a German immigrant who'd run out on a finance company. I told
them how I'd traced Frohman to Boston and how I'd run
over my own tracks having found the guy once before. I told
them how Charmain's scheme had come to grief. Then I
took them through the second act: Trilling, Carmody, Jenny,
my "parents" in Florida, and how that had blown up in
Charmain's face. And I explained about Peliac's article in
the university magazine, how I'd found Peliac and inadver-
tently got him killed. Lastly I told them about Peliac's notes,
and the snapshot of Frohman and him, about the idea of

identifying the lake in the picture, and how Carmody had used it to set me up. When I'd finally finished and stopped talking, my last words fell onto a pensive silence.

McAlister tilted in his chair and examined the ceiling as if he were trying to decide if white was really the best color for it. Dawkins, the blue-eyed rifleman, was looking the other way, head down, working a finger at a thumbnail.

"Jack," McAlister said, returning his gaze to me, "if I didn't know for sure that Ray Carmody had been on the edge of killing you, I wouldn't believe one word of that story."

"Neither would I," I agreed. I meant it. In retelling the story, the whole thing had sounded like a huge joke which, in a way, I suppose it was, although an extremely cruel one.

"They tried to beat the information out of you and in the process made sure you wouldn't be able to give it to them." McAlister had to struggle with it. His handsome face was mildly blanked by bewilderment. "It would be comical if the repercussions weren't so . . ." He stopped himself. I finished his sentence.

"Serious? I agree. It's very possible I've seen the last of my old memory."

"You don't know that. From what you tell me no real doctor's seen you, apart from the surgeon they hired to save your life. I think the first thing to do is get you down to Walter Reed." I didn't know who Walter Reed was, but I didn't want to discuss any possible treatment, and I didn't have to because McAlister was still trying to grasp how I'd been able to function.

"Without a memory, how in God's name did you make it this far?"

"I almost didn't make it this far." Dawkins seconded that with a confirmative nod of his semishaven head. I went on:

"Let me get a few things straight. For starters, how much of what Carmody and Trilling told me is true?"

"Most of it. Certainly everything about Werner Frohman. We know that he's working on something called Glitzenbak, or Glitterbug, and that it has a possible military application. Could be huge. We know the Chinese want him because of it, and that Acis are trying to find Frohman for them. We've been trying to find him ourselves, which is how you ended up in this pretty pickle."

"Then I really am a College boy?"

"Yes, indeed. You disappeared. We listed you AWOL, instigated a search, but couldn't come up with you. Hardly surprising, as it turns out. We've been watching the airports, car rental agencies et cetera, and one of Dawk's men got lucky today at La Guardia." McAlister nodded at his assistant who took his cue.

"We didn't intercept you. We waited to see if you'd check in with us, but you didn't. We tailed you to the hotel. When you came out of there with Ray Carmody, we knew something had to be up, but we didn't know what."

"I'll be honest with you, Jack," McAlister said. "I thought you'd sold out. It was the only explanation, gone all that time then turning up with Trilling's lieutenant. I hope you'll forgive me."

"I don't see why you should have known what was going on when I didn't myself."

McAlister liked my answer. "Very fair of you," he said.

"We were right on your heels when you went into that bakery," Dawkins continued. "Then the baker came out, a guy in a long apron and a paper hat, and he was practically shaking. I didn't like the look of it, the only store on the block that was closed, so I thought things had gone far enough and that maybe it was time to haul you in for a chat.

186

We went in armed because I figured Carmody would have a gun. When it turned out to be pointing at you, I knew you were still on our side."

"That's more than I knew. I didn't know which side was who. All I knew was I'd been eaten with a spoon. Twice."

"They're a bold, gutsy group," McAlister said. "And they have absolutely no heart. You were wide open, and they took advantage."

Dawkins concurred; I think they were trying to ease my embarrassment.

"Sure. Without a memory, why wouldn't you believe something if it sounded plausible?"

"Who are they anyway? Just who is Acis?"

"A bunch of international operatives left over from the Cold War," McAlister said. "When communism collapsed in the Eastern sector, an awful lot of state security people suddenly found themselves on the street. So Al Charmain, who used to be on the Czechs' payroll, rounded up a bunch of them up and took them freelance."

"That's basically what Carmody told me."

"He wasn't lying."

"He also told me about a new political alliance. Us and the Soviets against China and Japan."

"That's the way it's looking. There's nothing in cement yet, but I'd be surprised if it didn't work out that way."

"Carmody was smart to stick to the truth when he could," Dawkins said. "The truth is always that much more believable."

We were interrupted by the woman with the horn-rimmed glasses. She came in pushing a wheeled tray supporting some kind of electrical device I couldn't identify, a flat, circular thing with maybe fifty or sixty vertical slots around its edge. Dawkins got up and fiddled with it while the woman went over to the louvered blinds and cut the light. From a long metal cylinder Dawkins pulled out a stiff white screen, then plugged a power cord into a wall socket.

"We have a file on Acis employees," McAlister told me. "Sing out when you see a familiar face."

Dawkins squeezed a hand button and a man's face, wrinkled and elderly, filled the screen. I'd never seen him before. His features were replaced by those of a young woman with wiggy red hair, bending her head to an ice-cream cone. The shots followed one another in quick succession, men and women of various ages, the photographs taken from a hidden camera to judge by the candid attitudes of the subjects.

"Hold it right there."

It was Sharon with a drink in her hand at an outdoor table. She appeared to be agreeing with something that had just been said to her.

"That was my first girl. I knew her as Sharon Cole."

The slides were all numbered. Dawkins consulted a typed sheet, read out a name. "Jean Feltz. Only been with them a short while."

Five slides later I identified the guy who'd played my brother.

Two on from that was my "sister-in-law."

"That one," I said a minute later. It was Jenny perched on a park bench making a point to somebody only partially included in the shot. I wondered if it was Ray Carmody. "Jenny Halpern. She was my most recent paramour."

"She used her real name this time," Dawkins said, checking his list. "She does a lot of work for them."

"I'll bet she does, She's damned good at her job." I made the comment with a touch of jilted regret. Jenny was a wound that was going to take a while to heal.

GLITTERBUG

The slide show went on. The stars were all grouped together. Not surprisingly Al Charmain had been caught putting on pounds inside a McDonald's. George Trilling was gazing distractedly into a store window. Carmody, looking as sour as ever, was coming out of a bar. The next shot was of an Asiatic guy, then I got a brief look at a woman who looked Mexican. Dawkins flicked back to the first shot.

"You never ran into this man?"

He had sleek black hair, slashing sideburns, and freshly shaved shadow on his jaw; a young guy in his early twenties.

"No. Is he important?"

"I thought they might have used him in Florida."

"Show him the Florida file," McAlister said.

Dawkins took a minute to replace the slides with new ones. My "mother" came on almost immediately, frozen in midswing on a tennis court.

"Florence Hyde," Dawkins read out.

My "father" was three slides along. In his uniform, complete with hat, reflector sunglasses, and heavy holster, he was leaning his considerable weight against a police cruiser and laughing about something.

"Sergeant Ned Taws. They like using him," Dawkins said. "A tame cop's always nice to have on the payroll. And a lot of cops are damn good actors."

He went back to the local New York operatives, and I found the last of the people I knew: Wein, the guy who'd posed as my doctor, and the two nurses. I was glad I'd seen this light show, seen all the people who'd played a part in hauling me over the coals the last couple of months or so. Having them identified stripped them of their mystique, reduced the margin of their victory. It was a clever charade they'd put on, but, because it had been revealed, its flashi-

189

ness had begun to fade and the mean cheapness had started to show through. Dawkins opened the blinds, and we got down to some of the nitty-gritty. I related what Trilling had told me about Peliac's notes, that they weren't any help. McAlister was inclined to think he'd been telling the truth, pointing out that if the notes had explained what Glitterbug was, and how it worked, I would never have heard from Acis again. They asked me to describe the photograph of Frohman and Peliac, but I did better than that and produced the print in my pocket. Both of them examined the shot, both identified Frohman. Neither had ever seen Peliac before. I asked them how they'd go about tracking down the location, the lake and the mountains.

Dawkins fielded that one. "Lug that snapshot around town and see if we can get a response."

I made a face as I confessed something. "I'm afraid I gave Acis a head start."

I told them about my hunch that the shot had been taken in France and had something to do with cooking—and that I'd passed that information on to Trilling.

McAlister grunted. "One of your hunches, huh?"

I coughed behind my hand. This subject was a little embarrassing for me. "Let me ask you about that. Everybody was very careful to tell me what a terrific guesser I'd been in the past. Is that true?"

Dawkins spoke up again. He'd regained his chair and sat in it as if his compact body had nailed it to the floor. "I'm not sure they are guesses. They may be something more than that. We talked you into letting them run a few tests on you at Walter Reed. They said you have an ability that flirts with the paranormal. Flirts," Dawkins added quickly when he saw my reaction. "Nothing more. Nobody suggested you should be on the stage in a turban."

McAlister ran his large right hand over the bristles at the back of his neck. He spoke to the room in a growl. "The only para the Army recognizes is the kind that drops from a C Forty Seven. All you have, Jack, and it's a wonderful asset, is an ability to take a fact and extrapolate it. Nothing more. And if you'll take my advice, that's all you'll regard it as."

"Whatever you want to call it," I said, "the question is, is it going to work this time? And is it too late anyway?"

"Yes to the first question, no to the second. If you say that this photograph was taken in France, at a place that has some connection with cooking, then you've simply absorbed some facts that your subconscious mind has linked up."

I wasn't sure I believed that—what facts?—but I left it unchallenged and listened to McAlister continue.

"As for being too late, they have a couple of days on us, that's all. We'll have to play catch-up ball. It can be done if we start right away." He picked up the print, reversed it, and held it up to me. "You found the German once, Jack. And what a man can do once, he can do twice."

"That's what Acis was hoping."

Dawkins got up from his chair, took a second look at the snapshot, and made a suggestion. "I think we should give the TI boys a look at this. You see the boat here, moored off the point?"

McAlister creased his eyes. "By golly, yes. It's worth a try."

I asked them who the TI boys were, and got looked at as if I'd asked what year it was.

"You're going to have to understand something," I said. "I've forgotten everything I ever knew about the Army. I can't tell you one damn thing about it."

"Of course," McAlister said, although he looked as if he

couldn't conceive how a man could forget his time in the service.

Dawkins clued me in. "TI is Target Identification. The Air Force has a machine that'll show the collar on a dog at five thousand feet. If that ski boat has a maker's name on it, they'll be able to read it. Or the little town in the background here might be a match for one of their targets."

That raised my eyebrows. "The Air Force has targets in Europe? France? Switzerland? Italy? I thought we were pals with those countries."

"We are. Have been for years. But you never know."

I regarded the explanation as my first peek into the military mind. I didn't find it very attractive, and I was forced to wonder what kind of a soldier I'd been. And what kind I was now. We spent another couple of hours in the office, McAlister and Dawkins pumping me for details of my time as an Acis agent. McAlister sent the print off to be copied then told me there was nothing for me to do until they got some action on it and that I should take it easy and spend some time trying to adjust.

"Jack," he said, shifting his big body in his chair, "it can't have been easy adjusting to one life, losing that, then picking up another. And now you have to do it all over again. I'm wondering how much to tell you."

I was impressed by his perception. He was correct, I didn't want to know a lot of detail right away, but how could I escape it?

"Just the basics. If I have a girl or parents, I want to wait a bit before I see them. I don't think I can handle any more deep relationships for a while. But tell me anyway."

I waited on the information. If it turned out I was going steady with a lady wrestler or a trapeze artist, I don't think I would have been surprised.

GLITTERBUG

"No parents, they're both dead. Killed in a bus accident in Philadelphia four years ago. No brothers or sisters. An uncle in Seattle, if I remember correctly. As for a girl, how about that, Dawk?"

The blue eyes blinked as Dawkins's hard mouth relaxed a little.

"You liked to play the field. There was nobody special. But you do have an ex wife. Sarah."

"What?"

"And a daughter. Malinda."

I was dazed. Rocked all the way down to my shoes.

"I do have a daughter? Jesus!" When both men stared at me, I filled them in on a detail I hadn't yet given them.

"Acis told me I had a kid named Malinda, but they told me she'd been killed and that I was partly to blame."

McAlister's mouth clamped into a fierce line. "They're truly evil people."

"How old is she?" I asked.

"Nine," Dawkins said. "And a real sweetie."

I just shook my head. It was stupendous news and it was going to take me a while to get my mind around this flip-flop double reversal.

McAlister and Dawkins tried hard not to trade looks. I could see they were still trying to adjust to my handicap. A man who didn't know he had a nine-year-old daughter was going to take some getting used to. We talked about my big deficit, my total lack of knowledge of what Carmody had called Tradecraft, but McAlister didn't think it would be a hurdle.

"Dawk will be right beside you if things ever got sticky, but I can't see it happening. Acis are stubborn, but they're not stupid. They'll write you off as a lost cause."

"They'd already written him off," Dawkins pointed out.

193

I had to agree with that; I'd been headed for the Jersey Pine Barrens. However, I wasn't certain I'd seen the last of Acis, not if I got on to Frohman's trail. If they found out about it, those leeches would be right behind me.

The interview concluded twenty minutes later, and I left with just a couple of things in my pocket: some details concerning my ex-wife and my daughter, an office phone number, and the address of my apartment.

I found a bench in a tiny cement oasis and watched the office buildings empty; it was a little after five. I wanted to spend a few quiet minutes to give my head a chance to settle. Once again a thunderous waterfall of events had left me half drowned: I'd made a soul-crushing discovery, had survived, by the slimmest of margins a particularly sleazy attempt on my life, and seen a person gunned down right in front of me, my second dead man inside of forty-eight hours. The plus side of the ledger was that, barring further interference from Acis, I seemed to be out of the woods, back at last in my correct niche. Dawkins and Colonel Mc-Alister both had a military forthrightness that was hugely refreshing after the characters I'd been associating with. It was easy to see in hindsight that I should have suspected George Trilling's unctuous affability and been downright suspicious of Carmody, who'd been too busy disliking me to even attempt to win my confidence. But then that was being wise after the fact.

I dwelled on that for a while, then switched my thinking to the second big discovery, this one heart lifting. I was a father. I had a daughter.

What did she look like? Did she look like me? What color were her eyes, her hair? I dug out the details McAlister had given me. Her full name was Malinda Rebecca Penrose.

GLITTERBUG

Sarah and I had been divorced for two years. She had custody of Malinda, and I had visiting privileges twice a month.

I was overcome with a terrific urge to see my child, so I got up and began to trot through the crowds. I found a pay phone, called my ex wife's number, but there was no answer. I walked a few blocks, ambitiously looking for an empty cab, discovered a subway stop, and joined the crush heading uptown. I made it back to the hotel, picked up my bag, went down to Forty-second Street and caught the shuttle to Grand Central—one thing I'd learned from Carmody was the midtown subway system.

My apartment was in an old block in a section I think was called Murray Hill. It was a brown brick structure with handsome wainscoting in the foyer and old-fashioned multipaneled windows. I found the super's apartment. She was a chunky Italian woman who looked capable of fixing anything.

"Ey!" she greeted me, a wooden cooking spoon in one hand. "Lemme know next time you go 'way. You gotta mail box all stuffed up."

I told her I'd lost my keys. She went back inside, returned with a set of masters, and a plastic bag full of mail. She let me into my apartment on the seventh floor, gouged ten bucks out of me to have new keys cut, and waddled back to her pots and pans.

For the third time in less than ten days I walked into a new home. The difference was immediately evident. In the other two places, the painter's studio I'd shared with Sharon, and Jenny's Thirty-ninth Street apartment, the stuff Al Charmain had bought for me—books, records, tapes, personal things—had been too new, too fresh. The things in this apartment had a comfortable, used look, especially the furniture—the sofa looked like an old friend, and there was

195

a commodious winged armchair that fit my body as if it had been tailor made for it.

The books showed the biggest change. There was no *Firearms of the World,* no heavy tomes showing schematic drawings of Colt .45's or Stoner machine guns. Instead, there were hard-cover novels, travel guides, and some well-thumbed volumes of American history. There was a good quality CD player and a pretty extensive jazz collection. The pictures on the walls were prints of Hopper and Wyeth paintings.

The place had a lived-in welcoming feel to it; a feeling of home which the other two apartments had sorely lacked.

But what really excited me were two framed photographs on a coffee table. I picked them up and knew I was looking at Malinda. In one of the shots she looked to be around seven years old. The other was taken more recently. She was adorable. She wore jeans and a baseball shirt in one shot, a flouncy dress in the second one. But the dress didn't do a thing to formalize her cheery grin or tame her mop of brown hair. Mischief danced in her eyes. She looked like a little hellraiser. There were no photographs of my ex-wife, so it didn't appear that the breakup had left a large hole in my heart. But that didn't mean I wasn't curious about what kind of woman I'd married.

I tried her number again, and this time she was in.

"Sarah?"

"Yes . . . ?"

"It's Jack."

"Well, hello. You been out of the country?"

"Europe. Sorry I couldn't get in touch." I had to fib, I just couldn't face telling the truth—it pulled too much out of me.

"Malinda couldn't understand why you didn't phone. I

tried to explain about your job, your traveling, but you know Malinda."

"How is she?"

"Running on pure energy, as usual." It was a nice voice I was hearing. A little brisk but pleasing.

"Could I see her tonight? Could I come over?"

"Tomorrow would be better. She has a school holiday. Come around ten and have a regular day."

"That'd be great." The conversation teetered toward silence. "How are you, Sarah?"

"I'm fine. This is all very considerate of you, asking after our health. Have you had a religious experience or something?"

"No, just checking. I'll see you tomorrow."

I hung up. I was looking forward to meeting the woman I'd married. I wondered what had happened? Judging from that brief conversation the breakup had been an amicable one. But that wasn't the main thought in my mind: I was thinking that, while Sarah was no longer my wife, Malinda was still my daughter, and that simple, irrefutable fact I found very exciting.

I had the evening to kill so I roamed the apartment and poked into my former life. I found various things in my desk like bank statements—I was solvent, just—rent receipts, paycheck stubs from the US Government, some tax records —it struck me that I was paid by one section of the government only to give a lot of it back to another section—and some legal correspondence, including a copy of my divorce decree.

I cracked the mail next. It was mainly occupant junk mail, flyers, notices of one kind or another, some overdue bills, and a couple of book club mailings. There were only four pieces of personal mail: a postcard from Santa Fe

signed Bob and Megan, a letter postmarked Seattle containing an invitation to Patricia Prior and Arthur Brown's wedding, a cryptic and mysterious letter written in a man's bold
scribble about some kind of deal being on hold—it was
signed with the initial L—and another letter, this one
signed, Love, Sissy. It was a chatty letter about the differ-
ences between living in Atlanta and living in New York.

I gathered that we'd been close. I found an address book,
found a Cissy Clemson, a Manhattan phone number
crossed out, and a new one written in with a 404 area code
next to it. I found Patricia Prior and Bob and Megan Harris,
a Laurie and a Lisa, but no man's name beginning with L.

Leafing through the book, it occurred to me that there'd
been a similar address book at Jenny's belonging to me. I
assumed had I called those numbers I would have got
mostly answering machines or just ringing phones. But
some of the calls would have been answered by paid friends
and acquaintances. Sure. It demonstrated once again the
amount of time and money Acis had poured into the Jack
Penrose campaign, which in turn was an indicator of just
how important Glitterbug was.

I checked out the kitchen and found in the refrigerator a
pint of stale milk, a shriveled head of lettuce, an opened loaf
of moldy Wonderbread, and a can of Miller's in perfect
condition. I drank the beer while I defrosted a chicken pie I
discovered on a tour of the freezer, ate it in front of a TV
movie starring a world-famous actress I'd never heard of,
then fell asleep before the film had finished.

Another hard day at the office.

CHAPTER ELEVEN

When Sarah opened the door I saw why Al Charmain had chosen Jenny for my girlfriend.

He'd borrowed from real life.

She had the same petite stature, the same look of the gamin about her, except her hair was blond and frizzed out, and she didn't appear at first glance to have the same kind of high animation. She wasn't quite as pretty as Jenny, or as visually sexy, although the jeans and the blouse she wore did nice things for her pert little figure.

"Good morning," I said.

I watched her expression change as I knew it would: it would be a couple of weeks yet before I could remove my head bandage.

"What on earth happened to you?"

"Fell asleep behind the wheel. That's where I've been. Mending in a London hospital."

"But why wasn't I told?" Concern surged into her eyes, but she didn't move to take my hand or embrace me as she might have had she felt strongly toward me.

"I wanted to get all better. Besides, it's too far to go for a hospital visit."

She shook her head in mock disgust. She really was an attractive woman; I wondered what had gone wrong be-tween us.

"You never would let anybody help you, would you?"

We were walking into a living room that reminded me of some of the decorator stores I'd seen in my travels around town: track lighting, mirrored walls, a Chinese screen, a

199

blue-and-white rug from the same part of the world, furniture sculptured from grainy wood the color of butter. Sarah had remarried, according to my information, and had evidently done well for herself.

She wanted details about the accident, which were easy enough for me to supply, then I got off the subject.

"Anyway, *you* don't look as though you've had any accidents, you look great. How are you doing?"

She cocked her head, took a long quizzical look at me. "Are you trying for a good conduct medal? You want a favor? Is that it?"

"Nope. Just asking. How's your husband?"

"Fine. In Chicago on business."

"How's Malinda?"

"She's been ready for hours." Sarah crossed the blue-and-white rug, and called down a hall. "Malinda . . . Daddy's here."

I heard a yip, then, a moment later, a bundle of energy burst into the room.

"Daddy!" She ran to me, jumped into me, hugged me and held on tight. "Daddy, where have you *been*?"

Oh, what a moment that was! To hold my daughter for the first time in my living memory. What a stupendous feeling! She wriggled free, and I got a good look at her. So cute, with her long brown hair tied back and worn in a braid, and her mother's button nose. But I thought I could see myself in that delighted face, perhaps in the brown eyes, or the flat cheekbones, although I had an idea that most parents would claim to see their image in their offspring. I wouldn't have cared if she'd been cross-eyed and bucktoothed with one ear missing; she was my daughter and my heart soared.

"Why are you wearing that funny hat?"

"Lindy . . ." Sarah began.

"I've just been to a costume party."

"You go as a pirate?"

"Right. You ready to go?"

"All ready," Malinda cried, twirling around to show off a dress that looked freshly pressed. "Can we go to the zoo? I want the zoo."

"Lindy," Sarah said, "maybe Daddy's a little tired of the zoo."

"No, he isn't, are you, Daddy?"

I said I wasn't, which was a funny remark considering I had no idea where the zoo was or what it looked like. I didn't care where we went. I would have been willing to take her to the moon. Sarah got Malinda's coat, had a word in her ear about something, and saw us to the door. Malinda was pulling at my hand like a puppy. I asked Sarah what time she wanted us back. Five turned out to be the witching hour, so Malinda and I said good-bye to her mother and began our day together.

I can honestly say that it was, without question, the highlight of my new life by a factor of ten. I had a marvelous time. I'd had no conception of what it could be like to be with your own happy kid and watch her dashing around, full of interest in the world, innocent of its evils, aware only of its wonders. I ran a gamut of emotions. At one minute I felt fiercely protective, the next I was bubbling over with the sheer fun of being included in a child's life. It was a revelation, an epiphany.

We walked to the zoo, which I discovered was in Central Park, the huge green space I'd seen in my flight with Carmody from Peliac's apartment. I solved the memory problem with Malinda by inventing a game: she was a little girl washed up in a shipwreck, and I'd found her and didn't know anything about her. That way I was able to ask her questions about her life, about home, her school, her friends et cetera. I didn't touch on her new father, but I gathered they got along fine.

At the zoo she fed the ducks, held her nose in the lion cages inside, found her favorite, favorite goat in the children's section.

And she also rode the carousel. I tried to talk her into riding in the swan boat instead of on one of the plunging horses, but she scornfully told me that the swan boat was for little kids and that she always rode a horse. I know why I did it, of course: I still had that horrible fairy tale Acis had told me in the back of my mind and, as silly as it sounds, I worried every second Malinda rode that thing.

We had lunch at her favorite, favorite place, a Chinese restaurant, where she ordered her favorite, favorite dish: butterfly shrimp. Pretty sure of her answer, I asked her what her mother had whispered to her as we'd been leaving the apartment.

"She told me I wasn't to say anything about your head."

"Do I look very different?"

She bit into a shrimp and solemnly nodded. "Do you have a scar?"

"A big one. I call it Rodney."

"Rodney?" She cackled with laughter. "You can't name a scar Rodney."

"Well, I'll call it Alice. You like Alice better?"

"Dad-dy!" she said, knowing she was being joshed. "You can't name a scar Alice, either. You can't name a scar anything. They're just scars."

We went to the movies—Malinda chose it, a clever cartoon about two dogs. Malinda said she'd seen it three times. She kicked off her shoes, tucked her feet beneath her, and stared entranced at the screen. I kept sneaking glances at her profile, wondering what I could have been thinking of to give up a child like this. I assumed I thought it was worth it at the time. We went for a Häagen-Dazs later—with a name like that I expected anything but an ice cream—and got back around five as I'd promised Sarah. Malinda gave me numerous hugs and kisses, then ran off to catch a TV show.

"You look beat," Sarah said, walking me to the door. "Did she run you ragged?"

"She's a terrific kid. Can I see her again next Saturday? Her favorite, favorite goat is pregnant. It might have a little goat by then."

Sarah moved her hand in an iffy gesture. "Okay, but don't tell my lawyer."

I turned at the open door, wondering how to broach the subject of our marriage. I decided the frontal approach would be as good as any.

"Can I ask you a question?"

"Sure. No charge."

"What I'm gonna say will sound stupid, but stay with me, okay?"

"Go ahead."

"What would you say was the main reason why we split up?"

Her eyebrows climbed a quarter inch, enlarging her deep eyes.

"You're right, that does sound stupid."

"Tell me anyway. I want to get your view."

"It's not my view, it's simply fact. I got tired of your cheating."

I made some kind of bland comment, told her I'd see her Saturday, and left. Her answer hadn't really caught me unawares, I'd been half expecting it. I'd clearly had a serious fling with somebody, probably Sissy Clemson, the woman who'd moved to Atlanta, although not so serious that she'd stayed around to marry me. I couldn't help wondering what had brought that on—something lacking in Sarah, or something lacking in me?

I made my way back downtown in a mix of emotions. I was up because I was flying with the experience of the day, suffused with the charge of being with Malinda, somebody who was part of me. But I was down because of the knowledge that Malinda was going to be severely rationed out to me: seven hours twice a month, which came to a total of around one week a year.

I slow-dragged back to my apartment. A green light was showing on my answering machine. The message was delivered by Dawkins's firm, direct voice: his people had had some early luck; they'd found not one, but two people who claimed they could positively identify the locale of the Frohman/Peliac photograph.

I welcomed this quick development. It was exactly what I needed: action.

And I got it in spades.

CHAPTER TWELVE

The restaurant, a fancy place in the East Fifties, was being set up for lunch by a team of waiters laying out flatware, folding napkins, getting the room ready for the lunch session.

Dawkins had picked me up at ten-thirty A.M. and explained that his men had circulated copies of the print among the city's continental restaurants the evening before. They'd turned up a waiter and a chef who'd named the lake in the photograph. However, there were two problems: one, they didn't agree with each other and two, the waiter had identified the same shot the previous day when another group had showed him the same photograph. So it looked like Acis had gotten a step on us as we thought they might. But not being able to do anything about it, Dawkins chose to ignore it and press on with our own search.

"There aren't a tremendous number of French people living in New York," Dawkins told me, looking sturdily correct in gray suit, white shirt, and light tie. "But what there are seem to be working in the eateries. And seeing you figured an association with cooking, we could be on to something."

I wasn't sure if the cooking my hunch had put into my mind had anything to do with New York, but I didn't mention that. The main thing was to start talking to people.

We walked past a busboy handling a vacuum cleaner, past a woman scissoring flower stems, and out into an aromatic kitchen shiny with white tile and stainless steel. A variety of chefs worked in a kind of controlled panic.

Saucepans simmered, butter slid in copper pans, black-handled knives sectioned vegetables faster than the eye could follow.

The guy we'd come to see was a thin, intense young man with a mound of dark hair spilling out from under his chef's hat, a fine beak of a nose, and a wide mouth that moved energetically around his accented English. Dawkins gave him a mild story about a low-key government inquiry and showed him the shot.

"I understand you might know where this was taken."

The chef's long Gallic face moved in a quick nod. The name he gave us sounded like Talwah. Dawkins asked him to spell it, and jotted it down. It came out as Talloires.

"And it's in France?"

The chef's expression made the answer obvious.

"Where exactly?"

"In the Haute Savoie." The photograph bobbed. "This is Lake Annecy."

"You're certain of that?"

"Absolute. I stand on that jetty one thousand times maybe."

"You lived there?" I asked.

"For two years I am soo chef at Beece."

"What is that, beece?"

The Frenchman looked at me—another American for whom there was no hope.

"The restaurant. One of the great kitchens of France."

Dawkins didn't turn to me, but I could tell he recognized the breakthrough. France, and something to do with cooking—my prediction exactly, although prediction is not the right word. Dawkins asked the chef if he could identify anything else in the photograph, like the town that was just visible on the other side of the lake. There were no other close geographic details apart from a mountain rising out of the water, a notch carved out of its summit.

"Its name is Dwan," the chef replied. "And here, you cannot see it, here is a château on the *bord du lac*. Next to the mountain. The Château Monbell."

Dawkins got him to spell everything, wrote it down, and thanked the young man for his time.

Out on the sidewalk Dawkins's firm mouth softened at the edges.

He congratulated me without appearing to. "Better not tell the Colonel about this. He doesn't like anything that's not in the manual."

"It's looking good," I said, "but we still have the other guy to check, the waiter."

I was playing devil's advocate because France was a long way to go if I was wrong. Indeed, the man we saw next gave me pause because he was Swiss, and Peliac had been Swiss, and, on paper, the odds favored the lake being in Peliac's home country.

The waiter worked in an Italian restaurant on West Fifty-sixth, a handsome place almost as elegant as the French restaurant we'd just come from but not nearly as haughty. The waiter was from the Italian section of Switzerland. I hadn't known there was one.

"Ascona," he said, with a fair-headed nod. "That's where that was taken." His English was perfect; just a slight over-roundness in his vowels. "You're the third person I've told that to." I knew who the other two people were: our guys, and Acis. Dawkins asked the waiter if he recognized the dock. The man tapped the shot with a finger.

"I used to swim off that dock. Every summer for years. See the rocky point here? Behind that is a little cafe. My uncle runs it."

"And the town you can just see in the distance?"

"Locarno. I was born there. That's the lake in the picture. Lake Locarno. And the mountain with the notch in its peak is Mount Sasso. It has a grotto halfway up with a statue of the Virgin."

Dawkins got it all down, then we took our leave.

"He was pretty positive," I said.

"So was the French guy. What we need is some comparative reference. Washington's digging some stuff out for us, but I think we can do a little research ourselves."

He took me over to Fifth Avenue, to the Swiss Tourist Office, which shared space with the national airline. They had all kinds of brochures on the Italian part of Switzerland, the Tercheeno as they called it, and there were several views of Lake Locarno, but there was no way the little town in the shot could have been Locarno as the Swiss waiter had claimed; Locarno had prominent spires and bell towers, and was way too big anyway. That left us with the French Tourist people, just a block north. They were helpful, too, and came up with a large poster of the lake the young chef had claimed was Lake Annecy. It was a magnificent piece of scenery: snowy mountains hugging a stretch of water so still it was a mirror image of itself. But it was an aerial shot and no good for our purposes. As for the town, Talloires, the office had no photographs, although in a brochure of the area, there was mention of the restaurant the chef had talked about. What he'd pronounced Beece I saw was spelled Bis.

We needed more than this, and the young lady who was helping us suggested we try a place that handled rentals in France.

We went straight there. It was on the West Side near a

gigantic building that looked like the pictures I'd seen of Greek temples.

Dawkins said it was the main post office.

The rental place was called Vacances des France. When Dawkins explained what we were looking for, there were no negatives, it was all go. The Annecy area, we were told, was very popular in the summer, popular, too, in the winter for the nearby skiing. The agency had something like a dozen villas for rent around the lake, including a little apartment in Talloires. The woman who ran the place showed us some photographs—she had snapshots of all her rentals, and their towns or villages. There was one of her, taken in Talloires, standing on a stone quai, the lake behind her, the mountains rising in the background.

We both knew this was it, Dawkins and I, it was all there in front of us: the rocky headland on the left, and the by-now-familiar shape of the notched mountain.

"Is there a wooden dock somewhere near where you're standing in this shot?"

"About a hundred feet along the quai," the woman told me. "The ferry stops there in the summer."

It was Dawkins's turn. "Is there a town opposite with a castle?"

"Dwan. It's another stop for the ferry."

And that was that.

Riding back uptown, Dawkins made a slightly nonplussed confession.

"It would've taken me weeks to get this far, but you, a couple of days. How do you do it, Jack? Do these things just leap into your head?"

Dawkins was a nice enough guy, if a touch stiff, and I didn't want to be rude to him, but I'd grown wary of this question, mainly because I was uncomfortable with the answer. I didn't want to feel different from everybody else; I was already different enough being a man without a memory. I pleaded ignorance and took the conversation into a fast U turn.

"I want to leave for France as soon as I can while we've still got a jump on Acis."

"They can't be far behind," Dawkins said, "but we could probably keep our noses in front if you left today."

"Can I move that fast? Don't I need a visa and stuff?"

"No. What you'll need most of all is somebody to go with you. A French speaker, which lets me out."

"Who do I get?"

"That's up to the Colonel. He handles staff assignments. We'd better call him," Dawkins said.

Even though I had my passport I thought that getting away the same day would be pushing it, but I got a good demonstration of what military efficiency could be like. By eight P.M. I was airborne with a suitcase, a pack of travelers checks, two thousand French francs, and, sitting next to me in a window seat, a brand-new partner.

Her name was Joyce Benavides, a Peruvian American.

We'd met for the first time at the airport thirty minutes before the flight left and had got to know each other over the Atlantic. She'd been fully briefed about Frohman, Peliac, and the enigmatic Glitterbug, and she also knew about my condition. That became evident by the diplomatic way she stayed clear of the past. She never asked me who I knew, or where I'd served, but instead volunteered information about herself. She was a lieutenant, and had taught at the Army's language school in Monterey, California, before being assigned to Fort Dix in another capacity. The College borrowed her on loanouts from time to time. Her father, a

businessman, had been transferred to Paris when she was
five years old, and French had become her first language
until the family had moved back to the States when she was
sixteen. She'd gone into the Army on a college program.

Had I been told, before meeting Joyce, that it was a
woman French speaker going with me on the trip I would
have envisioned somebody dark-haired and statuesque, like
the girls I'd seen at the French Tourist office. By contrast
Joyce was slim to the point of being skinny, and although
she did have beautiful black hair, her complexion was poor,
and a prominent jawbone pushed her mouth a little too far
forward. She was no raving beauty. She was a little shy with
men, I felt, and perhaps a little anxious or uncomfortable
with one she'd only just met. I couldn't help but think that,
had Acis succeeded in fooling me all the way, and I'd pin-
pointed the location of the shot for them, the French
speaker they would have supplied me with for the trip to
France would have been a voluptuous sexpot.

The disappointing realities of life.

As far as I knew, it was my first transatlantic flight and,
after dinner, a movie, and a short nap, I was fascinated to
find the sun coming up at what was midnight New York
time. I also found it interesting the way the cabin staff
served us breakfast at three A.M. as if everybody always
breakfasted at that hour.

We landed, not in France, but in Switzerland, in Geneva,
because it's a lot closer to Annecy than Paris is. Customs
and Immigration was a breeze, then we picked up a reserved rental car and got going. The airport seemed to be
just on the edge of the city because ten minutes after we left
the modern new terminal we zipped down a short, curving
hill and out on to one of the quais that border the lake, Lake
Geneva or Leman, as Joyce said it was called. We drove

across a low, flat road bridge toward the other side of the city and into another downtown section fronted by elegant buildings, all of which carried huge neon signs for either banks or watches. The city was a pretty sight in the high morning sunshine, the wind-whipped lake the star of the show. A jet of water from a spectacular fountain spumed a couple of hundred feet into the clear air. Closer in, white swans glided on the bright, choppy water, miniature versions of the antique, high-decked steamers moving against the green hills of the far shore. The traffic was compact but easy-flowing and very well mannered compared with Manhattan, and we made the French border, on the western outskirts of the city, in less than fifteen minutes.

It was a double border, Swiss control first then, two hundred feet farther on, the French version. We were waved on through at both stations.

We hit the turnpike and some spectacular scenery: magnificent deep valleys on our left, sweeping up to a frosty and jagged mountain range and, on our right, rolling green fields patched with snow and dotted with enormous wooden farmhouses.

We swung onto another highway under a sign pointing to Lyon, spent thirty fast minutes on that, then took the Annecy North exit, and paid some money at a toll gate. We drove through an urban area of no particular attraction, were squeezed into a one-way system and, accompanied by a phalanx of convening cars, rounded a low modern building fronted by a sidewalk cafe.

What a revelation!

Facing us was a large grassy park, and beyond that a breathtakingly beautiful lake, blue-green, fading away to dark mountains that folded into one another like the mountains of China I'd seen in a painting.

"My God," I said. "This is absolutely gorgeous."

Joyce, who'd been to Annecy before, laughed and told me that everybody had the same reaction the first time they saw the lake, partly because the stunning vista suddenly popped into view after the closeness of the unimpressive streets.

The road followed the curve of the lake, allowing us to look back at the imposing château looming over the old medieval part of the town. Joyce said this section was a place of ancient arcades, cobblestone streets, and five-hundred-year-old houses set in the middle of placid canals. I was half in love with Annecy already. The drive to Talloires took maybe fifteen minutes winding through several small lakeside villages then climbing and leaving the lake behind. To the east massive overhangs of granite rose like threats against the sky, and above these massive heights, where it was still winter, sun-sparkle bounced off snow and ice. The road reached a junction, one part of which looped up toward a craggy pass. Joyce took the other fork, followed its precipitous swoop downhill where, after the road horseshoed left, the lake was once again revealed, a panoramic marvel.

If I'd had the remotest doubt that this was the location of the snapshot, I had none now. I could see clearly the small green mountain growing out of the lake, the angular notch sliced out of its peak, the little white town to the south of it, and a romantic, water-lapped château that had to be the one the young chef had told us about.

I felt tremendously confident that I was close to Frohman's trail again, heartened by the feeling I was getting as we dropped down, turned off, and crept along a narrow, one-car-width street that meandered through the quiet gray village of Talloires. The road descended all the way to lake level, ran along a small, tree-bordered quai, and finished abruptly at the walls of a very large and very lovely stone building. The sign, worked in fanciful wrought iron across the opened gates, said, L'Abbaye. We had reservations here. The wife of the owner, a pretty woman who spoke English with a charming accent, checked us in and showed us up to our rooms.

I didn't even bother to unpack. I went straight back downstairs, past the hotel's glassed-in cloisters, out through the gates, and along the quai to the dock I'd spotted on the way in. In back of the dock was an imposing structure, a gabled inn above, an expansive and luxurious restaurant below. It was where the young chef had said he'd worked, Père Bis.

I walked past a handful of strolling tourists out to the end of the dock. Its weathered brown boards were bare except for a quaint wooden shelter housing a couple of benches and a painted sign showing a diagram of the ferry route. Over to my right a half dozen small sailboats slept at anchor on the quiet little bay, while ahead, farther out into the lake, the surface quivered under a gentle breeze, a reflected sun dance popping into my eyes. I was astonished at the clarity of the water. There were no weeds, no murk, certainly no garbage, but then it was an alpine lake, something like fifteen hundred feet above sea level and fed by melted snows.

I checked the photograph of Frohman and Peliac. Both were smiling in the sunshine, relaxed and comfortable, taking a pleasant little time out from their work. They looked as if they hadn't a care in the world. And maybe they hadn't had one then. But because of their experiment, the lives of several people had been radically changed. Peliac's had been brutally snuffed out. Frohman had become a hunted man. I'd lost all memory. And Ray Carmody had ended his days in a pile of flour and a pool of blood.

What could Glitterbug be that made it worth such easy slaughter? What did it do that called for such a colossal outlay of money and manpower?

I heard footsteps on the planking: Joyce coming up to join me.

"I thought you'd be here," she said.

I passed her the shot, and she seemed to catch my mood. She hadn't got much sleep on the plane, no more than I, and she looked tired, but she could tell I wanted to get down to it right away. She asked me if I wanted to start in the village.

"Sure. Where to first?"

Joyce plumped for the post office on the theory that, in a small French village, the postmistress knew who came and went better than anybody else.

We found the place at the top of the hill, on the village's tiny main street, a pleasant, two-story cottage containing a couple of phone booths, a counter, two women behind desks, and a short-haired dog that barked at us. The women, both in their forties, both good-looking, shushed the dog and said bonjour. Joyce replied in kind and followed it with a burst of rapid French. I caught the names Frohman and Peliac. One of the women came to the counter, accepted the photograph from Joyce, and conferred with her associate. This woman viewed the shot, took another look at me, and appeared to have a revelation. More French flew back and forth, Joyce made a note of something, thanked them, and guided me outside.

"They recognized them. They rented a villa up the hill about a year back. I got the directions."

It was the first confirmation that my guess had been right, and Joyce congratulated me. She suggested my hunch about Frohman being here was something like the hunter's affinity for his prey, but I rejected that analogy, although I wondered about it. It wasn't the only thing I wondered about. As we walked through the village, up the winding one-way road, I noticed uncertainty in Joyce's face. I knew that she'd learned something back there at the post office, and I put it to her.

"What else did they tell you? Something about me, correct?"

"They recognized you. They said you were here asking about the two men about three months back."

My reaction to this news was excitement, not surprise. It was what I'd been hoping to hear. It meant I'd done the right thing coming to France because that had to be how I'd traced Frohman the first time.

I was back on my own trail.

"You had a woman translating for you," Joyce added uncomfortably.

"They describe her, this woman?"

"In her fifties. Spoke French with a Swiss accent."

I got the impression Joyce had been a little thrown by this hard and fast evidence that she was partnering somebody who was living two lives. Her unease was understandable: it was probably the last thing a military person would ever be expected to handle.

"Then I probably hired her in Geneva, huh?"

"Most likely. With the UN there, it's not hard to find a language service."

We walked single file along a track cut into a grassy bank, the lake appearing below as the village's main street joined a higher, far busier road. I asked Joyce something I didn't understand. "If I was here before, why are there no records of it? Why doesn't the Colonel know I made the trip?"

"The College doesn't work that way. You're given an assignment, you're expected to carry it out to the best of your ability and report when it's been accomplished." Joyce turned her head to give me a piece of a smile. "The Army doesn't want to hear how you do something, just that you've done it."

We were walking on the main road now, moving past a splendid Gothic mansion with a tower and a tall, narrow, gingerbread chalet set into the incline above us. The house we were making for was down a rocky little lane off one of the horseshoe bends the passing cars had trouble negotiating. It was a substantial brick residence sited on a couple of acres of steep and freshly mown lawn. The front door was approached via a stone balcony that gave on to a stupendous view: the southern end of the glistening lake which, from this angle, was backed by a spectacular chain of white-capped, saw-toothed mountains. Far down below I could see the rocky point and the brown roof of the restaurant Père Bis, and the wooden dock tonguing out into the perfect stillness of the lake. No craft moved on its glassy waters, just the soft flight of cloud image bounced down from the sky.

The woman who answered the door was strikingly handsome, her beautiful silver hair painstakingly brushed and set around her head in an elegant coif, her makeup very professionally applied. I wondered if she'd been a model in her younger days. Joyce started off in French, but when the woman realized we were American, she replied in English, which she spoke achingly well, and with a classy accent. She recognized the two scientists and verified that she'd rented her house to them last spring while she'd been away in Austria. She also recognized me. She told me I'd come to see her some time back asking about Frohman.

"You couldn't contact him at that address I gave you?"

"Address?"

217

"The forwarding address he left. The private post box in New York."

So there it was. I'd got an address from this woman, returned to New York, and waited for Frohman to pick up his mail. It probably hadn't been the one he'd been going to use for the university magazine, and he was certain not to be using it any longer, but that didn't really matter; what mattered was I knew, at last, how I'd found Werner Frohman.

I gave the woman my, by now, patented story of losing my notes and having to start from scratch again. Like everybody else she thought it was strange, a person being so sloppy, and was surprised I'd come all this way to do the whole thing over, but she agreed to tell me what she knew a second time.

It wasn't much.

Frohman and Peliac had rented the house for four weeks and had apparently spent almost all their time in the basement where they'd set up a workbench. The woman had been concerned about the possible dangers of flammable chemicals, but the two scientists had insisted they'd only be working with some pots and pans, a small heating device, some glass lab equipment, some harmless powders, and several flasks of prepared nonvolatile fluids. What had bothered the woman most were the rats they planned to keep down there, but the two men had assured her that the rodents would be caged at all times and could never get loose.

At my request she took us down to the basement. It was as immaculate as the other parts of the house we walked through. The furnace had been silver-frosted and shone like a valuable piece of furniture, and the floor was a pristine sheet of white-painted cement.

The woman had nothing more to show us, but she did fetch Frohman's forwarding address for me. As I'd suspected, it wasn't the one he'd given to the Boston librarian.

Showing us out, the woman suggested we check with her neighbor, who'd looked after the house for the duration of the scientists' stay. We thanked her for her time, took her advice, and went next door. The neighbor was yet another pretty woman—I was beginning to wonder if all Frenchwomen were good-looking, or if it was just in Talloires. She invited us into her charming house: blond marble floors, some wonderfully colored African birds mounted in glass cases, and that same spectacular lake and mountain view. She spoke English, too, sweetly accented, as did her husband. She remembered the scientists who'd rented her friend's house, and she'd closed the place up after them when they'd left. All she knew was that they'd bought their chemical supplies in Lyon. They'd never bothered her for anything, had turned down an invitation for a drink, and seemed to want to keep to themselves. She'd seen them from time to time shopping in the village, but they'd always been deep in conversation, as if they hadn't left their work behind. If we wanted any more details she suggested we try her neighbor, who was very much involved in the life of the village, so that's where we went next.

I was expecting yet another good-looking woman in this remarkable town, and found not one but two: a delightful extrovert whose French ranged a full octave, and a fine-featured pal of hers who I think was Danish. The French-woman told us, as Joyce translated for me later, that she'd often seen the two foreigners down on the quai when she'd been taking her grandchildren out in her little rowboat. They were always carrying saucepans down to the lake, but just what had been in those saucepans she was at a loss to say. This had been in the afternoons. She'd never seen them venture out in the mornings.

That was our last house call. Joyce went into the village to ask some more questions, and I returned to the hotel to think and do something about my jet lag.

We met downstairs for dinner in a room hung with seventeenth-century tapestries and lit by flickering candles. We were sitting by a window overlooking the spreading plane trees on the front patio, strings of fairy lights twisted through their newly budded branches winking like fireflies. It would have been easy to have been seduced by the rich cooking, the fine wine, and the languorous evening, but we were both rehashing the events of the day. Joyce had made a call to the Colonel, who'd checked on that forwarding address, but, as suspected, that one had been canceled, too.

"Not much to go on," Joyce said. "I talked to several people in the village, but nobody can offer anything more than we know."

"How about those chemicals, the ones they bought in Lyon? Could we check that?"

The candlelight played on Joyce's Hispanic features, flared in her eyes as she shook her head. "It was a year ago, and Lyon is a big city. Who's going to remember a small cash sale that far back?"

"Then how about the rats? Where did they get those from?"

"I don't see how it would help us if we knew."

"I guess not. They'd hardly tell anybody what they needed them for."

"That's self-explanatory," Joyce said.

"Not to me it isn't." I gave her a smile. "Remember who you're dealing with here."

Joyce fiddled with her napkin, sensitive about what she

might have regarded as a gaffe. She explained that rats were used in lab experiments because, after chimpanzees, their metabolisms were the closest to the human kind.

"Then they were feeding those rats something, or injecting them."

"Almost certainly. A bug of some kind."

"You figure it's a germ weapon? Glitterbug?"

"Has to be, a name like that, Glitzenbak. The Colonel thinks so, and he's plugged into some pretty heavy Pentagon brass."

I studied the wine bottle, picked at a corner of the florid label, tore off a tiny strip in a straight and even line. I was trying to imagine the two men in that immaculate basement.

"They brought saucepans down to the lake, something they'd maybe boiled up on that heating device the woman said they'd had. What were they doing, emptying stuff into the lake? Why not simply tip it down the sink?"

Joyce allowed that those were both good questions. "I don't see how we're going to get them answered if none of the locals knows anything."

"We have to solve it," I told her. "Otherwise we'll come away with nothing."

We went outside after dinner, walked along the quai in the soft night. Several other couples were out strolling, the only other sign of life being the blaze of light coming from Père Bis's glassed-in veranda.

We headed for the dock, a place I didn't seem to be able to stay away from. It was the one spot that photographic evidence definitely placed Frohman, and I gravitated to it as if I could evoke his shade by simply being there. However, the setting was too romantic for any receptions of that kind; the lake was a still, dark presence, totally black all the way to the glow of the little town on the opposite bank. Past our hotel, past a private quai fronting some stately lakeside villas, the sharp rise of the headland bulked against the night sky, black on black. No stars shone down; it was perfect high-altitude darkness, the way the whole world must once have looked before the discovery of fire.

I rested my forearms on the rough wood of the rail, the same rail that Werner Frohman had leaned against twelve months back.

"We have to figure out why he came here. To do some experiments, okay. But why here? Why Talloires?"

"It's quiet, out of the way," Joyce proposed. "He came because he wouldn't be bothered."

"It's got to be more than that. I've got to believe he came here for a reason that's not that obvious. If we can't figure what it was, there's no way of tracing him back to the States."

Joyce didn't respond. We listened to our thoughts wrestling in the middle of all this calm.

A splash sounded not far away. I glimpsed the quick shape of an aquatic bird, popping up briefly then disappearing forever. Like Frohman was going to do if I couldn't get a handle on what he'd been up to.

I was pondering the probability of this when something completely unexpected happened: a dazzling cluster of glowing lights appeared from behind the slanting cliff of the headland, moving slowly from right to left at a languid, dreamlike pace. There was no accompanying noise; the lights moved silently, gliding just above the dead flat skin of the lake.

"For a moment I thought it was the Enterprise," Joyce said.

I wasn't sure what she meant, something unearthly, I assumed. The faint thump of engines came to us, then the form behind the lights took shape: a lake ferry, a glass showboat, the thump and splash of its paddle wheel getting louder. With great dignity it made a wide, slow turn, circled the little bay, traveling on its own white reflection, then winked out as it slid behind the dark headland on its way back toward Annecy.

So unexpected, so ethereal, it had been a magical sight. There was something special about this place, Talloires— gorgeous scenery, the quietude, the pure mountain air, the fairytale castle on the lake. Maybe Frohman and Peliac had come here for no other reason than because it was beautiful.

It was a possibility.

But one I didn't believe for a moment.

I was up early, and out into the warmth of the young day.

The only person who looked to have beaten me out of bed was a teenage girl getting some rental rowboats into place. I made myself understood, rented a boat from her, and pulled out into the middle of the sleepy lake to a sand-bank marked by a tall red flag. I wanted to see if a new perspective would nudge any great ideas. I could see the house Frohman and Peliac had rented, white with a brown roof, nestling among its neighbors on the grassy slope that descended all the way to the quai. Behind the houses a line of tall trees marched up one side of the precipitous head-land. In the other direction the slope became a leaning hill, which became a hulking white mountain twirling up into the blue.

I brought my gaze back to the brown-and-white chalet. What the hell had those two guys brewed up in the immaculate basement of that lovely house? Something hideously lethal that they'd then fed to a rat and watched the thing keel over? But why bring whatever it was down to the lake?

To see the effect it had on the water? Possibly. But would that tell them anything?

I was groping in territory as unfamiliar as the snowy reaches of that looming mountain. I needed another expert with me, not just a French speaker like Joyce, but a scientist who might have been able to get close to some answers.

I spent some time drifting over the sandbank, crystal clear beneath the boat, waiting for a hunch to arrive, but my body appeared to have got up earlier than my brain.

I rowed back in and found Joyce on the hotel terrace. We had coffee together, then she decided to have another crack at the village. I went with her and listened to her question three women—in the butcher's, the baker's, and the little photography store—and a bearded man who ran the gro-cery-cum-winestore-cum-vegetable-stand. Everybody was as polite and as sweet to us as if we were valuable customers of long standing, but nobody could add anything to our skimpy knowledge: the German and the Swiss had kept to themselves, two foreigners who'd come and gone.

We trooped on through the village past stone houses with intricate lace curtains hung behind open-shuttered windows. We crossed a tiny bridge that spanned a rushing stream cascading down from the mountain snows; pure, icy water rushing down to the lake. The road twisted up to the junction, then higher still toward the crossroads, and we took the fork toward the sky-high pass. We made it a thousand feet up a tortuous road to a little church cut into the side of the mountain rock. A wall plaque informed us that a mystic had spent thirty years living in a cave here, gazing out at mountains and lakes and meditating. Thirty years. At that moment I felt it might take me at least that long before I got a decent idea.

I suggested to Joyce that we give it another day, then pack

up. I was loath to leave Talloires, I loved the place, but we seemed to have done all we could. Also, I wanted to get back home and see Malinda. I didn't want to miss next Saturday. In my mind I'd already let her tug me to the zoo, waved to her as she spun by on the carousel, ordered her favorite dish at that Chinese restaurant, watched her take renewed delight in her fourth visit to the same animated movie. I think she could have been part of the reason why I was having so little success conjuring up an idea about Frohman. She'd taken over a large part of me and I couldn't have been happier about it.

I'm not sure, but it could have been that, sitting on a bench on the side of a steep mountain road and thinking that my delight in Malinda had sapped my hunch reception had the opposite effect—because something happened when Joyce and I got back to the lake that radically altered the whole picture.

Hungry after our climb, we'd stopped to have lunch in the flower-trestled garden of a small hotel just below the post office. Walking back along the quai, a ball came bouncing over the road and dropped into the water. It belonged to the child of a couple from New York, nice people we'd chatted with briefly the night before.

"Oh, great!" the husband said. "There I go polluting the cleanest lake in Europe. The ugly American strikes again."

I fished the ball out of the lake, tossed it back, and didn't hear the guy's thanks; I was staring at the water on my fingers, staring out at the lake.

Joyce must have seen something in my face. "What is it?"

I didn't answer. I was gazing past her at the sparkle dancing on the water, the afternoon sun bouncing rays off the surface, a million tiny golden flags waving a message at me.

My thoughts were tumbling, too many and too fast to

separate, but I knew, looking at the diamond-bright water, that I was looking at Glitterbug.

"Jack?"

I nodded at Joyce, although I was nodding more at my scattered thought process that was slowing its mad whirl. "That woman you spoke to, the neighbor, the one with the rowboat, she said she only saw them in the afternoons. Never in the mornings. That's why."

"What's why? You're not making sense."

I stooped down to the water, scooped up a handful, watched the fat drops run through my fingers. "I took a boat out this morning, rowed out about a mile. The water's cold out there because of the mountain streams that feed the lake. But in here, in this still little bay, after the sun's had all morning to work on it, the water temperature's way up. That's what they wanted, Joyce. Lake water heated by the sun. They weren't bringing anything down to the lake in those saucepans, they were taking it back up." I knew I was right because I remembered Trilling telling me what Peliac's article had been about: the effect of heat on liquids. For some reason they needed pure, clean lake water for their experiment, water that had been brought to a certain temperature naturally.

I explained all this to Joyce, perhaps a little too fast. And it didn't help my hurried explanation when I got a flash. Of all the times to get one, I got one right then, right in the middle of trying to sound logical.

"He's in New York, Joyce. Frohman. Not the city, he's in the country. Somewhere in New York State. And if he's still working on Glitterbug, he'll be at a lake like this one. An alpine lake." I took Joyce's arm and hurried her down the quai toward the hotel. She didn't give me an argument. I must have sounded so confident I think she allowed herself to be swept along by my certainty.

Twenty minutes later we'd packed, paid our bill, and were heading toward Geneva Airport.

And, I was pretty certain, Werner Frohman.

CHAPTER THIRTEEN

We were too late to get a flight to New York, which was an unexpected blessing because, as we discovered, New York was not where we wanted to go.

We found this out when we bought a New York State road map at an American bookstore in downtown Geneva. A quick glance was all it took to see that the alpine lakes were all grouped together way up north in an area called the Adirondacks, a huge area that was something like a national park. Joyce knew it. She told me it was an all-year vacation spot, and that the Winter Olympics had twice been held at Lake Placid, one of the major towns. If that's where we were going, Montreal was far closer than New York or Boston, so I called Bob Dawkins and gave him a verbal telegram. I told him I couldn't guarantee anything but there was a chance I had a lead on Frohman, and to meet our flight in Montreal. When he asked for some details I told him we'd be heading south a hundred miles or so and left him with that.

We'd missed all of that day's flights and had to cool our heels till the next morning. We left at eleven, made the short hop to Zurich, changed planes there, then took off for the long haul. We managed three seats for the two of us, and spread out the road map on the seat tables. I hadn't got anywhere with the map the night before, so now I had around nine hours to try to figure out exactly where we should head for after Montreal.

Adirondack Park was about a hundred forty miles long by ninety miles at its widest, and home to maybe two hundred lakes of various sizes. The eastern part of the area was bordered by two huge ones: the long, stringbean shapes of Lake Champlain and Lake George. I ruled out these two because they were far bigger than Lake Annecy. I figured Frohman might want to duplicate Lake Annecy's size—about nine miles by three—but even given those parameters there were a whole lot to choose from: Racquette Lake, Forked Lake, Long Lake, Loon Lake, Cranberry, Tupper, Saranac, Meacham . . . the list went on. The worst of it was there weren't going to be any clues. I had to either close my eyes and stick a pin in the map, or hope I got one of my flashes and that it turned out to be a good one. It didn't make me feel too confident. I wasn't sure I could produce a hunch just because I needed one.

Certainly nothing was jumping out at me from the map, but then I'd learned that these guesses of mine needed time to marinate in my mind. I also learned that they needed more than two hours because, when lunch was served, the lakes on the map were still just looking back at me.

"Let's try shapes," Joyce suggested. "Maybe Frohman chose a lake with a similar shoreline to Lake Annecy."

She had a brochure of Annecy in her carry-on bag. The lake was shaped like a peanut shell with the top part leaning to the left. We searched our map. Chazy Lake was close, as was Lake Kushaqua, even though it narrowed too much in the middle. Tupper Lake was another possibility, Silver Lake also, although it bent the wrong way. But none of the lakes sang to me.

We discarded the shape theory and tried narrowing it down to lakes with superior elevation, but that didn't do anything for me, either. Four and a half hours after we'd left Zurich, Joyce took the map away from me. "It's not working. Let's just talk for a while, about Frohman and Peliac. If nothing's coming in through the front door, maybe it'll come in through the window."

I liked Joyce. I was sure she didn't believe I could do the swami trick, but I was also sure she'd been briefed on me, given a profile that had perhaps portrayed me as exceptionally intuitive. She was going along with it in spite of the way she must have felt.

"What do you think happened between them?" she asked. "Why did they split up?"

"Who knows? But let's say they worked at Talloires, then both came to New York. Maybe they split up because, I don't know, maybe Glitterbug wasn't finished, but Peliac didn't want to take it any further. Maybe he got cold feet. So he took some of what he'd learned about heat and fluids and wrote a paper on it, and that paper was published in Boston. Frohman heard about it and wanted it. So he requested it from the library."

"Then why did he cancel it?"

"Because by that time he no longer needed it. When he returned to New York he got together with Peliac and persuaded him to tell him what he wanted to know. That's one huge guess, but it's a possible scenario."

"It doesn't sound bad." Joyce unfolded the map, laid it out again.

"Where is he, Jack? Tell me the name of the lake."

It was a good idea switching me on, then switching me off again.

But it didn't work.

Two hours out of Montreal I knew I was in real danger of making an idiot of myself. Dawkins would be meeting me at the airport expecting a destination, and all I'd have for him would be a shrug and a red-faced fixed grin.

An hour out, people were lining up for the washroom,

getting stuff together, getting rid of the junk they'd accumulated during the flight. All I was doing was staring a hole through the map.

"Let's try something else." Joyce was pulling out a small notebook and a pen. "We used to do something like this with playing cards in college, just for fun."

"Do what?"

She pointed the pen at the map. "Read out the first lot of names, the lakes that are similar in size."

I went along with it, read out the names I'd been staring at for the last eight hours. "Racquette, Forked, Long, Loon, Cranberry, Tupper, Saranac, Meacham." I added four more. Joyce wrote each name down on a separate piece of paper, shuffled them, then held up a page with the blank side toward me.

"What's it say, Jack?"

For two dollars or the Taj Mahal I couldn't have told her. It was just a piece of blank white paper.

"This one?"

"I don't think it's the way I work, Joyce. That's like a magician's trick. I need a medium of some kind, like this map, only it's just lying there."

"I'll be your medium. I'll read them to myself. See if you can get anything from me."

"I'm not a mind reader. I just sometimes have good hunches."

Joyce wasn't about to give up. She had a stubbornness that I'd never have guessed at in so placid a personality. "Okay. I won't think, I'll just look, and you go ahead and hunch." She held up all the pieces of paper, one after the other. All I got was what I saw: a blank.

On the PA the captain's voice announced our descent into

Mariel Airport. A stewardess asked us to buckle up and put up our tables.

"One more time," Joyce said to me.

She held up the pieces of paper, went slowly and deliberately through the first, the second, the third.

Blanks.

The fourth, the fifth.

Nothing.

She held up the sixth one.

Wham! There it was. So strong. I saw the word Saranac as clearly as I saw the Fasten Seat Belt sign. Without turning it over, I took the piece of paper from her and put it in my lap. I didn't bother with the rest.

Joyce, watching me and wondering, said, "Is that one special?"

"Could be."

Green fields came up into the windows, farm land outside, then a sea of concrete. The aircraft juddered as the landing gear telescoped, brakes squeezing on, the roar of reversing engines. I turned over the piece of paper in my lap.

Saranac.

CHAPTER FOURTEEN

Joyce had a connecting flight to New York, so we said good-bye in the terminal.

"Is it permitted to hug a soldier?" I kissed her cheek. "Thanks, for everything."

"Good luck with Frohman." She gave my hand a quick squeeze, then headed toward the transit lounge.

Nice woman. We'd made a pretty good team. Just how good I'd know pretty soon.

I got my bag from the carousel, passed quickly through the Canadian formalities, and found Bob Dawkins waiting for me. Seeing him standing there, getting every inch out of his compact, five-feet-eight-inch frame, it struck me that he wore his tight-fitting, three-piece suit as he would a uniform.

"Welcome back. Good flight?"

We traded pleasantries as we moved toward the exit. A white Ford was waiting there, one of the help standing next to it, a tall man in a topcoat. He nodded at us, then walked to a van parked behind it, a van with smoked-glass windows and deep-tinted windshield.

"Where are we going?" Dawkins asked.

"Saranac Lake."

"Is that where he is?"

"Maybe. And that's about as definite as I can get."

Dawkins made a claw of his hand and raked it through his brush cut. "Good enough." He didn't quiz me or question the basis of my suggestion, he just got in behind the wheel and checked a Rand McNally.

I climbed into the rear seat and stretched out, apologizing
to Dawkins, but I was dead from nine hours of map reading.

I saw nothing of Montreal, nothing of the thirty-mile
drive through Quebec to the border of New York State. I was
wakened up to pass through the checkpoint where I got out
and joined Dawkins in the front seat. We picked up speed,
still heading south on the Interstate. Now and then I caught
glimpses of a wide blue reach of Lake Champlain to the east
and the timbered hills of Vermont, smoky in the afternoon
light.

Dawkins asked me how I was feeling.

"Better. It was a tight couple of days."

"Any sign of Acis?"

The question took me by surprise; it was something I just
hadn't considered. I told Dawkins I hadn't given them a
thought over there.

"You should have. If they got to that young chef in that
French restaurant we went to, and he ID'd Talloires for
them, they could've had a man in place and waiting for
you."

"How could they have done that? We left New York almost immediately."

"By making a phone call," Dawkins said. "They could've
called somebody in Geneva and given them a description.
You would've been picked up the moment you got to Talloires. Who was assigned to you? Joyce Benanides?"

"Yeah."

"A big guy with a head bandage and a tall, thin Latino
woman. They couldn't have missed you if they were there."

I tried to think back. Had anybody looked at us twice?
That American couple with the kid whose ball I'd rescued
from the lake? There'd been a couple of dozen French-

speaking people in the hotel, quite a few tourists in the village. Acis could easily have had somebody there. And yet Joyce would have been trained to spot a tail, and she'd noticed nothing like that. When I pointed this out to Dawkins, he had a disturbing answer.

"It didn't have to be a physical tag. Were you out of the hotel a lot?"

"Practically all the time."

"It doesn't take long for a good operator to get into a hotel room, plant a beeper in the lining of your suitcase, the heel of a shoe."

Listening to Dawkins's hard, even monotone it began to sound dismayingly possible. Given that Acis had found out about Talloires soon after we had, wouldn't that have been exactly what they would have done? Sure it would.

"What should I do? Strip down to my underwear? Get rid of my suitcase?" Dawkins drove the way he stood, straight-backed, shoulders square. His bullet head moved in the barest of negatives. "If they're behind us, it's not such a bad thing."

I didn't understand, and said so.

"Al Charmain needs a lesson. If we do find Frohman, and his men try to outflank us, they'll get their asses well and truly kicked."

I checked the rear window. The backup van was a hundred feet behind.

"Who's in the van?"

"Kaufman, Davis, and Ralph Hale. All of them won range medals with a carbine."

The van was a blue color, but lighter than the color of the sky. It appeared icily impersonal, the smoked-glass windows lending it a cold, indiscriminate look.

Dawkins, silent and hard-mouthed now, slowed the car,

took an exit, came out on a road that swung west through flat green fields. Trees began to dot the fields, multiplying in bunches as the road started to rise. The bunches became long clumps of pines that thickened into a forest. For the next twenty miles the road snaked and meandered past several small towns that had seen their heyday thirty or forty years ago. A rushing river played tag with us, wide and brown, the water coming down from the mountains that appeared on the skyline. The road took a dip, then began to climb, the forest hemming us in, thick, pythonlike power lines looping from high poles each side of the road. Ski-area signs began to multiply: Paleface, Whiteface, Wilmington Notch. We rose up toward the sky, the van like a silver blue leech in our tracks.

The brown river vanished, appeared again on our right this time, a narrow chute peppered with sharp boulders. The forest receded for another small town, the houses white or mustard-colored clapboards, penguins and flamingos stalking the front yards in a curious display of the wood workers' art.

The forest returned, closing out the world, then was defeated as we came over the brow of a hill by the quick appearance of a massive mountain in the faded distance, a pale, wide scar dividing its summit, ski trails zigzagging down its eastern face.

Ten minutes later we rolled into the town of Lake Placid, past an impressive-looking high school and a flag-bedecked white structure whose flashing electric sign proclaimed it the Olympic Center. There was a pretty main street of stores and restaurants, a steep hill, a double row of serious motels; then the road curled through more of the forest before it split a golf course and arrived on the outskirts of Saranac Lake.

I can't say that the town spoke to me; there was no memory lunge when we rolled down the main street with its 1930's stores and bars and hardware emporiums, painted brick and leaning second-floor verandas. But I had no doubt that Frohman was near. It wasn't as if I could feel his presence, I couldn't. It was more like walking down a familiar street and knowing what was around the corner before you got there.

We checked into the only downtown hotel. The van, I noticed, had stopped at a nearby motel—separation of officers and troops. As soon as I got to my room I called Sarah, said Hi to her, chatted about this and that, then asked for Malinda.

"Daddy? Guess what?"

"I give up."

"We had a spelling bee. I came second. Almost first, but I said soap was S.O.P.E."

"Then you are a D.O.P.E."

"D.O.P.E.? That spells . . . Daddy! I am not either."

We talked for five minutes. I loved hearing her; she just bubbled over with enthusiasm for everything. She asked me to come early on Saturday so we could see if the goat at the zoo had had a baby. I told her I'd try my very best, blew her a kiss, and hung up. Today was Thursday. If I found Frohman tomorrow I could make it. I caught the flippancy of that thought. I'd been hunting him for the best part of two weeks and yet, strangely, I was confident that I'd find him within twenty-four hours.

I went back to thinking about Malinda, and I was still chuckling over our conversation when Dawkins called me. We went downstairs for a drink. I briefed him thoroughly on the trip now that we could relax a little, and explained why I figured Frohman was here, although I omitted how

I'd come to choose this particular lake—I didn't think he'd appreciate the swami bit. I simply said that Saranac was the nearest to Lake Annecy in surface area, and he accepted that.

We discussed tomorrow's strategy—nothing more than checking the local realtors—then had an early dinner after which I took myself off to bed; for me it was two A.M. French time. I felt drowsy and jet-lagged, but good. I'd find a realtor who'd rented to Frohman, drive out to his cabin, verify that he was still there, and that would be that, mission accomplished.

No problem, right?

CHAPTER FIFTEEN

The realtor was tall and meatless, with the sad eyes of a beagle hound.

He didn't look happy to see us—perhaps because it wasn't yet nine and he hadn't had the morning coffee that was perking on a little corner stove. His office was small and square, brochures on a counter, a fan on the floor, a planter with some limp greenery, a sign offering insurance and appraisals. Pinned to a green baize board behind him were Polaroid shots of houses, most of them in the white grip of winter.

"Nope," he said, examining the photograph of Frohman, the original one, "I never rented anything to this dude."

When I asked if he was positive about that, he flung a bony hand at the shots on the green board.

"Mister, I ain't exactly Donald Trump. I know who's in my properties and who ain't. And one of the many people who ain't is this gentleman here in this photograph."

We left him grumpily waiting for his coffee, walked down the block, and tried another realty office, this one bigger and politer.

The woman who ran it couldn't help us, but she suggested somebody who could. "Try Wally Gillet. He doesn't have much of a business, but he knows everybody else's."

Gillet's place turned out to be a brick-and-glass storefront with several copies of the same publication fanned out in the window, *Homes for Living* and the *Free Trader*. Most of the houses in the photographs on the rental board looked in urgent need of a skilled carpenter. Wally Gillet looked as if he could have used a little structural repair himself. Elderly, bent over, he seemed not so much to sit in his office chair as to be leaning against it. He flicked milky eyes over me, then settled them on my bandaged head.

"That the latest thing in Noo York these days?"

"How did you know I'm from New York?"

He flicked a look at Dawkins. "Anybody wears a suit like that round here's gotta be from Noo York."

I showed him Frohman's photograph, told him I was a friend, asked him did he know him.

"Sure I know him. Ought to. I'm renting him a cottage."

So there it was, as simple as that.

I'd found Werner Frohman.

Curiously, it didn't give me a charge; I'd expected to find him.

Dawkins, however, had a tiny note of excitement in his normally flat voice.

"He still there?" he asked.

"Damn well better be. I ain't picked up this month's rent yet." Dawkins asked him where the cottage was. The realtor lifted an arm and pointed in a vague direction. "Take Route Three twelve miles toward Tupper. Take 30 and watch for the Wawbeek turnoff. Mile 'n a half on there's a roadside stand, sells honey, strawberries in the season. Take the dirt road right next to it. There's a shack down the end of that right on the lake. That's where he is. You plannin' on goin' out there now?"

"Probably."

"Good luck."

"What do you mean?"

The realtor rubbed at his flank, as if scratching was one of his serious interests. "I mean he won't be glad to see you, 'less you're a real close pal. He don't like callers. He's got one of them walkie talkie things set up at the end of the road. I go out there to collect the rent I have to ID myself every time. The wife figures he's a 'centric millionaire. It's anybody's guess."

We left him on that note, walked back to the hotel, and got the car. When we hit the road the smoked-glass van fell in behind us. Dawkins was smiling. I think he might have punched my arm if he'd been the type. "Congratulations, Jack. Great job."

"Thanks, but let's see if he's there first."

"He's there. If he'd left, that old guy would know about it."

We took Route 3 out of town, following the realtor's directions. Checking the map, I saw that Saranac Lake was actually three lakes looped into a U: Lower Lake draining off into Middle Lake, which in turn linked up with the main body of water, Upper Saranac Lake. I swiveled in my seat to look back. The van appeared around the last curve, but I could see nothing following it. However, there was a large black car ahead and I wondered if it were possible to tail somebody from the front, pulling ahead where there were no turnoffs, slowing a little when the car behind you had an option. I asked Dawkins if anybody in the van had seen any sign of a tag.

"Nothing so far. But if Acis are around they won't be making their move till after we pick up Frohman. They'll let us do the donkey work for them, then, after we've got him, they'll move in and try to take him away from us." He craned forward to peer up through the green part of the windshield, checking the sky. I hadn't thought about a helicopter, but I could see it would be the perfect way of staying with somebody.

Now that we were so close to the German, a pedestrian

thought occurred to me. What if Frohman didn't want to come with us? What if he was perfectly happy where he was and indifferent to the thought of Acis?

"He'll come," Dawkins said when I voiced this possibility. "He knows about his partner's murder, his security setup tells us that, if you have to ID yourself by radio. All we have to do is point out to him that if we found him, Acis can, too."

"You think he knows about Acis?"

"Maybe not by name. But he's got to know that there's a whole bunch of people who'd kill to get their hands on Glitterbug."

Dawkins broke off. "Dammit!" he said. He was frowning at the dashboard. The gas-gauge needle was leaning against the E. We got lucky: we found a Mobil station a mile farther. Dawkins got out to pump his own gas, the van pulling into a turnout a little way ahead. Several cars passed going east, some heading west, then the road was empty.

The gas station was a quiet little spot off by itself.

Near the little office a man in a quilted vest was repairing an inner tube. Next to him a black cat was scrupulously cleaning behind its ears. The sun climbed higher into a clear sky, bridging the peaks of the forest, driving the chill from the air. I had a funny taste in my mouth, had had it since breakfast. I'd got up early at the hotel and walked through the sleepy town dropping into a pancake place for breakfast. The bacon had been greasy. I checked the glove box and found a pack of gum. I unwrapped a stick, chewed out the first burst of flavor, then rolled the gum into its wrapper and pulled out the ashtray.

Outside Dawkins had paid for the gas and was getting into the car. I put the gum into the ashtray and closed it.

Dawkins shot me a blue-eyed look. "You okay? You don't look so hot."

"I had a lousy breakfast." I don't know how I got the words out without stumbling on them.

Dawkins started the car and drove off.

I opened my window and leaned my head out. I had to take a couple of deep breaths and fight down, not a feeling of nausea—it wasn't food that was bothering me, but a combination of swirling emotions: rage, a feeling of crushing ineptitude, and an immense despondency. In quick successive waves they slashed through me, my mind in a furious fast forward/reverse mode playing back the events of the last few days.

What had brought on this extraordinary reaction? This despair and anger and teeth-gritting, fist-slamming frustration? A very small and seemingly innocuous thing.

A cigarette.

The one that was in the car's ashtray.

It had been partially smoked, stubbed out, and broken in half. And very, very recently. The tobacco was still crisp and golden-colored. The cigarette paper still stiff.

Such a tiny item, but oh how huge the ramifications!

It meant that this whole episode was a fake—the Army recruiting office, Colonel McAlister, and Dawkins, the guy sitting next to me.

It meant that my apartment was a fake. And Sarah was a fake.

And, by far the cruelest blow of all, it meant that Malinda was a fake.

The realizations left me winded, flattened, beaten, every nerve and sinew like a piece of jelly. This was the low point for me, the plunging nadir, the deepest part of the trough since I'd woken up in that bogus hospital room. I should have been used to my gullibility by now, but I found this third demonstration of it staggering. What made it even worse was that they'd made a mistake in that "recruiting office," and I hadn't caught it. When Dawkins had been running the slides of Acis operatives—he'd been careful to take himself and McAlister out—he'd left one in that shouldn't have been there: the Hispanic woman I'd glimpsed before he'd hurried on to the Florida file. I'd thought she'd been Mexican, but now, too late, I realized that she was from a little farther south than that—Peru. It had been a photograph of Joyce. Through the spinning fog of my shame, my hurt, my overwhelming embarrassment I was aware of a hand-painted sign swinging into my vision —Strawberries, Honey—and a shuttered roadside stand. The car slowed, turned, bumped over a rutted track cut into the forest.

I sat there like a bloodless thing and let the car's suspension jounce me around. The right front wheel slammed into a pothole, and the car reared wildly. I'd unbuckled my seat belt at the gas station and I was thrown skyward by the sudden dip and recovery. My head hit the roof with a bang.

"Hold on there," Dawkins said.

In some of the medical books I'd studied I'd read that a sudden blow to the skull could jog an errant memory back into place. It didn't happen to me.

Frankly, right then, I wished that blow had robbed me of what memory I did have. However, the instant pain did have an effect: it literally jarred me out of the paralysis that had gripped my heart and mind.

I knew what I needed: a gun. But they'd been careful to keep one out of my hands. Dawkins had told me that it was too much hassle to carry one on board a commercial flight, and that I wouldn't need one in France anyway.

I sure could have done with one now.

Something else I could have used was a little of the very things my tormentors majored in: cunning, guile, deception. Because without them I was more than certain I wouldn't be around to see the end of this warm and sunny morning.

The winding track at last threw off the clutch of the forest and opened into a clearing. A ruined fence stumbled across a patch of ragged grass and, beyond that, 150 feet away, a small cabin was framed by high pines. Behind the pines came the glint and flash of sun-riddled water.

Dawkins pulled the car up against the fence, the van stopping—for reasons that were now obvious to me—thirty feet away from us in the shade of some trees.

"Strategy session," Dawkins said, getting out. "Be back in a minute."

He marched over to the van. With its cold, dark windows and deep-tinted windshield it could have contained robots, although I knew perfectly well who was inside.

I made the first part of my move right then. I didn't have much of a plan, but at least it was simple. The way I saw it I had a big thing and a little thing working for and against me: the negative was a stunning lack of street smarts, which, when boiled down, left a thick and gooey residue of stupidity. The positive was surprise, something I'd thought I'd had once before. But this time I was sure I could count on it. I reached across, hit the trunk release, got out of the car, and went around and opened the trunk all the way. Inside was my bag. I'd put it in this morning on the chance that we'd be finding Frohman and wouldn't be returning to the hotel in Saranac. Next to my bag was the carbine I'd noticed, and a box of shells. I unzipped the bag, took out a sweater, and put it on underneath my jacket so as to give Dawkins and the van's occupants a reason for me going to the trunk. I put the carbine and the box of ammo into the bag. It was one of those long nylon sports bags, and it took the short-barreled rifle with an inch to spare. I closed the trunk just as Dawkins made it back.

"Okay," he said. "We're all synchronized. Let's see if we can't winkle him out peacefully."

I was about to reply when a voice crackled out of a supermarket box nailed to a leaning fencepost.

"Who are you? What do you want?"

The accent was heavy, the W's pronounced as V's. These past couple of weeks, Werner Frohman had been just an image on photographic paper for me, almost a phantom who existed on other people's sayso. But this was his voice. I knew it. He was real and alive.

Dawkins lifted his chin at me. "You handle it."

I went over to the box. Inside was a two-way radio. I lifted it out, pressed a button under the word Speak. "Mr. Frohman, my name is Penrose. I'd like to see you, please."

"That is not my name. Who are you?"

"I'm with the US Government. I just want to talk with you."

"I have a gun. Go away or I shoot."

I came back to the car, popped the trunk.

Dawkins frowned. "What are you doing?"

"I want to make him think I've got something for him." I pulled out my bag. The rifle bulked slightly at one end, but it could have been a shoe or something. I slammed the trunk before Dawkins could see that it was empty. I checked the van. Two topcoated men stood beside it, carbines carried loosely in their hands. I went back to the radio.

"Mr. Frohman. I have something for you. I brought it from Talloires."

"Talloires?"

It was said with surprise. If Frohman knew me, he would have known I'd been to Talloires, wouldn't he? So we'd never met. I must have traced him to this little cabin, but not revealed myself.

"Let me bring it, Mr. Frohman. I'll come alone."

"No. Do not come. Do not come here." The words were laced together by fear, warbled in that strange, lisping inflection.

"I just want to talk. I'm not armed. Can you see me?"

"I see you plain. I have Zeiss glass."

"Binoculars," Dawkins murmured to me.

I opened my jacket, lifted up my sweater, revolved slowly, spoke into the radio. "I have a lock. Can you see it?" I held up the little padlock from the bag. "I'm going to lock my bag and put the keys in my pocket."

I did as I said, making slow, big movements of it: got the two metal tags together, slipped the U of the padlock's arm through both holes in the tags, and clicked the padlock home.

"I'm coming in now, Mr. Frohman. Just me. Nobody else."

The answering voice lifted, tinged with panic. "Do not come. I shoot."

"He could be bluffing about the gun." Dawkins had his eyes narrowed against the eastern light, peering unwaveringly at the cabin. "But if he does have one, take it away from him gently and bring him out. Don't waste too much time."

"I'll see what I can do," I said to him, the last words I ever spoke to his face.

With the bag in my right hand I started the long, exposed walk toward the cabin, very much aware of the irony of the situation: the man I'd hunted in several different locations on two continents was now my only hope of salvation. I had to keep them from getting him because, once they did, they wouldn't need me to winkle him out as Dawkins had put it. So I had to gain access to the cabin and use it as my fortress.

It didn't appear to be exactly impregnable. It looked like a child's drawing of a witch's cottage: a door bracketed by two windows and a crooked stone chimney jutting through the roof. A combination of age, neglect, and bad weather had ruptured the fly screening on the porch, which, shored up by chipped cinder blocks, sagged to one side like an old car that had lost a wheel. The trees, heavy and thickly grouped on each edge of the clearing, stopped short at the sides of the cabin as if the earth around it had refused to nurture anything.

The hillocky ground I was crossing was clear all the way to the leaning front door, and I was an easy target if Frohman had been serious. There was no sound except for my shoes scuffing over the scrubby grass and a light breeze swaying the tops of the pines. It came off the lake, fresh from the mountains, and raised goosebumps under my shirt.

Thirty feet from the ruined porch, Frohman's high piping voice reached me.

"Stop. No more forward."

The breeze would have carried my voice back to Dawkins. I had to get closer. "I can't talk to you from here. Let me come to the door."

"No! Stay there!"

I began to walk slowly forward. "I've just come from France. From Talloires. I have something for you in this bag."

I could see him now, a dim outline to one side of a window, a rifle at his shoulder. I didn't think he'd shoot

250

unless I tried to enter the cabin. I made it to the rickety steps.

"Listen to me." I kept my voice low. "The men I'm with are hunting you. And not for the US government." I heard Frohman grunt as if he'd taken a blow to the stomach. "They used me to get to you. If they get you, they'll kill me. We have a chance if we make a stand together. In this cabin."

I took a breath, climbed the steps, walked over the warped boards of the porch, pushed through the half-opened door.

Frohman had backed up against a wall, a fine trembling moving through his body. He held the rifle as if there were a bayonet fixed to the end, his arms extended.

I put down the bag, dug the key out of my pocket, placed it on top of the bag, stepped back several paces, and fessed up. "I don't have anything from Talloires. There's a rifle in that bag. I'm going to need it against the people I brought here." The German was staring at me, shaking his head as if to deny what he was hearing. I recognized him from his photograph, but just. He'd lost weight, and his hair was thinner, and some nervous complaint had blotched the skin of his narrow face. He was almost as tall as I, but a stoop robbed him of commanding height. He'd grown a mustache. It looked like a dark and ragged Band-Aid applied to a cut beneath his nose. The tartan shirt he wore slumped on his thin shoulders, his blue work pants bagged, and his old-fashioned dress shoes were scuffed and busted.

"Who are you?" His voice was as thin and shaky as the rest of him.

"I'm a man who's been lied to. Open the bag."

He watched me like a bird keeping an eye on a cat, but he went to the bag and did as I'd told him.

251

The carbine gleamed dully. Frohman didn't touch it, and when he saw that I was keeping my distance, I think he believed what I'd told him. He folded in on himself, the rifle drooping. He mumbled something in his own language, a despairing tone cracking his words. When he looked up at me again, a tiny curtain of sweat opened along the sparse hair above his discolored forehead.

"How did you find me?"

"I traced you to Boston, then back to New York. I found Peliac's name in a magazine you requested, found a photograph in his apartment of the two of you at Talloires. I thought you might be at a lake like Annecy, and got lucky with this one."

Frohman was straining for comprehension, perhaps wondering if his English was letting him down. *"Bitte?* Peliac gives you this photograph?"

"I found it in his desk. He was dead when I got there. These people killed him. They're working for the Chinese."

Frohman found a stronger voice, a stiffer backbone. "They offer me money. For Glitzenbak. The Chinese. I say no. But I never work for them if they hurt Gerard. They know that. It was the other that kill him because he could not tell them I am here."

"What other? Who?"

"Die Japonsie."

It took me a few moments to understand but when I did I understood everything. I almost chortled. I was *still* learning. Carmody and McAlister had both told me about the new alliance, that China and Japan had secretly shaken hands. And they'd been telling the truth; Frohman had just confirmed that. But I'd had a strong suspicion for some time that there were other players in this game besides Acis and their Chinese clients. And there was only one group that qualified: the people on the other side of the handshake.

And I had absolutely no doubt as to who was being paid to run the show for them. Who else but Carmody? The ace liar. The all-time champion deceiver. A perfect choice to work both ends against the middle. And I would've bet a year's salary that Dawkins didn't know it. Of course he didn't know it. If he had, he really would have shot Carmody in that bakery.

Over near the window a radio crackled. Dawkins's voice. "Jack? You okay?"

I crossed the room, picked up the device "I'm fine. No problem."

I clicked off and turned to Frohman. "Are you any good with that rifle?" It didn't look like much of a weapon. It was too light, too slim. Frohman's thin shoulders moved in a doubtful shrug.

"I do not know."

"Well, we'll find out in a few minutes."

I took a fast tour of my fortress. The inside was as dilapidated as the exterior: one large room with a rough board floor, a couple of fat armchairs, their torn vinyl cushions patched with yellowed sticky tape, a cast-iron cooking stove in one corner, a mussed camp bed in another. It was a fifty-year-old fishing cottage, a slum, but I was sure Frohman had snapped it up because of its isolation and its proximity to the lake. I went out the back to a room with linoleum curling off the floor and damaged screen windows repaired with fishing line. This was Frohman's laboratory as I saw by the long, collapsible table holding a collection of liquids and powders, plus a delicate array of glass equipment all connected by thin rubber tubes. A squeaking noise came from one corner: rats in a wire cage, two of them lying on their sides. This part of the cabin was practically in the lake. It had been raised on stilts sometime in the past, and water lapped just a few feet from the rotting supports. The rear door opened on to some steps leading down to a nervous little dock, its busted walk practically awash. Moored to the end of the dock was a battered aluminum rowboat, the wooden oars floating in six inches of rainwater. Beyond the little boat a couple of miles of sun-dazzled lake rolled away to the dark-green forest of the opposite bank.

As a defensive position it could have been worse; I didn't have to know anything about warfare or tactics to see that. It was impossible to approach from behind unless you had a boat, and anybody trying to sneak up for an end run could be spotted from the front windows because of the lack of trees on both sides. But the cabin was so skimpily built, and in such poor structural condition, I was certain those rifles out there would be able to bring it down around our ears.

I turned to find Frohman standing beside me, his tortured eyes sweeping over his workshop. He'd lapsed into despondency, far more sad than afraid now.

"Mr. Frohman, we're going to have to defend ourselves. We're going to need some protection."

I went back into the main room to the iron stove, brought my foot down hard onto its out pipe. The old tin burst apart and came away. Like a drugged man Frohman wandered in and helped me with the stove. It weighed a ton, but we managed to walk it across the floor and bump and shove it in front of the right side window. I got the carbine from my bag. After Frohman's rifle it had a comfortable solid weight to it. I pumped up a round without even thinking, an instinctive skill I didn't have to rely on my memory for.

"Jack? What's the holdup? You okay?"

Dawkins getting impatient.

GLITTERBUG

I picked up the radio. "We're just having a little chat. Be out in five." It was such an effortless lie, such a facile piece of deception, and it had just tripped off my tongue. But then I'd had good teachers.

I placed the opened ammo box on top of the stove and indicated Frohman's rifle, asked him if he had extra ammunition for it. Almost absently, as if I'd requested a matchbook, the scientist pulled a small red box from his pants pocket. It held four narrow bullets.

I borrowed Frohman's binoculars. I couldn't see the van, obscured as it was by a stand of trees, but I could see Dawkins clearly, waiting in front of the car. The two topcoats had joined him, their barely visible carbines held beside their legs. There were supposed to be three of them.

I knew where the third man was.

"How many?" the German asked.

"Two rifles. And almost certainly a handgun."

"We are overmatched," Frohman said mournfully.

I didn't tell him we'd be overmatched against just one of those rifles. I'd have to look after the scientist when the shooting began, which would cut my effectiveness right down the middle.

"Get down behind the stove."

Frohman stayed where he was, stoically ready to accept whatever fate was warming up for him. He gazed through the discolored window glass, squinting against the distance separating us from the car down by the fence.

"Who are they? Who are those men?"

It wouldn't have made any difference had I told him: Acis, consummate liars, champions of deceit. I could have humbled myself and told him how they'd made a monkey of me not once but three times, each time getting a little smarter. Clever, cleverer, cleverest. The third go-round, but

255

for a slim, busted-in-half cigarette, would have been a masterpiece.

With grim humor I recalled considering the circumstances surrounding Peliac's grotesque death. That was one thing that had been for real. I'd actually said in my head that a faked death would more likely be a simple production, like a fake gunshot wound and some fake blood.

And when I'd seen it in the bakery I hadn't tumbled.

I could have told Frohman that. And I could have told him how smart they'd been with the woman the third time around. No sexy, hot-breathed paramour this time; instead a polite, arm's-length ex-wife. And in place of ready sex they'd substituted instant love—they'd given me a beautiful daughter.

And I hadn't tumbled to that, either.

I picked up the binoculars and the radio. What I was about to do, I was fairly certain, would result in the death of three people. I had to weigh that against the death of two other people: me and Frohman.

It was no contest.

"Dawkins?"

"Right here."

With the binoculars at my eyes I could see that was true. He was still standing in front of the car, the radio in his hand, his two confederates next to him. All three were shading their eyes as they looked into the bright slant of the morning sun.

"Mr. Frohman isn't coming out," I said.

"Why the hell not?"

"He's decided it's safer where he is."

Through the double lens shape masking the group I saw Dawkins react to that, annoyance pinching his mouth.

"Tell him he's wrong. If he stays there Acis could find

him. He could end up in Peking faster than he could turn around."

"I've explained that to him." I raised my voice a little, certain that the reception on Dawkins's radio would carry to the van. "I've also told him that it's already happened."

"What's already happened?"

"Acis has found him."

I could see the jolt on Dawkins's face, the look he passed to his two lieutenants, who immediately swung up their rifles. I savored that moment; my first little triumph over my adversaries. It was so wonderfully satisfying to know something they didn't for a change, and I put that thought into words.

"What's the matter, Dawk? You didn't know I knew? I have news for you. I know something else you don't know. You ready for this?"

Dawkins had his feet planted, his hands in front of him, his body a clenched spring ready to go in any direction.

I delivered the clincher. "The guy in the van's only working part-time for Al Charmain. The rest of the time he's working for the Japanese."

It poleaxed Dawkins, but only for a moment. He and his men spun toward the van, guns flashing up. They'd reacted with exceptional speed but it didn't save them.

An instant later, slowed by wind and distance, the popping chatter of an automatic weapon slashed through the forest quiet.

"What is that?" Fear had surged back into Frohman's eyes.

I told him.

"That was the odds changing."

I know that might sound a little tough, but fifteen minutes back, down at the gate, when we'd known for sure we'd found Frohman, those three men had been as good as dead.

Besides, remorse would have been a luxury: I had a five-shot Remington carbine and Frohman's squirrel rifle up against a machine gun. From the fence came the sound of an engine starting up. The smoked glass van rolled into view, stopped beside the bodies on the ground. An arm reached quickly for the radio Dawkins had dropped. Something told me it was not a percentage shot, so I didn't use the carbine. I snatched up Frohman's rifle, and my instincts did the rest. The butt rammed into my shoulder, left hand gripping the stock, master eye focusing past the front sight, right hand working the bolt, squeezing the trigger. I repeated the sequence four times, so fast it astonished me. There was no recoil. The rifle made little barking noises. I could practically see the bullets in their slow, parabolic ride.

A figure raced for cover from the driver's side of the van. A moment later the radio next to me coughed to life.

"Hey, Jacko. You mad at me or something?"

"Yeah. I thought you were dead."

"Not lately you didn't. You spot me in the van or what?"

"Dawkins's car. Still trying to kick the habit, huh?"

There was a soft chuckle. "Shit, did I do that? Bust a Marlboro and leave it in the ashtray? Getting sloppy."

Even when he talked about himself the sneer stayed in Carmody's voice; the same tired, superior tone.

"Where'd you get that rifle, Jacko? Coney Island?"

"That was just to show we're armed."

"With that? A fucking pea shooter?"

"It'll do the job from fifteen feet."

"Come on down and prove it."

"I kind of think you'll be coming to us."

"Goddamn right. And I'll be bringing this little Socime I

got here. Only weighs four pounds but hits like a Thompson."

As if a hurricane had leaped against the house, the windows above us caved in, shattered and blown apart, the hammer of the machine gun faint against the crash and splinter of the fragile panes.

"See what I mean?" Carmody asked.

Frohman's face had blanched and he was breathing through his teeth. Shards of glass lay on his shoulders and in his hair, and a thin smile of blood appeared on his cheek where he'd been sliced. The wood of the rear wall looked as if some monster had savaged it. It was Carmody's idea of a morale-sapping message, a fast, three-second burst to demonstrate the flimsiness of our shelter. I didn't need a reminder, I already knew it wasn't in my power to outmuscle him. I was going to have to outsmart him.

His voice crackled again. "I'm coming in a little closer, guys. It's lonely down here all by myself."

I couldn't see any movement because the forest was too heavy down by the gate. It petered out thirty feet from the house, but Carmody wouldn't have to cross any open space to get to us; he could park himself somewhere close and tear the cabin down around us. I stayed where I was, crouched behind the iron stove reloading the little rifle. Frohman was slowly recovering from the awed shock of having the window shredded over him. I pulled him down next to me and thought about escape, thought about that dented little rowboat moored to the dock. It would be the slowest getaway vehicle of all time.

I tried to figure something else, but Carmody's voice interrupted the thought flow.

"What do you say to an early day, Jacko? Bring him out and you go free. You're a schmuck, but I got nothing against you. In fact, I owe you one. Without you I never would've found the Kraut."

"You're indulging in your favorite hobby again, Carmody." That brought a piece of a dry laugh. "No point in pulling your leg now, kid. Send him out, huh? He'll be okay. My bosses want him alive."

Beside me Frohman was vigorously shaking his head trying to influence his fate.

"Tell you what I'll do; I'll make you an easier exit." Carmody's offer was followed by a devastating barrage, a colossally destructive burst that tore through the upper part of the thin plank door, blew away the rusty top hinge, and sent the door flopping sideways at a forty-five-degree angle. Fat chunks of splintered wood scorched around the room as a second burst chopped away the bottom hinge. The door turned on its front corner like a dancer spinning slowly on a point, then toppled and crashed to the floor.

I knew then that Carmody wasn't just having fun. He had to know that to get Frohman alive he'd first have to get me dead. This was merely the softening-up process to get me spooked.

"Hold up, Carmody. You've got too much gun. I'll send him out."

"No!" Frohman clutched at my arm. I shook him off.

"But I want something in exchange," I said into the radio.

"Name it."

"I want the truth."

"You're better off without it, Jacko."

"That's the deal."

"Throw out the pop gun. Then we got a deal."

"You lied to me all the way. I'm supposed to believe you now?"

I was risking little peeks over the shattered window. I figured Carmody was off to the left somewhere, but all I could see was the silent forest, the scruffy clearing, the car and the van beyond the fence, and the crumpled bodies.

"I had reason to lie to you before. I got none now. Ain't nothing left to lie about."

"Sure there is. I'm a loose end. You go back to Al Charmain and you tell him that the Japanese decided to get in on the act. You were all set to grab Frohman when a bunch of them came out of nowhere. They must've had me tailed in France then picked me up in Montreal. There was a firefight and Dawkins and the other two bought it. Me, too. They belted you on the head, and when you came around Frohman was gone."

"You learned a little, huh? Hanging around with me? That's close to what I'm gonna tell him. Only I say that the Japs grabbed the both of you. If you turn up later in New York, so what? The Japs didn't need you, that's all. It'll play."

I listened to the static on my radio. Carmody's voice wasn't getting any closer, but I was certain he was moving, picking his way through the pines, taking a roundabout route toward us. "So I'll trade you," he said at last. "Throw out the .22, push the Kraut through the door, and we'll leave you to get in a little fishing." Frohman was trembling, desperately afraid I'd go for Carmody's deal. "It's the best offer you'll get all day, Jacko."

"I want a sweetener."

"Like what?"

"What I asked for, the truth."

"You won't recognize it."

"Let's start with the little girl. How did they get her to act like that?"

"Trilling dug her up from somewhere. Her real dad died or something and she went a little nuts. Show her a guy and say that's your daddy, and she believes you."

In a way it was a relief to hear that. If Malinda had a psychological problem it could well be overcome one day with some expert help. But if she'd just been a clever young actress, willing at such a tender age to fool somebody, to lie to them and fake love and affection, I think that would have been far worse for her. It certainly would have for me.

"Next question. Who am I?"

"Your name's Jack Peck. You were Army, and you transferred to Intelligence only not the Defense College because the College doesn't have a clandestine arm. We made that up. You came to Boston looking for Frohman, which is where I come into the picture. You came to see me."

"Why you?"

" 'Cause I'm a spook, what do you think? Worked for the E Gees until they went out of business."

"The who?"

"The East Germans. You and me had known each other for years. Spooks have a kind of weird relationship even if they don't all work for the good guys. They trade info all the time. You wanted to know what I knew about Glitterbug. Offered to trade me for a future favor. I didn't know shit about Glitterbug, but I sure as hell wanted to. So I took it to Al Charmain who'd just started up Acis. And he took it to the Chinks."

"And they hired him . . ."

"Like a shot. Then I went across the street and offered it to the Japs. They didn't want their new buddies to have anything they didn't have so they put me on the payroll. They pay better than the Chinese and I get to keep it all."

"So you tailed me until I got close to Frohman. I'm talking about the first time around."

"You got close, but no cigar. I had you tailed to France, and from there to Montreal. But that's where you spotted the tag."

"I think I can take it from there," I said. "You pulled me in and tried to beat it out of me, but you hit me too hard."

Carmody snorted. "That was another little invention. You didn't lose your memory because of a shot on the head. We took it away on purpose."

"What?" I'd heard him perfectly, but the meaning behind his words refused to register.

"The Japs got hold of a tame neurosurgeon. He went to work on your head and scooped out your memory. In medical terms, you should pardon me showing off, your amnesia was surgically induced."

I couldn't speak. Could hardly think. I was horrified. A blow with a lead pipe, some serious head damage, that was one thing; but the image of me lying in a pristine operating room, a masked and gowned surgeon peeling back the flaps of my scalp, boring the holes, trepanning my head, then taking gauze-wrapped instruments and an icy scalpel and going to work, lifting the fragile frontal lobes, slicing with exquisite care; paring, exorcising—that was a horrible and hideous picture I wanted to reject and deny, refuse to even consider.

"They knew you'd still be left with your gift, your hunch ability," Carmody went on. "You'd find Frohman again because what a guy can do once he can do twice. Only this time I was going to be tagging on your sleeve."

I found some words, pushed them out of my dessicated mouth. "It's not true. You're still making things up."

"It's true and you know it." Carmody sounded impatient

now, as if he'd given me too much of his expensive time. "Come on. Frohman'll be an old man by the time you give him to me. So let's move it, huh? Throw out the .22, and push him out the door."

I didn't answer. I was still struggling to reconcile everything I'd heard. It meant my memory was gone forever, thrown out with the detritus of a surgical operation. But it meant other things as well, things that might also be permanent that I'd welcome. I checked Frohman. His tall body was pretzeled in behind the stove, a fearful anxiety eating into him. I wondered what he'd made of the Jack Peck story, or if he even realized that his fate was inextricably bound in with mine now.

"Okay," I said into the radio. "Let's do it. He gave me some trouble, I had to slug him. You want to give me a hand with him?"

"C'mon, Jack, you're a big boy. Put him over your shoulder and bring him out."

"I can't. He got me in the leg with a kitchen knife. Last thing I expected."

"Last thing *I* expected with hands like yours. Don't bullshit me, fella. Just send him out."

"I can't do that."

"Why not?"

"Promise you won't be offended."

"I won't be offended."

"I don't trust you."

"I'm offended."

"Toss out the machine gun. Then you can have him."

"Hey, c'mon now. I'm out in the woods here. There are snakes maybe. I don't wanna be entirely defenseless."

"You won't be. You've got your piece in your belt." It was

just a guess on my part, but I was sure Carmody would have his pistol on him. He was a gunman.

"You're still short on tradecraft, Jacko. When you got a weapon fires twelve hundred rounds a minute like the Socime, you don't need a handpiece. If you got a baseball bat you don't carry a twig as well."

"I'm gonna offend you again, Carmody."

"Hey, let's get square here. If I give up the machine gun and the pistol, I'm left with what I can find lying around. I'm good, but you're better, goddamn you. You'll waltz the Kraut right on by me."

"That's true. But if you keep the pistol you could kill me."

"I tell you I won't. No percentage in it."

"You may figure one."

I listened to an open mike, Carmody thinking to himself. Then he spoke again sounding conciliatory.

"Look, let's get this disarmament conference on a better footing. We'll do it tit for tat, in sections. You give up the .22, I give up the Socime. Agreed?"

"Okay, throw it out."

"You first."

"It was my idea. You first."

"Uh uh. You've got the superior weapon."

"You better be on the level, champ."

"Waiting on you, Carmody."

I was still peering past the jagged edge of the shattered window, but I couldn't see any movement in the trees except the trees themselves, their tops slow-dancing with the wind. Then something gleamed, the sun flaring darkly on something black arcing through the air. It landed on the grass about fifty feet away, a short, evil-looking thing with a short barrel and a long magazine.

"Get it!" Frohman hissed at me. "The machine gun."

I ignored him and threw out his rifle. It hadn't finished bouncing before the left side window blew inward, five shots bursting through the tattered screen, taking out the filthy glass panes and matchsticking the wooden frames.

I knew what the weapon was: a carbine, exactly the same one as I had. Carmody had simply gone back to the van while he'd been keeping me talking and got it. I should have figured that and covered the fence with the binoculars, but I hadn't. I was so mad at myself for letting him outsmart me I lost my cool. And my advantage, so I thought. I snatched up the carbine and sent five shots, an entire clip, winging into the forest, bracketing the area where I thought he might be.

All I achieved were puffs of grit as the bullets chunked bark and tore off a small branch.

As the echo of the two fusillades died, Carmody's leering voice once again came into the cabin.

"I wondered if you might have a Remington. I didn't think you went to the trunk just to put a sweater on, but I wasn't sure."

I slapped the heel of my fist against the cold metal of the heavy stove. I was getting mad. Carmody had been a dozen steps ahead of me and he was still in the lead. I reloaded the carbine knowing that the man in the woods was doing exactly the same thing. I breathed deeply, forced my anger down. I had to do something a little smarter. I snapped on the radio.

"We're at an impasse, Carmody, so to break it I'll give you an edge."

"An edge? I'll take it."

"We both throw out the carbines, but you keep the pistol,

266

the Brownie Hi-Power. Thirteen rounds in the clip and one up the spout. You told me that in the bakery."

"So I did. I get to keep it, huh? What do you get to keep?"

"There's nothing left for me to keep."

"Doesn't sound kosher, sporto. Why leave me the pistol?"

"Because you don't get to keep the magazine. Drop the clip and toss it to me. I'll leave you the round in the chamber."

"Now that's interesting, you give me a handicap. Unless Frohman's got a second gun."

"He only had one. And I only had one."

"Now I'm gonna offend *you.*"

"Ray, you've been away from the truth so long, you can't recognize it. I'm betting I'm better than a piece of crap like you even with a one-shot gun."

"I gotta think about this."

"Go ahead. But you can forget about another trip to the van or any of the dead men. I got Frohman's binoculars here."

"Okay. Gimme a minute. Let me think."

The radio went silent.

Frohman had followed most of the exchange and looked to be aghast by my proposal. "You must not give him the rifle. Then we are without defense."

"No we're not." I'd seen the strange-looking object when I'd first taken a look around the cabin. It was over on a shelf lying on top of a bunch of tattered paperbacks. Keeping low I duckwalked across the floorboards and reached for it. I didn't know what it was, but I recognized it as a weapon. It was made of strong dark wood cut in a Y shape. Attached to each arm of the Y was a thick red rubber strap with a little leather pouch in the center. Next to it was an old tobacco

267

5

can containing half a dozen roller ball bearings the size of my thumbnail. When I brought everything back to the safety of the stove, Frohman fluttered a hand in panicky dismissal. "A catapult. A toy for the children."

I didn't think it was a toy. I could see that the rubber, when stretched tight and released, could launch one of those ball bearings at considerable speed. I was only guessing at its possible effectiveness, hoping, too, because I needed a weapon and was dead without one. There was no way I was going to talk Carmody into total disarmament, but I was sure he'd be attracted by the idea of keeping his gun, even if it did have only one round in it. A single bullet at close range would be all it would take to make a mess of me.

"Jacko? I'll buy Frohman only having the one rifle. He ain't a pistolaro. He'd buy a .22 and feel safe. And I know you only have the one piece because that's all there was in the trunk of Dawkins's car. But you've found something else in that cabin, and I'm sitting here in the middle of all this Mother Nature shit and wondering what it is."

I decided not to lie. I wasn't much good at it.

"I'm wondering about it, too. I don't know how effective it's going to be."

"Yeah? Thanks for the hint. I'm gonna think some more."

Beside me Frohman let out a sigh that was studded with pain. Confusion seemed to have stolen over him, mixed in with fear and a sinking depression. He'd twisted around on the floor and was gazing toward the rear of the cabin at the glass apparatus set up on the folding table. He muttered something I didn't understand.

"Zwei wochen."

"What?"

"Two weeks. I need two weeks."

I twisted around, too, peered at that innocuous-looking setup in the back room. It looked like a bright child's Christmas present.

"What is it, Mr. Frohman? What's Glitterbug?"

He turned to me, but there was no comprehension in his sagging face. *"Bitte?"*

"What is Glitzenbak?"

"I cannot tell you. I can tell no one."

I put it as simply as possible, and it wasn't hard. "The reason why I'd like to know is I might be dead pretty soon because of it."

The German responded to that. He propped himself up on one elbow and appeared to be getting words together in his head. In his semisupine position, with his hair in disarray and an expression of suffering draining his color, he looked like the sole survivor of some dreadful calamity.

I said something to get him started.

"I think I know what you needed. Pure mountain water heated by the sun."

His mouth opened. I'd floored him. "You know that? How?"

"I guessed. I think that's why you and Peliac went to Talloires."

Frohman's head began to nod as if it were too heavy. "It is my fault he is dead. He never had his . . . heart in the project. I had to always tell him not to give it up. We came back from France close to success. Gerard refuse to continue. He had fear. Such a terrible weapon."

"But it didn't bother you?"

Although the scientist didn't move, he seemed to rise up. Something incredibly intense lunged behind his eyes.

"They destroyed my parents."

"Who did?"

269

"*Das Russisch.* My father, my mother, my sister. They fled from Munich because they were Jews. They went to Moscow where they had family. After Stalin sign the pact with Hitler they are sent back to Germany to the camps. It happened also to Gerard's father. He was German. Sent to Russia. Sent back. They knew they send them to their death."

"All that was long ago," I said quietly. But Frohman wasn't listening.

"Twelve million people died because of Soviet Union. Millions more under Khrushchev, Brezhnev. Sent to the gulag. Russia is an abomination. A terrible mistake."

For a moment there was only the sound of Frohman's labored breathing, the high squeak of the rats in their cage in the back room, the slap of water beneath the broken slats of the boat dock.

He began speaking again in his lisping English, lost in a reverie of failure. "It was my idea. A superweapon based on a hundred-year-old theory. A man name Wynzinski. A Pole. A substance that could produce a change in the body."

I didn't get it. When I thought of a superweapon I imagined some kind of colossal laser beam or an undetectable, deep-space missile launcher. And he was talking about changes in the body.

"I don't understand. What do you mean?"

But the German was lost in the weird honeycombs of his brain.

"Ten, twelve men could deliver it."

"Deliver what, Mr. Frohman? You're not making sense."

"One teacup of the solution in the water supplies of the big Soviet cities. Done in the summer, in the afternoon when the sun glitters on the water, heating the surface to the exact temperature to combine with the solution."

Glitterbug was some kind of incredible potent poison. It

would make the water in the reservoirs undrinkable. Is that what he was saying?

Frohman's gaze lost its focus. God knows what he was seeing.

"An enzyme change," he said. "It would produce an enzyme change."

I didn't know what an enzyme was, but even if I had, I would never in a million years have guessed the horror of what he had in mind.

"A human being can eat almost anything," he said, as if I'd voiced my ignorance, "because of enzyme flexibility. But what if they no longer had that flexibility? What if they had the enzyme makeup of a ruminant?"

"A what?"

"A horse or a cow."

I stared at him, only just beginning to grasp the appalling thing he was getting at.

"Glitzenbak in the water, the Soviets drink it. A year's time they are intolerant of meat, fish, vegetables, cereals. All they can eat is grass. They would dig through the snow, root up the grass, strip the tundra like ants in the Amazon. But there would not be enough. They eat it faster than it could be grown. In ten years, eighty percent of Soviet Union starves to death."

I couldn't look at him, this wide-eyed madman who seriously planned to wipe out a couple of hundred million people. I was standing next to the greatest potential murderer in the history of mankind.

I couldn't help but think of the photograph of Peliac and him taken on the dock at Talloires, the loveliest, most peaceful spot you could find. Werner and I take a break, it had said on the back of the print. From carefully thought out, meticulously researched genocide. I couldn't encompass it.

Frohman turned, rolled his eyes in the direction of the forest. "If that man takes me, the Japanese make me finish the work. They will have Glitzenbak. And maybe one day it won't be Russia starves to death. Maybe America."

I lied to myself. I made out I hadn't heard that last sentence. I refused the thought admittance and concentrated on saving just two people in America.

Carmody's voice intruded.

"A kid's air rifle. Left behind by a family in a hurry. Am I close?"

I answered him: "I told you. Besides the carbine I don't have a gun of any kind. Let's get to it, okay?"

"Okay. I'm gonna take a chance on you, buddy boy."

"Toss out the clip."

"How do you know I ain't got another one?"

"Because a wise jerk once told me that if you have a baseball bat you don't need a twig as well. Toss it into the cabin."

Something spun out of the trees, skidded in the dust in front of the ruined porch, way short.

"Sorry," Carmody said. "Guess I don't have my stuff today."

"You'll have to go for it," I said to Frohman.

Fear stressed his body, wobbled his voice. "He missed on purpose. He wants to shoot me."

"No. If he wanted you dead, you'd be stretched out by now."

"Capture me then. If I go outside."

I raised the carbine. "He knows I have this. He won't risk it."

Like a man going to the scaffold, the scientist uncurled

his thin frame and stood as if he were suspicious of his legs. He measured the open ground he had to cover. If I was wrong about Carmody Frohman would be a target like a duck in a shooting gallery. He moved uncertainly to the door, stepped out onto the porch, hesitated, then went slowly down the steps to the grass. The area he had to traverse was alive with sunshine blinking off the hard pressed steel of the machine gun, the barrel of the .22, the dark finish of the pistol's magazine. I thought Frohman would make a clumsy dash for the clip, dash back again, but he didn't. He went on moving with funereal gravity, stopped with the clip at his feet, and looked over toward the trees around where Carmody had to be. He raised his head to the cloudless sky as if it were the last sight he'd ever see. I found that I was keeping my breath inside my lungs, my cheek hot on the carbine's stock, one eye focusing on the spot in the forest where the clip had been thrown from.

Frohman stooped, retrieved the clip, straightened, stood there. I thought he was offering himself to a self-ordained fate, but then I saw what was in his mind.

The machine gun.

It was only a couple of strides away, the stock facing him, inviting his hand.

He was going to go for it.

"Frohman! No!"

My yell iced him. He swiveled his head, turned wide eyes to me. Sweat darkened the collar of his shirt, his sparrow chest rising and falling.

"Bring the clip back. Now!"

He wavered on the edge. Then his shoulders fell and the tension seeped from him. He made it back inside and collapsed beside me panting like a dog. I couldn't decide if what I'd seen had been simple bravery or extraordinary foolishness. He was still clutching the pistol magazine. I took it from him, and sprang the rounds. It was a full clip: thirteen.

"Finished counting, Jacko? Let's keep going," the radio said.

"I'm ready. Throw out your rifle."

"We'll toss 'em out together on the count of three."

"Fine. Except you throw yours out on the count of two."

"You're some horse trader, Captain."

"One . . . two . . ."

The rifle cartwheeled in a high loop, flumped down on the grass.

"Three," Carmody said. "Go ahead."

I didn't want to do it. I hated the idea of giving up the carbine, but if I didn't, if I couldn't tempt Carmody out into the open, he'd camp out there till nightfall, then go down to the car, milk the gas, douse the dry wood of the cabin, and burn us out of there. I hurled the Remington through the smashed window. As it hit the grass Carmody said, "Okay. Send him out."

"You want him, you have to pick him up."

"You want me to swing on by? Sure, why not? Do me good to stretch my legs."

I knew Carmody well enough by now to recognize a hard edge of gloating triumph in his voice. It chilled me, and even before the splintered remains of the left side window crashed in under a storm of gunfire, I knew I'd made a huge mistake. And I knew what it was. When Carmody had sneaked down to the fence to get a rifle, he'd brought back not one, but two.

He emerged from the trees, sauntering in that insolent way of his, an infuriating grin on his lopsided face, a winner's grin full of contempt for the loser.

Frohman started jabbering at me, grabbing at my arm. I thought he said, "He must come! He must come inside!" But I thought, with his off-and-on English, that he meant he *will* come inside, so I didn't understand what he was getting at.

And I wish I had.

But I was fighting against myself right then, trying to tamp down a freezing numbness as I watched my executioner approach, casually reloading the carbine he carried.

I hunched down behind the stove and fumbled with the catapult, got the ball bearing nestled into the leather pouch. It was going to have to be a potshot. I'd have to show myself to use the thing, and the moment I did that Carmody would try to blow me away.

I had to be fast and I had to be accurate. Try for an eye, a head shot, then get out there and take that rifle away from him. Frohman was still babbling at me. I don't think he knew it, but he'd switched to German and couldn't make sense in either language. He was pulling at me, spitting something about *verschtoken* and *farlah*. I had to fight him off, shove him so hard he tumbled over. Carmody, much closer now, had the rifle at port arms.

"C'mon, Jack Peck, let's see what you got. You gonna throw shoes again?"

It occurred to me that this was the second occasion I'd played guns with this man, only this time he was going to be shooting to kill.

I squeezed thumb and finger around the loaded leather pouch, gripped the catapult's handle low in my left hand.

"Maybe it's boots, huh? You find a pair of boots in there? Throw the socks this time, will you? The ones I'm wearing are—" I shot to my feet, swung the catapult up in line with Carmody's mocking mouth thirty feet away.

He matched my movement, the rifle muzzle strobing around. The ball bearing zipped across the space with phenomenal velocity but way off line. It cracked into his left shoulder punching his aim off. The slug dissolved a remaining shard of window glass and smashed up a shelf on the rear wall.

Carmody yelled out, half turned trying to grab at his shoulder with his gun arm, but the shot hadn't done me any good—he was still on his feet, still had the carbine in his right hand, and one hand was all he needed to blow my head off if I'd even thought about rushing him.

I ducked down, snatched up another ball bearing, then saw it wouldn't be going anywhere: the catapult's red rubber strap, unused for too long, had snapped at the sudden tension and now dangled limply like a piece of old rope.

"Fuckin' *bastard*!" Carmody yelled at me, pain scrunching his face. "You're dead, cocksucker, dead!"

Frohman had come up off the floor and was jabbering at me again in his back-of-the-throat English. "The trap! I have a trap!"

It was my turn to grab at him. I shook his skimpy shoulders, chopped words at him. "What trap? Where?"

He wriggled free, took a couple of paces to the middle of the floor. He pulled at a section of the rough boards.

A piece the size of a small table top came away revealing a shallow hole dug into the moist black earth.

I understood then what he'd meant about getting Carmody inside the cabin, but I thought that the German, reflecting his unstable thinking, was hoping that Carmody would rush in and stumble into his pathetic trap.

I'd badly underestimated him.

"I made explosive. I put it in the wall. Get in!" He was

276

pulling at my wrist, his thin arms trying to muscle me into the hole.

"Get in!" he implored. "I go to the lake. *Brauch die antenne!*"

My thought processes unscrambled finally and I got it— Frohman had booby-trapped the cabin.

He rushed toward the back door, perhaps heading for the little rowboat. I called after him. What had it been, an instruction, that last snatch of German? But my voice was flattened, masked by the crash of the carbine, the heavy slugs ripping through the thin front wall, saucer-size chunks of wood rocketing past my ears. I caught a glimpse of Carmody clutching at his ruined shoulder, dropping the carbine, walking away. I thought for one gloriously foolish moment that he was quitting but, of course, he was making for the machine gun on the grass, a far lighter, easier weapon for a one-armed man.

The rifle was fifty feet away from me. Carmody was twenty feet from the machine gun. I didn't even consider it.

I crouched, lowered myself into the hole, scrunched my knees up, pulled the trapdoor over me. I found myself squeezed into dank semidarkness, the smell of earth and fresh sawn timber in my nose, a clammy coldness on my sweaty back. I was ferreted in there like some kind of burrowing animal hiding from an aggressor, but hiding wasn't going to be good enough. Christ! What the hell had Frohman meant, *Brauch die antenne?* What antenna? What did it mean? Was I supposed to set off the booby trap or would Carmody do that the moment he stepped into the cabin?

A fearful volley drowned out my silent screaming questions, a long lead fist of slugs smashing into the stove, behind it the steam hammer whomp of that vicious little machine gun. Then Carmody's grit-toothed obscenities cussing me out as he fought against the agony of his broken bone.

He was on his way. He wanted me dead. He wanted that Italian machine gun in close and chewing up my innards in great, hungry bites. I groped in the dark, flushed with relief as I felt two thick wires. Something told me that all I'd have to do was touch them together.

Carmody's footsteps clumping over the porch, his pain-stiffened voice.

"Sonofa*bitch!* I'll fuckin' blow you in *half!*"

I almost died. What I'd thought were detonator wires were two long grass roots.

The floorboards shook as he stomped through the ravaged doorway. I could see him clearly through the wide cracks, his left arm dangling, his nostrils white and flaring, mouth jerked back on his teeth. He saw instantly that the room was empty, that there was nobody behind the stove barricade. His head whipped up toward the rear door, and the dock and the lake beyond it. I was frantically feeling around me trying to locate some kind of switch, knob, or handle, and in my squirming, my shoe belted against the wooden trapdoor.

Carmody whirled, thinking that I'd somehow got behind him, the little machine gun in his good right hand blasting a fiery arc. I was trying to lash my brain into an answer. What in God's name had Frohman meant about an antenna? Or was that a German word that meant something totally different?

I was staring at Carmody, my hands flailing the dirt each side of me. I tried to shut my eyes, close out visual contact, but it was like trying to look away from a coiled snake.

Pulled down by my fascinated gaze, his furious eyes locked on to mine. He would have been able to see pieces of

GLITTERBUG

me through the trapdoor, the daylight sectioning me in pale stripes.

An amalgam of hatred and victory banished his pain. His lumpy jaw fixed his mouth in a pastiche of a smile as he planted his feet, practically astride me.

"Well, lookee here. The fucker dug his own grave."

My groping hand hit something.

My fingers closed on it.

Hard metal, like a transistor radio.

Radios had antennas. They received signals and they sent them. *Brauch die antenne.* Pull it? Push it? Turn it? I wasn't sure I could do any of these things: I was trapped by my hiding spot, caught in it like a wrapped mummy in a sarcophagus. I fought against the constriction, tried to suck in breath and squeeze my left arm across my body, but with Carmody standing on the trapdoor there was no play in the boards, no room for me to get my hand on to the signal sender.

Carmody, bestride me like a ton of meat and bone, was going into great detail about my short future, how he was going to carve me into bits and pieces as he had the windows and the door. He squatted, shoved the barrel of the machine gun down through the widest crack in the trapdoor. The steel blip of the barrel was an inch away from my body.

"Say good-bye to your leg, cunt face. I'm gonna take it off right *here*!"

The muzzle speared into my hip. I yelled, I couldn't help it, and he liked the sound of that.

"Did I hurt you, dear?"

The barrel rammed down into a rib. I felt it go as I cried out again. I couldn't see now—sweat from my forehead and tears of pain—but I could feel. The same nerve/brain func-

279

tion that shot agony through my rib cage, my hip bone, also allowed my fingers to feel the cold hard sides of the radio, the milled knob at one end, a knob the size of a pea, a tiny stalk of metal beneath it.

I thumbed it down.

Nothing.

I turned it between thumb and forefinger. Once, twice. A third time.

Dead.

It had to be pulled, jerked out of its telescope. But I needed two hands to do that, and I just couldn't get my other arm across my chest. But I could maybe get my right hand, the one holding the little radio, close to my face, close to my teeth.

I yelled as a hot, lancing pain chopped viciously into my side. I could have partially blocked that mean barrel with my right arm, but I was inching it over my body leaving my side exposed.

"How a-*bout* it!" Carmody grunted, savagely bayoneting my shrieking muscle a second time.

I battled the fire in my body, battled the thought of the killer sadist who was having such a wonderful picnic above me, tried to ignore the long, sharp splinters from the underside of the floor planks needling into my wrist and forearm.

It was costing Carmody, too, those hard, stabbing jabs, jarring his busted shoulder. He straightened, stepped back, not wanting to chance a ricochet.

He was going to finish the job now, watch my trapped corpse jounce and shudder from a twenty-bullet puncture.

His weight transference gave my pincushioned arm an extra inch of space. I got the radio to my chin, bit down on the antenna's tiny metal ball. I stretched my hand away, fingers laced around the radio's tiny shoulders. The antenna, less than eight inches long, began to snake out of its tight little recess.

The machine gun waved toward my face, down toward my groin.

"Where do you want me to start, pal? Top or bottom?"

I didn't get a chance to answer Carmody, and he wouldn't have heard me if I had.

Vision fled, hearing bolted, both senses chased by a whirling white cyclone, a godawful explosion that ripped into my underground world and stunned my ears and sucked at my eyeballs.

A second later the massive weight that had thumped down onto my chest, pinning me against the dirt, rolled away, taking with it the paroxysm of silver fire that had torn my visible world apart. As focus returned it was the color blue I was seeing—half the cabin's roof had been blown away.

Then the pain arrived; not the pain of Carmody's metal attack, but the sear of flames dancing in over the floorboards a few inches from my face.

I shoved at the burning trapdoor, kicked it off, scrambled out into mad destruction. The iron stove, bowled over on its side, was the only recognizable thing; all the other bits of furniture were either missing or were blackened, twisted ruins. I staggered toward the remains of the rear room, but my legs weren't ready for action and I fell onto flames. I rolled, got my feet under me, then ran, clothes smoking, past the shattered glass residue of Frohman's experiment, down the steps outside, belly flopping into the lake.

I pressed my burning skin into the cooling mud, let the icy water lick my wounds. I would have drowned if I'd passed out, and I was on the edge: my head felt like an expanding balloon. My hand reached for the dock. I levered myself up and saw, at the end of it, the half-sunken rowboat and a pair of legs sticking up.

The old-fashioned dress shoes needed new soles.

I moved over the dock thinking resuscitation, trying to remember what I'd read about life-saving drill. I grabbed at Frohman's shoulders, lifted him, then forgot about mouth-to-mouth. He didn't have one, his face had been scorched away. The blast had hurled him into the boat he'd been trying to launch and caved in the back of his neck.

He was way beyond help, but I couldn't worry about him anyway, I had to concentrate on keeping my senses. I knew I was concussed. If I lost consciousness I might not wake up again.

I weaved my way back to the grassy bank, climbed out past the exploded cabin. Blue chemical flames fluttered along the blackened roof beams, red ones attacked the stumps of wallboards. Gray smoke was beginning to spiral, the breeze fanning it westward. Splattered over what was left of one of the walls was what was left of Ray Carmody. The undertaker was going to need a hose.

I walked unsteadily over the grass down to where the two carbines lay. I picked up the one I'd handled and continued to the fence.

Dawkins was lying on his side like a man who'd got close to the ground to search for something. The other two men were on their backs. Dark badges of arterial fluid had spoiled the crisp tan of their topcoats.

I searched the car's glove compartment, found a rental agreement from a firm in New York. My focus was awful, but I made out the rentee's name: Ralph Hale. I checked the IDs of the two riflemen. The second one was Hale. I did something then that was a first for me, as far as I knew: I robbed the dead. I took his ID and gave him mine. I found a handkerchief in his pocket, which I used to wipe my prints off the carbine, then dropped the rifle beside him, got into the car, and drove it back down the dirt road to Route 30.

I was in no shape to be behind a steering wheel, but I had to distance myself from that lake scene because I couldn't have explained my presence to any law enforcement group. Plus, I had nobody to vouch for me. I was my only witness to the whole affair, and who would have believed my story anyway?

I drove slowly, keeping one eye on the double yellow line of the curving road. I must have strayed over it from time to time because I was loudly honked by several cars heading north. Fire simmered under my skin, and I was beginning to shiver, a reaction that I suspected was not a result of my soaked clothes. My brain kept on wanting to close down, but I held on as I hit Route 3, and turned west. I followed it toward Saranac Lake and, a few miles outside of town, spotted what I'd been looking for: a lonely forest road that looked untraveled. I turned into it and kept going around a bend where I couldn't be seen from the main road. I stopped the car on the edge of the shoulder. The road fell away into a ditch. At the bottom lay a placid swamp full of the ghosts of trees, their naked trunks sticking up like stiff hands calling for help.

I maneuvered the car as close as I could to the dirt edge. Picking my spot, and going in at an angle, I hung the left front wheel in space. The car lurched and teetered, got ready to go. I struggled out the high side. It was a hell of an effort; I wanted to forget about it and just lie down on that leaning front seat. I had to make saucer eyes to keep my lids open.

I removed the cap of the gas tank then used the last of my

strength to push the car. It toppled and rolled, and crashed down the rocky bank finishing up on its back.

Gasoline had sloshed out, streaming down the left rear fender. I had a matchbook in my pocket taken from the glove compartment. I lit the cardboard corner, flicked it down at the automobile, and got what I wanted, which was the last thing I needed: a concussive whomffff! of an explosion.

The air around me collapsed. The hot wave of expanding gas was like a pair of harsh hands boxing my ears. My legs wavered, but I stayed upright because I knew that if I fell down on this lonely little turnout I'd be staying there.

I started back down the forest road meandering over it like a drunk. In my zapped confusion I began to wonder if I hadn't started in the wrong direction. But the highway finally appeared around a bend, and I made it to the shoulder where I stood swaying on my planted feet. Not surprisingly, given my drenched and shoddy condition, five vehicles went by me, showing not the slightest inclination to answer my signal. But a sixth car did. It braked, and when the driver saw I wasn't going to trot to it, the car backed up to me. It was a large station wagon, a woman behind the wheel, a small child in the rear seat.

"What happened?" the woman asked.

I meant to say "I ran off the road," but the skin around my mouth was starched into place. "Accident," I got out, then climbed in beside her. She mashed the gas pedal.

The little kid hung over the front seat fascinated by me. "Is he gonna die, Mommy?" he asked.

I slid into luxurious oblivion, wondering about the answer to that myself.

CHAPTER SIXTEEN

Coming out of it.

Light popping as if a kid were playing with louvered blinds.

The kid in the car that had picked me up?

Focus brought me white sheets, white walls, the white rod of a bed rail, a figure in a crisp white uniform: a nurse. I wondered if it was still going on, wondered for one crazy moment if the woman in the station wagon had been paid to pick me up; if this was an Acis nurse in front of me, a fake Acis hospital room I was in.

But everything was real this time: real nurses, real doctors, real sulphur wrap on my arms and legs, real lake and pines outside my window. Even real television reporting my mishap.

The medics and I agreed on what had happened. I'd run off the road and totaled the car. It had burst into flames, and I'd had the presence of mind to dive into the swamp, thus lessening the effect of the burns covering fifteen percent of my body.

No smiling brothers or concerned, loving girlfriends came to visit. Nor did I see any severe-faced heavies in dark suits, or overweight fatties with poor eating habits. No agreeable cherubs, no straight-backed, militarily correct brush cuts, no dyspeptic, lumpy-jawed con men. Nobody was posing as anybody they weren't, except me. I was Ralph Hale, and had a driver's license to prove it, even if the photograph on it was a little scratched up. I made out a report for the rental car company, and had a friendly chat

285

with the local police. What was found on the southwestern edge of upper Saranac Lake when the fire watch responded to a pall of smoke, made large headlines in the area's newspapers. The police were clear on what had happened but couldn't even guess at why. Dawkins and his two confederates were identified as employees of the Acis Corporation, a New York City security firm. A spokesman for the company, whom I assumed was Al Charmain, claimed to be mystified as to why his men were there. Frohman was identified finally as a recent immigrant, a reclusive type who appeared to have been caught up in some kind of Mob vendetta, judging from the bomb that had destroyed everything. That theory was further supported by the fact that he was a chemist and the finding of the remains of some lab equipment in the cabin. It was suggested that he'd been manufacturing crack, and once that element entered into it, I think the whole affair was regarded as just another spectacular drug wipeout.

The remains of a fourth person had also been discovered, but identification had proved impossible as there'd been no fingers to print and no teeth to check against dental records. I mended quickly but still had lots of time to figure things out. I came to the conclusion that Frohman had probably welcomed his death. I think that along with the immense disappointment of not seeing his work finished, he'd also had to battle with a suspicion that he wouldn't have had the guts to use it anyway. And that would have made him a double failure. Plus there was the guilt of having indirectly caused the ugly demise of his best friend, Gerard Peliac.

Anyway, Glitterbug, and its inventor, were history now, and I was only interested in the future.

The day I was released from hospital I flew to Washington and went straight to the Pentagon. It took the best part of a morning to struggle through security procedures and finally get to see somebody who recognized me.

I was officially debriefed—I had a lot of explaining to do. But, in return, I got the truth which made for a welcome change.

Much of it I knew anyway, because Carmody hadn't been lying in our showdown at the lake. Army Intelligence were aware that Glitterbug was some kind of superweapon, knew that Frohman hated the Russians, and were worried that he'd use it against America's new ally. I'd been detailed to find the German and stop him. And I guess you could say I accomplished my mission even if it was done in what might be charitably described as a roundabout way. But I found out something, during that intense debriefing, that Carmody had neglected to tell me. And I couldn't have asked for a better piece of news. It had to do with my personal life: I was happily married—to a woman named Sarah—and the proud father of a nine-year-old daughter, named Malinda.

And so it proved to be.

They're both terrific, and both very special to me. And very understanding with a guy who can't remember a single thing past a couple of months back.

Will it ever come back, my memory?

Probably not. But I don't really care if it does. Living with Sarah and Malinda I'm collecting a whole new set of memories. And they'll do just fine.